AFTER GLASS SHATTERS

CINDERS IN MIDNIGHT GLASS

BOOK V

J. DARLENE EVERLY

Hardcover: ISBN 978-1-954719-47-7
Paperback: ISBN 978-1-954719-46-0
Ebook: ISBN 978-1-954719-45-3
First paperback edition August 2023.
Edited by Jupiter Alley.
Cover art by Miblart.
Layout by Wishing Well Books.

J. DARLENE EVERLY

AFTER GLASS SHATTERS

CINDERS IN MIDNIGHT GLASS 5

For the artists

My fellow theater kids, actors, writers, painters, sculptors, dancers, and all other people gracing the human experience with their artistry to help us all express ourselves and understand ourselves: the world and humanity will always need you. And contrary to the beliefs of others, no computer will ever replace or express that piece of your soul you put into your work. Thank you for creating in a world that doesn't have respect for creators or recognize the value of it. The next time someone tells you that you can be replaced by an algorithm, hand them a sci-fi novel and remind them that we've seen the end of that story before.

INTRODUCTION

After Glass Shatters is the fifth book of the six in the Cinders in Midnight Glass series. The sixth book, After Ashes Fall, is coming soon! If you would like to be the first to hear about the next books in the series, get an exclusive prequel to this story and more free books, as well as see what else the author has written and is writing, please go to jdarleneeverly.com and sign up for her newsletter.

CHAPTER 1
CATALOGUE OF PAIN

Cinder

Everything hurt, and I felt like I was dying.

Still.

Being awake was a punishment for every crime I committed on my brother's behalf, including lying to myself to pretend we were righteous.

"Cinder," Tristan said, leaning down to rest his forehead to mine, and letting out a tight sigh. His arms wrapped around me, and his hands grasped at my hair, "I'm so relieved. You didn't stop breathing this time."

Dragging in breaths, I was thankful the action managed not to send agony arcing through my back and my ribs as he held me up, and maneuvered around to curl up behind me on the bed again. I couldn't answer. Not at first. The words would have been too hard to eke out of my mouth even as my pain ebbed away, and I settled into him. Allowing him to support my weight kept me from hurting.

"It's getting better," I finally managed to say, sinking into his arms, and letting my eyes fall closed.

"Good," Gus said, bustling into the room with Jacquetta on her heels, both carrying more of Jacquetta's ingredients for her lotions and potions.

"How much better?" Jacquetta asked, coming to the side of the bed where I already spent too much time, putting her hand to one of my eyelids as she stared into my eyes, and moving her head around.

Not enough. That was the honest answer.

"She can breathe when she's on her own power now," Tristan said from behind me. The way his voice rumbled in his chest paired with the heat of his body pressing into mine felt just as healing as a therapeutic dip in the pools under my home in Lehar.

I ran a hand along his fingers. The movement was small, and didn't hurt at all, as long as he supported the rest of me.

He wrapped my hand up in his, threading his fingers through mine, and I hoped he understood that my small gesture was meant as a sign of gratitude.

A thank you for being the perfect man for me, and for bringing me back to the palace when I fell from the air on the back of that damn crow.

Saying the words, putting voice to my deep and true appreciation, was something he refused to accept. Still. But I could show him in the little ways I was capable of at the moment. In the future, as soon as I was able, I planned to show him exactly how appreciative I was as often as I could.

Jacquetta stepped back from the edge of the bed and nodded, turning to Gus, who stood in the doorway to the bathroom.

Gus set to work drawing a bath and preparing, but before another round of soaking and their ministrations, I had some questions.

"Why do you keep checking my eyes?" I asked.

Tristan kissed the top of my head.

"Because," Jacquetta said, her tone almost like her mother's when Madam was close to scolding, but not yet there. A warning floated in it that she was seconds away from getting angry at me for getting hurt, which didn't make much sense to me, "When you and that Corvid fell, its body did not entirely shield you from damage."

I furrowed my brow, about to interrupt to point out the obvious. I was in pain. I knew I was injured. But she raised a hand, and kept talking.

"Not just your body was hurt. It did something to your brain that I have never seen happen to you before. Your eyes were not reacting to the light properly, nor were they tracking the movement before you quite right."

She shook her head, and looked down at the floor for a second before returning her gaze to me, the steel in her softening to something more like gold—malleable and only hard on the outside.

"The things I know how to treat do not include injury to your brain."

It took something out of her to admit she didn't know how to heal everything that was wrong with me. The way she held herself told me that much. But it wasn't her fault.

None of it was.

"Jacquetta," I said, hoping she heard my concern for her in my voice before she heard the worry over myself, "you help me so much already. Just tell me, is that injury to my brain any better?"

Maybe it was something that would never be right. Maybe it was something that I couldn't recover from. I wouldn't let it stop me. Somehow, I would train to fight with the new realities of my inconsistent vision, but I wasn't sure how to deal with the news either.

"From what I can tell, it is getting better." She lifted an imperious finger at me, and one of her eyebrows rose along with it. Every bit her mother's daughter now, she managed to tamp down the relief that shot through me in response to her diagnosis. "But you need to be careful, even after we heal your other wounds."

"Why?" I asked. Her eyes narrowed while Tristan's arms tightened around me, and his grip on my hand became almost painful.

"Because," he said, and she nodded before he finished speaking, "you are not invincible, and we all need our queen."

There was no arguing with either of them. I knew that. They wouldn't hear it. But they were wrong. What we all needed was to end this war. And I could help us do that. If I got healthy again.

"So, what's the plan for my other injuries? How long will it take for me to heal?" I asked. The time it would take me was the most important question, as far as I was concerned. The faster I got better, the faster I got back on the battlefield.

"Cinder," Gus groaned from the bathroom, poking her head out the door, "you know they'll both keep you out of the fight for as long as possible. Don't ask them that question. It isn't fair to make them wonder if they should lie to you or not."

"I am not going to lie," Jacquetta said, her nose in the air.

"Fine," I said, even as Tristan made a rumbling noise of disapproval in his chest, "then how long?"

Jacquetta sighed and deflated before she shrugged, and said, "I am not sure. You heal differently than most people. Much faster. And with your training, I know your recovery will go more swiftly as well. But your injuries are extensive."

"Why won't any of you just tell me what the injuries are? All of you just keep saying 'wounds.' I deserve to know the extent, and the specifics." This was getting ridiculous.

Tristan acted as if it was too painful for him to talk about.

Even now, he sucked in a breath behind me, and held himself far too still.

Gus winced where she was emptying jars into the bath.

Jacquetta just froze, showing nothing on her face.

"Please, my flame," he whispered in my ear, running his free hand along my cheek.

"Well, then, is the bath ready?" I asked, choosing to bide my time until I could ask Jacquetta and Gus when he wasn't around.

"Yes," Gus called from the bathroom.

"If this hurts, tell me," Tristan said, shifting me so that I was laying across his arms, one supporting my back, and one under my knees. He twisted and brought his legs over the end of the bed, keeping me as close to him as possible as he stood up.

There was an ache, but it wasn't outright pain yet. That always came when he wasn't behind me, when my body had to hold itself up, or even hold itself together. Not understanding exactly what was causing the pain that arced through me by just breathing when he wasn't with me was part of the reason that I wanted to know exactly what was wrong.

Part of me thought my breathing problems and the passing out could be explained by the brain injury, but I wasn't sure.

"You should let her take this bath alone," Jacquetta said, her voice soft as Tristan reached the edge of the tub.

"But..."

He had yet to leave me for longer than was necessary to relieve himself.

"My King," I said, looking up into his tired eyes, the short beard growing along his jaw made him look every inch the war-weary sovereign he was, and did nothing to hide his concern for me, "you should go take your own bath, and get changed."

Tristan sighed and tilted his head to kiss me, the force of his love sweeping through me on fiery tides of heat, reminding me that I needed to get better as fast as possible. If for no other reason than I didn't want to be yet another thing that wore him down. He needed me to be healthy and whole right now.

Breaking the kiss, he touched his forehead to mine as he lowered me into the water.

Not until I sunk low into the warmth of the fragrant water and all the herbs and flowers that floated in it did Tristan pull his arms away from me. The leather of his battered sleeves, still bearing the marks from the battlefield, dripped as he stood next to the bath.

I smiled, even as the muscles around my chest and back screamed. He needed a break, and I was going to give it to him. No matter how hard it was.

Curling in on myself, hoping it would relieve the pain some, I said, "I'll be fine. I love you. Go."

But a line appeared between his brows. He knelt at the edge of the tub, reaching out a shaking hand to dip it into the water, and ran a finger along one side of my spine. The heat of his hand was scorching, even compared to the steaming water. It was enough to make me suck in a breath.

"Jacquetta," he said, his voice tight and cracking.

"Oh, Cinder," she said, appearing next to him. She shook her head before she darted to the counter and her many containers of items she used for her remedies.

"What's wrong?" I asked, hating the way Tristan's eyes wouldn't meet mine as he ran his finger along the other side of my spine, then traced every rib along my back even though I wasn't sure how he knew where they were since many couldn't be seen through the muscles.

"King Tristan," Gus said, looking up from helping her wife mix something, "we have something for that. You can go. She'll be fine."

Finally, he looked at me, placed his palm on my back before he bent again, and kissed me.

"I won't be long, my Queen," he said, his voice shaking. He

jumped up, splashing water that sluiced from his leather sleeve as he darted out of the room.

I waited a minute, my breathing shallow again until I was sure he was out of ear shot to avoid the arcing agony that ripped through my torso with each normal breath I attempted to take.

"He's gone now," I said, my voice low and thin without the full support of my lungs, "you can tell me what's wrong."

Gus looked at me and swallowed as she nodded while Jacquetta hunched and doubled her efforts at mixing.

"You do need to know," Gus said, and I braced myself for bad news.

CHAPTER 2

PAINTED IN NEED

Tristan

I didn't care about the dripping mess I left as I sprinted down the hall, down and up across the top of the grand staircase, through the royal wing's hall, and up the stairs to my room as fast as I could.

My dash through the palace earned me odd and worried looks, but I didn't have time to give them more than a passing thought. Whatever the people assumed based on my brief, disheveled appearances could be sorted out later. I needed to do as Cinder wanted me to, and get back to her as fast as I possibly could.

Every single bone in her back, her spine, and her ribs, was outlined in bruises on her skin like some macabre and terrible satire of a painting of the human skeleton.

When she landed on the battlefield, on top of the already dead Corvid, the impact shattered the giant bird, turning it into a mess of gore and feathers that I only knew was a crow because I saw it whole before it plummeted from the sky.

Picking her up from where she lay sprawled on top of what was left of the corpse, everything in me rebelled at the idea that she was dead, that her injuries were grave enough to kill my Flame. When she took a breath, spoke, opened her eyes, touched me—did all the things that proved she would live if I helped her—I refused to let her go. I naively believed that, as long as I was there, and the proof of her continued life was in front of me, it somehow meant that she wasn't hurt *that* badly.

Jacquetta told me while Cinder was passed out in my arms that she thought it was likely Cinder broke bones, but I wouldn't move so Jacquetta could see her back. I couldn't. Holding her, feeling her breathe, it was the only thing keeping me from losing my mind with worry.

And I didn't *want* to believe her.

Instead, I spent every day with Cinder for a week while the war waged on. Meetings were held in her bedroom, whether she was awake or not, while she was wrapped in blankets in my arms. I blocked out the worst possibilities.

Not now.

All of Jacquetta's whispered worries stabbed me in the heart when I saw the visual evidence of how close I had been to losing her.

There was nothing I could do now. That was the worst part.

Jacquetta was better equipped to help Cinder with this. She and her baths and medicines were the reason I had the opportunity to hurry back to her.

So, I stripped down the second the water started pouring into the tub, and climbed in long before it was full.

Maybe it didn't make any sense. Maybe I should stay away. But I couldn't. Not when Cinder needed me to hold her up to make the pain less intense.

With my mind in Cinder's room with her, my hands made

the quickest work possible of scrubbing off too many days spent in the same attire, too many days of not washing anything other than my hands, too many days of barely dipping myself in the water to hold Cinder up while keeping my clothes on.

By the time the bath was full, all the dirt was already off me, and I released the drain as I jumped out. I skipped shaving in favor of drying off, and throwing on fresh clothes.

"King," Rath yelled, barreling into my room, "your Flame must be better, huh?"

"No," I said, shoving my feet into my boots, and tugging my shirt into place, "I need to get back to her."

"General Pace and I need to speak with you," he said, stepping aside so I could walk past.

"Fine," I said while he followed me out of my room and back down the stairs, a fraction slower than I came up so I didn't leave him behind. Moving slower frustrated me enough that I curled my hands into fists, "But you're going to have to get the General, and come to Cinder's room. Cinder will want to talk to her about Lehar anyway."

"Maybe you should take a break," Rath said, his voice was careful. Still, it took a physical effort not to whirl on him, and say something I would regret.

"Whether I should, or not, I can't. Not until she doesn't need me anymore." While I had to say it through clenched teeth with a voice that sounded like that of a growling animal, I did manage to speak.

"King, you don't sound like yourself," he said, putting a hand on my shoulder.

Rath was right. I didn't sound like myself, and I definitely didn't sound like a king. But I had lost the capacity to care, and sure didn't possess the will to change it. Not while she was hurting. Not while she needed me. And certainly not while my blood burned in my veins every second that I was away from her. Worrying about her made the heat in me rise higher than the damn crows could fly.

"I almost lost her, Rath," I said, my voice still wrong, every muscle in my body still tight as if I braced myself for a blow.

"She seemed fine when I was in there last time," he said. "Hurt, but healing."

"That's only because she's stronger than either of us. She has been through so much already." I swallowed. There it was, the hard truth I kept running from. I was still unable to look at it head-on. Instead, I could only confront it with Rath at my back.

After what she went through, the years of abuse and pain at her brother's hands, she was supposed to be safer with me. Instead, she was closer to death now than I imagined she had ever been.

Her bastard brother told her she was an investment. But she was so much more than some cold investment to me. She was my queen. And I didn't protect her.

"But she's going to be fine, right?" Rath asked, worry dripping from his voice that only made me speed up as I ran up the stairs toward her hallway.

"She has to be," I said, breaking out in a sprint as I got closer to her.

I needed her to recover. And then I needed to find a way to keep her safe, to protect her better than I did before.

Pulling open the door of her rooms, and darting inside, the dread coursing through me was almost enough to make me sick.

Because, even as I made it past the servants making her bed, to her bathroom where I found Jacquetta and Augustina painting her back in a thick paste while the water around her in the tub was blue, I knew that she would chafe and fight against every attempt I might make to keep her from harm.

"My queen," I said, kneeling beside her, and taking her hand off the edge of the tub to wrap in mine while I cupped her face.

Her eyes were pressed tightly shut, but there was no other sign of pain on her face. Watching as her body moved with her breath allowed me to breathe, too. The mere fact that she still drew breath relaxed every muscle in my own bone-weary body. When she sighed like my presence allowed her to do the same, I never wanted to leave her side again.

"She did well," Jacquetta said, and Cinder made a snorting noise that caused a smile to tug at the corner of my mouth.

"Flame will be back out there destroying our enemies in no time," Rath said, leaning against the doorframe, and smiling in her direction.

"Rath," she said, turning her head to look over her shoulder as much as she could without twisting her torso at all while Augustina and Jacquetta leapt away from her and whirled on him, "get out of my bathroom."

"What?" He looked back and forth between Augustina and Jacquetta as they herded him out of the room, leading with their hands smeared with whatever they put all over Cinder's back. "Fine. I'll go, but I'm coming back with the General."

"Your friend needs to learn that people on land have different boundaries than people stuck on a ship together," Cinder said, her voice still small, her eyes closed again. But a smile played with her mouth, and her grip on mine was strong. "Did he say the General was coming?"

I nodded, "You can ask her then."

"He needs to learn manners," Jacquetta said, getting back to the work of coating Cinder's back.

"Don't worry," Augustina said, walking back into the bathroom to wash her hands, "he won't be coming through that door again."

"Gus?" Cinder asked, a careful quality to her voice as she opened her eyes and narrowed them at her lady.

"And you have a little bit before he and the General knock on the door to the apartment for whatever meeting he thinks you need to have," Augustina said, grinning as she returned some of the items Jacquetta used to their rightful place.

"What exactly did you do to him?" I asked. "He *is* important. And my friend."

For some reason, even though Cinder's ladies were only gone for a moment, I pictured Rath skewered on a thousand hair pins.

"Nothing," Augustina said, but her smile said something else. "Nothing permanent."

"Oh, Gus," Cinder said, shaking her head and sighing.

"Hey, all I did was make a mess out of his pants to make the point that he shouldn't get in the way of the Queen healing." Augustina raised a self-satisfied brow, and her smile turned into a smug smirk. She looked every bit like a cat that caught a delicious mouse.

I laughed. I couldn't help it. Although, if Rath found out, he would find a way to make me pay for it.

"May I know how you did both of those things in just a handful of seconds?" I asked while Cinder simply rolled her eyes.

"She smeared her hands on his...um..." Jacquetta furrowed her brows, pursed her lips, and redoubled her focus on Cinder's back.

Looking to Cinder, I thrilled to see some mischief in her eyes as she bit her lip on a smile, and I laughed even harder.

"Thank you," I said through my laughter, "now I can hold that against him for a while."

Cinder's eyes widened in a moment of glee that was too rare since her fall.

"He already said he was going to use things against me," she said, letting out a laugh, and then cringing as she breathed through the pain it caused before looking at me again, "I'm going to enjoy having a little arsenal against him."

CHAPTER 3

BETTER

Cinder

"So, are we finally going to plan how to use Rath's information?" I asked, out of the bathtub, a wrap around me that held one of Jacquetta's grass-smelling poultices in place, and wearing a nightgown for the first time in a week. Tristan was at my back in the bed with his arms around me, and a blanket over the top of me.

"I don't know," Tristan said, running a hand along the back of my fingers, "but I want to know how you're doing now."

Taking a deep breath that was shockingly free of pain, I closed my eyes and smiled, my body relaxing further against the hard planes of him, enjoying the softer clothes he wore, and the smell of his soap.

"Better," I said, my voice a sigh. Sleep clawed at me even though I wanted to stay awake for the meeting with Rath and General Pace.

So much better. His warmth made everything better.

"Sleep, my Flame," he whispered, kissing my temple.

"No," I said, turning my face toward his, even though I didn't open my eyes. I wasn't any less likely to have my dreams claim me than before. But I didn't want them to. I needed to hear about Lehar. What I wished for more than anything in that moment was to feel his lips on mine.

Finally, he shifted, and the heat of his kiss intensified the warmth coming through his clothes, and soaking into the rest of my body.

I hummed a sound of approval and pressed to deepen the kiss, but he pulled back, and looked into my eyes, his own shining golden and soft.

"Cinder," he said, his voice low as my heart sped up, "please rest, and allow yourself to heal."

He lifted a hand, and brushed a wet piece of my hair behind my ear, pulling it away from my face.

"My King," I said, relishing the way his eyes squeezed shut, and a tremor ran through his body. Only two words and I could prove to myself that he missed being able to kiss me with abandon as much as I missed kissing him.

Opening his eyes, the gold in them shifted in the low light of the setting sun streaming through the windows. Regret showed right alongside the love shining from him.

"Flame, please, we have the rest of our lives. You need to get better."

But we were at war. And the rest of our lives might not be very long. Well, the rest of his would be no matter what that meant for me. I would see to that even if I had to defend him while in this pitiful state. But he didn't want to hear me say that again.

"No matter how long we have," I said, lifting a hand to run my fingers through his hair, "it won't be enough time with you."

"I love you," he said, pressing his lips to mine in a chaste kiss that still managed to make the blood sing in my veins. My hand tangle in his hair.

"You must be feeling a lot better," Rath said, and Tristan broke the kiss to lean his forehead against mine with a groan while I smiled at him.

Damn it, Rath. He had terrible timing.

"Hello, Rath," I said, not taking my face away from Tristan, but letting him pull back from me before I turned my head toward Rath and General Pace. I nestled into his chest, "No, I'm not that much better. But you're lucky Gus and Jacquetta even let you into the apartment."

General Pace turned a flat, unamused expression on Rath standing next to her.

"What did he do to Lady Jacquetta and Lady Augustina?" she asked.

Even though she kept her voice calm, I knew asking the question was a warning to him.

And so did he, because he swallowed, and looked away from her level gaze. Without Madam Valentin around to protect her daughter and daughter-in-law, it was more than clear that our General was taking up the role.

"Nothing," Rath said. "I didn't do anything. I just showed up." Eyes wide, he whipped his head around to look at the General.

I couldn't help smiling while Tristan laughed behind me.

"He walked in on me in the bath," I said, earning me a look of utter betrayal from Rath.

General Pace burst out with a harsh bark of laughter, drawing every eye in the room, before shaking her head, and stepping away from Rath.

"What?" Rath asked, his voice tight.

"You should worry more about what Duchess Cinder will do to you if you try that again when she is healthy," the General said, grinning at him. "Or what the King will do to you when he is finally willing to let her go."

"King?" Rath said, turning to look at us both, actual fear in him this time. "Flame?"

"Oh, Rath," I said, enjoying this a little too much, "remind me to spar with you as soon as I'm able to. It will be good…practice."

Tristan laughed again, and kissed my head.

"Maybe we should…um…get back to the point here." Rath ran a hand along the back of his neck, and swallowed, shuffling his feet.

When I first met him, I didn't think he was capable of becoming flustered. But this side of him was fun. At least for me.

He said he wanted to use things against me before. Maybe he would think about that a little more the next time he decided it was a good idea to make me the butt of his jokes.

"Fine," Tristan said, shifting to get us both a little more upright in the bed. He gestured for General Pace and Rath to take seats in the chairs that were a fixture in my room since Tristan took so many meetings there during my recovery.

"Before we get to whatever you need the King for, General, how is Meg doing?"

"You chose well," she said, "and the people are more than happy with the Guard troops we sent to patrol just outside the border."

"Good," I nodded and let out a tension-filled breath.

I didn't doubt Meg—it was why I chose her—and I didn't doubt how angry my people would be when they found out about Ash's betrayal of them. But I did worry about how we could successfully protect them from Ash and his army marching in and claiming the land again. Hearing they solved the unbreathable air issue by stationing Guard troops along the border outside the area where the ashes fell alleviated some of my worry.

"So, is this meeting about how we're finally going to use

your tip from Amethyst?" I asked, not bothering to dither around anymore with Rath's bad manners. I was the only one in the room waiting for details of Lehar. Tristan cared, but he just took the General's word that she was handling things while I was unable to.

After being nothing but a hindrance for too many days, I was determined to get back to helping defeat my brother.

Just knowing my brother caused so much death and destruction made me ache in a way that none of Jacquetta's remedies would fix. The only way I knew to lessen it at all was to kill him, and end this war.

"Yes," Rath said, then shook his head, and looked at me as he leaned back in the chair. "I mean no."

He smirked, and I was sure I looked like I wanted to punch him, because that didn't make any sense.

"William is already with our ally on the other side of the border, and they're blocking Duke Asshole's path to retreat. Even though our ally isn't willing to send his troops across the border—he can't afford to get that involved—he's more than willing to have his troops do some 'training' along the border, and make it clear to that asshole that crossing into Amethyst would be bad for his health."

"Our ally?" I asked.

"Second Prince Nevan wishes you a speedy recovery," General Pace said.

At that, I almost sat up, but my body froze instead as a defense mechanism.

"But his family," I said, knowing exactly how much risk he was taking on even just amassing his troops like he did.

"The royal family of Amethyst is very concerned about their missing niece, and hope that she will be found soon," General Pace said, tilting her chin up with a small smile on her face.

"Prince Nevan's cover story to all the other countries is that...what?" I said, trying to puzzle it out as I spoke, and not believing he could keep this going for more than a minute. "The Marquessa vanished in the middle of a war? How careless do they think we are with their family members?"

Visions of revenge plots from the Amethyst royal family swam in my head and my stomach roiled. This was bad. There was no way this wouldn't end terribly.

"On the contrary," General Pace said, "this betrayal by Corvid on Amethyst—the plot to crown your brother in Onyx and Amethyst—has turned every royal against the crows. The last of the reticence to leave their lucrative trade deal with them is gone."

Rubbing a finger along my brow, I tried to figure out what Nevan's whole play here was.

"But what is he going to do when we kill her or capture her?" I shook my head as a pain began in my temple. Nevan's games were too much to think about right now. "We can't give the snake back to them."

"I think he told them the truth," Rath said, and my headache grew worse.

"Then why are they lying?" I asked, squinting now through the pain. "Should we be worried about a plot against us from the royal family in retaliation for her loss?"

"From what William reports," Rath said, leaning forward to rest his elbows on his knees, "they don't want to face the tidal wave of problems if the world knew one of their own was part of this war, and planned on taking over Amethyst as well—even though the Crown Prince was devastated to find out she's married. And the best part is..." Rath paused, grinning like he could taste our anticipation. I raised a brow, and he finally went on. "...the lands just on the other side of the border from Mariposa belong to our best, purple friend."

Letting out a breath of a laugh, I shook my head, and rested against Tristan again, my headache finally lifting.

"Nevan's lands are across the border from Mariposa," I said, wondering why I didn't know that already. But I never really asked him for additional information, and doubted he would have given it to me at the time if I did. He was still hard to keep up with because he was so much better at the small, suspicious aspects of court life.

"But wait," I said, cocking my head at Rath, and wondering how trustworthy this information was, "who is William?"

CHAPTER 4

WITHOUT ANSWERS

Tristan

"Oh, perfect," I said, laughing and shaking my head, knowing exactly where this was going. "Don't get him started on the complicated way his crew works."

"Your crew?" Cinder asked, sounding more interested than was healthy if she didn't want to have us all stuck here for the next two days while Rath tried and failed to explain it all to her. I had known the man forever. That meant I received regular updates while his crew was forming. And I still didn't understand it all. "William is a part of your crew? Is he part of your spy network?"

"William is my second mate," Rath said, getting that overly proud look in his eye he always did when he spoke of Will or Heddy, his first mate. "He doesn't usually do this kind of work, but I'm here with King."

"And your second mate? What does that mean on a ship?" Cinder asked.

General Pace opened her mouth like she was going to answer, but I had a feeling she would have provided Cinder with a concise description of the way the military ran crews. Which wasn't at all how Rath ran things.

Rath laughed, leaning forward, his elbows on his knees, and a wide grin on his face.

"You see, Flame," he said. I groaned, burying my face in her neck, not knowing what he was going to say, but having zero doubt this was going to be embarrassing somehow, "on my ship, I have a first mate—her name is Heddy—and a second mate— his name is William. On my other ship, I have an under captain. Most of that crew is of my father's old ship, and they run theirs like their own duchy. I am king of both."

"Oh…okay," she said, sounding like she still wasn't following at all. I braced myself for the overly-detailed explanation that was bound to be the embarrassing part. "But why wouldn't your first mate be the one in Amethyst, then?"

I laughed into her shoulder, and she twisted to look at me, her brow furrowed.

For one second—not that it was a word I ever associated with her—I thought she was cute.

"King hasn't told you anything about me, has he?" Rath asked, his grin turning into a smirk.

She looked at me again, and there went the cute. She snapped back to dangerous, with a fire in her eyes at the thought that I was holding anything back from her, just like Rath wanted.

"Cinder knows all about your connection to me, Rath," I said, for his knowledge and her benefit. I put emphasis on his name, just in case he got any bright ideas about trying to get me in trouble again. "Besides, we should focus on the important thing here. Which is the ongoing war."

"When this war is over, Flame, and you finally come spend some time on my ship, you'll meet Heddy and William, and you'll be able to see for yourself what having mates means to a pirate." Rath winked at her, and I decided I would do everything in my power to ensure that never happened.

"Rath," I said, my voice harder than I expected it to be.

"Hey," he said, raising his hands, and softening his smile to look as harmless as possible, which for a man the size, shape, and look of Rath, was surprisingly effective, "she asked."

"Back to the point," I said, trying to sound as if giving the command of a king, but landing somewhere closer to irritated.

Cinder lifted a hand to run her fingers through my hair, which was more than she usually moved. After everything she did today, I kept expecting her to fall asleep in the middle of a sentence as she had been doing since she fell. But my Flame was as strong as perfectly forged steel. I kissed her shoulder.

"The point is," General Pace said, "we should move forces to flank the Duke's."

"Yes," Cinder said, her voice like a knife. "Box him in. Don't let him and his crows dictate where we meet them on the battlefield."

"I like having you back to normal, Flame," Rath said, grinning wide.

"We all do," General Pace said. I let out a long breath, knowing Cinder was still so far from normal, but more than relieved that she was closer to it. It was clear she was headed that direction, no matter how awful her back looked now.

"How long will it take to get the Guard regimens in place?" I asked, trying to figure out if Cinder would be well enough by then for us to visit them to tell them how important they were to what we were doing.

"Not long at all," General Pace said, "But that is not the biggest problem. They will be in place in a matter of a couple days with little fuss. Supplies are easily transported to them, and the leaders of Breakwater and Tavis are more than willing to let us use their lands to support them from the rear of their positions, should it be needed."

"Then what's the biggest problem?" Cinder asked. Although she tried to keep that steel in her voice, the edge of her exhaustion was finally showing through her will to keep it at bay. Her hands stilled in mine, and her head rested against my chest.

It was as if knowing the kingdom needed her to heal forced her to rest.

Even though we were talking about challenges, of which there never seemed to be an end, feeling her relax into the safety of my arms was enough to make me smile.

General Pace's gaze went toward the window as if she were looking for crows instead of staying on us, which made me brace myself for what she was about to report. "Right now, the biggest problem is that the crows are no longer with Ash's forces."

At that, Cinder's relaxed posture stiffened. She lifted her head, her body going still and hard where she lay on me.

"What does that mean?" she asked, her voice low and careful. "Where are they? Have they attacked somewhere else on their own?"

"So far," General Pace said, looking back at both of us, meeting my eyes and then Cinder's, "they were spotted gathering over the Marshlands."

"Fuck," I said, chewing on my lip, and wishing I could know what was happening in my Kingdom at all times without the delay in news. Throughout the war so far, it felt like we were behind no matter how hard we tried to be ready.

"I don't understand," Cinder said, drawing me out of my frustrated thoughts, and back to the conversation.

"One of the things you missed," I said, trying not to make it seem like it was a bad thing that she was not very aware the previous week, "is that because of the guards moving all over the country, and the people trying to tuck themselves away for their own safety, some of the clergy are struggling with their holy places."

"But they don't like people. They hardly speak," she said, and I understood the confusion if that was her experience with the clergy she encountered.

What must she have thought of our Shield Elio? He was a far cry away from the kind of solitary figure some of the clergy were.

"Not all of them live alone at their shrines and holy sites," General Pace said.

"I know that." Cinder sounded annoyed, but also confused. I realized that she may never have spent any time with the High Sect.

"Cinder, the Marshlands are not a part of any duchy," I said, running a hand along her arm, "they belong to the High Sect. The entire connected waterways of the Marshlands are considered holy sites for them. One of the ways they live there on their own, far away from the charity that is given to the clergy at their little springs and pools, is from donations of people who go to the marshes and pay for their prayers, their healings, and to harvest blessed fish and the like."

"Blessed fish?" she asked, sounding more than a little skeptical that anyone would put stock in such a thing.

"Many people believe in the divinity of water," Rath said, pointing a finger at her with a smile like she should know better than to question it too much.

She let out a small laugh and nodded.

Of course, Rath, the pirate who lived on the sea his entire life, believed in the divinity of water. None of us faulted him for that. Cinder was just a lot less likely to believe in anything she couldn't see or touch beyond her own instinct.

My Dragon Queen didn't even believe in the Dragon King

powers—which I thought hilarious whether they were ever real or not.

"Fine," Cinder said, and Rath grinned, "so that's what the clergy is upset about? That all the people have hidden themselves away, so they aren't providing the clergy with money?"

"It is more than that," General Pace said. "Even the clergy in their little ponds and pools are struggling without many people remembering to venture out enough to drop off food and supplies while the threat of the crows hangs over everyone."

"We need to get them the things they need," Cinder turned her head to look at me as if I didn't already put that intention into practice. I kissed her temple.

She proved to me every day that she would make a good queen, and she didn't even realize it.

"Already in motion," I said. "The problem is that if the clergy and the High Sect get too frustrated through this war, they could turn public sentiment against us, and make a play for a more prominent role in the court."

"Their only Shield is already at court often," she said.

"But he has no real power," General Pace said. "Some in the High Sect want our country to work more like Algodona."

Cinder groaned, and I had to bite my lip to keep from laughing.

"If we were," I said, tightening my hold on my fierce Queen, "you would have won your crown in a minute."

"And you would be a strange hermit draped in robes," she said, her voice full of distrust. "And you would not be my Archer King. No, thank you."

Her Archer King. I liked that. It made me wonder if she found something about my archery attractive. I knew she liked my formal clothes, and it was true that I had never heard anyone speak of the Conduit of Algodona as ever being seen without the hooded robes that covered him from head to toe.

I was going to come back to this topic with her later when

we were alone, and she was feeling good enough. For now, I just kissed the top of her head.

"Flame," Rath said, shaking his head, "you need to get better fast because you two are both far too easily distracted right now. It isn't healthy for the country."

She laughed. It was a contained sound, so she didn't hurt herself. But I smiled, too.

"Right, then," she said, her voice lapsing back into seriousness, "so what do we do about the High Sect and the clergy? And what does it mean that the crows were spotted over the marshes?"

"There is the problem," General Pace said, and I agreed.

"We don't know the answer to either question," I said, wondering if I would get to stay with Cinder until she was fully better, or not.

CHAPTER 5

TAKE IT SLOW

Cinder

Getting out of my bed the next day, Tristan refused to let go of me as I shuffled. I tried to remember falling asleep while they reviewed scenarios for dealing with the crows in the Marshlands, and the pressure from the High Sect. But, no matter how I ran through it all in my head, I couldn't remember.

Clearly, whatever injury Jacquetta thought I sustained to my brain hadn't fully healed.

Fantastic.

A sharp stab flashed across my ribs in my back on one side, and I grunted.

"Just let me carry you," Tristan said, his eyes bright green, scanning me head to toe. "You don't have to push yourself this hard."

"My King," I said, my voice still too thin, which only served to make me want to keep trying as he squeezed his eyes shut for a moment. Pain flashed across his face on my behalf. "Everyone needs me to get better, faster. You can't pamper the Queen when the country needs her."

I swallowed. I almost never referred to myself as "Queen" out loud. The word still felt wrong in my mouth.

But Tristan's eyes flew open, and the green gave way to molten gold in the center.

"You are beautiful," I said, forgetting for a moment about the ache in my body, and the reason we were having this discussion.

He smiled, soft and perfect, which only made him even more gorgeous to me.

With one hand supporting my arm, his other cupping my elbow, my hand grasped his forearm. He let go of my elbow to tuck a piece of hair behind my ear, revealing the scar on my cheek that he ran a thumb down before he placed his palm along my cheek.

"Nothing is more beautiful than my Queen," he said, leaning in and kissing me.

For the first time since the fall, this kiss held nothing back. I almost pulled him down on top of me.

But I had a purpose today. As much as I hoped it would soon lead to me pulling him tight to me so I could feel him inside me again, I needed to focus on getting out of the bed first.

"Do you want me to stand next to you as Queen?" I asked after I broke the kiss, touching his forehead to mine.

"More than anything," he said, which I knew wasn't true. He wanted peace more than that, but I smiled anyway.

"Then I need to get out of this bed," I said, and he sighed.

Pulling his face back from mine, he set his jaw, and braced my other arm with his before he nodded.

Ready.

I planted my feet, and used my legs, digging my heels into the floor, to scoot forward, closer to the edge of the bed.

My back didn't scream at me. It was a low aching, and I took the chance to breathe deeply before I reset my feet, and relaxed my back.

Saving my core muscles as much as possible, I pushed up, my leg muscles complaining about going far too long without use.

But they were strong. They would recover fast. I just needed to use them. My muscles could do all the yelling they wanted to, but they were going to help me get better no matter how much they griped about it.

Finally, I was upright, holding tight to Tristan's arms, my back straight, my core only throbbing instead of arcing in agony.

Tristan scanned me again, his gaze darting all over me, as if my injuries were suddenly all over my body, not just on my back.

"I'm fine," I said, my voice stronger now that I managed this much. "I can do this."

"You can do anything," he said, his chest rising and falling in deep breaths even as he stood tall, looking every bit the King before his kingdom.

"Ready for the next part?" I asked, smiling and lifting a brow, pretending to be cocky just in case it might help me hang onto a little bit of confidence.

"Just don't be afraid to tell me when you're done," he said.

"Fear? I don't know him," I said, and Tristan let out a huff of a laugh.

"Don't push yourself too hard, Cinder, please."

I leaned forward, and pressed my forehead to his chin. He shifted to lean his forehead to mine.

"Tristan," I said, keeping my eyes closed so he wouldn't spot a bit of fear in me, "Stop. I know. I'll be fine."

He laughed as he pulled away before ducking to put his lips to mine.

"Sure. I'll stop now."

We smiled at each other, and I let go of one of his arms so he could step to the side while I gripped tight to his other forearm with my other hand. He squeezed my elbow in reassurance as he shifted to support that arm with both of his hands.

My first step sent a sharp stab up my back. So did the second. By the time I made it to the door, the edges of the pain were blunted enough for me to continue into the main room, and toward the table.

"Cinder," Gus yelled, running into the room from her old room.

Jacquetta appeared in the doorway behind her, and shook her head, her eyes tightening.

"I thought we talked about this," Jacquetta said.

"You talked," I said, as Gus hovered on my other side. I walked around the table, and headed back toward my room, "I just didn't argue."

"But you can't even stay awake, yet," Gus said, sidestepping along with me, staring at me as if she would catch me before Tristan did, even though he was still holding my arm.

"Maybe," I said, "but I can't just wait until everything is perfect to try and do what I can to get better. I have things to do."

"Just because you want to get naked with the King," Jacquetta said, "doesn't mean you should rush this."

Even though Tristan ducked, turning his face away from Jacquetta, he couldn't hide the grin on his face from me, or the way his shoulders shook with laughter.

"I'm not doing this so I can be with my King," I said. "That's just an added benefit."

"Cinder," Gus said, trying to sound serious, but she laughed without stifling it like he did.

I smiled fully because for the first time in a while it felt like I could get back to fighting soon enough to help win this war. I kept on my track back through my doors toward the bed.

For some reason, making a joke about being naked with

Tristan was enough to get them to stop haranguing me. Which, if I were honest, I was very much looking forward to. All this time spent in bed with him—having him love me in all the ways he could except making love to me—was making my want of him almost as acute as the pain in my back.

Plus, I wanted to marry him. And I wanted to be well enough to enjoy my wedding night.

I couldn't get better fast enough.

We made it to the bed, and Tristan shuffled my arms, turning so he faced me again with both my arms braced on his.

He nodded, and I took a deep breath before using my legs to lower myself down to the edge of the bed.

Once I was finally sitting, he moved a hand into mine, threading our fingers together before he climbed behind me on the bed, and slipped an arm around my waist.

"You did so well," he said, kissing my shoulder.

The warmth of his chest on my back soothed the growing ache from using it so much that it allowed me to breathe deeply as I relaxed against him.

"Does this mean you are going to want to go back to fighting?" Jacquetta asked, her hands on her hips, clearly gearing up to give me another lecture.

"Not yet," I said, trying to hide my grin as she deflated.

"Good," she said, recovering well even if Gus shook her head, and shot her a loving and long-suffering grin.

"But," I said, holding in my laughter while Tristan shook me with his, his face still in my shoulder, and both Gus and Jacquetta braced themselves, "I do want to put on real clothes."

CHAPTER 6

BACK TO WORK

Tristan

Walking with Cinder down the stairs took longer than she probably thought it would. Not just because she needed to take each step carefully, refusing my offer to carry her, but because half the palace lined up to greet to her, to celebrate her being whole and alive.

She kept her face as full of smiles as possible, but the tightness of her lips along her teeth, and the way her eyes widened a fraction every time she looked my way were dead giveaways. I knew she hated it.

My Queen detested this kind of attention. The social kind was torture for her. When she couldn't get away, no one else was a proper distraction, so she had to speak, and keep herself contained at the same time—to her it was painful.

I offered words, interjections, things that would help her as she was greeted and complimented again and again.

But still she hated it.

This was part of why she didn't think she would make a good queen. Yet I knew that her determination to do what was best for the people, combined with the people's love for her, meant that she was wrong, and I was right.

Queen Cinder, the Flame of Onyx, would be a better queen than she could imagine.

Leaning down, I kissed her hand, surprising her and the Chamberlain, making them both stop in their conversation.

"My King?" she asked, her voice merely a whisper.

"Everyone," I said, letting my voice carry down the stairs and to the line of people, "forgive me, but we must make quicker progress to accomplish everything we wish to today."

Cinder beamed, and her joy caused everyone else to smile even through their disappointment.

"First," she said, turning back to the Chamberlain, who I was surprised to see was more than willing to take her offered other hand, "I need to speak with you privately later. Will you come to my rooms to meet with me?"

"Yes, of course, Duchess Cinder," the Chamberlain said, chest puffed, and smile proud.

She let go of the Chamberlain's hand, and nodded before we went down another step.

With a nod, a hello, or a hand clasp, she acknowledged everyone who waited on the stairs, still giving them what they lined up for, if not for the duration they wished.

Rath thought it was a good idea to tell the people she died when she plummeted to the ground, but this was why we couldn't. The blow her death would be to the people—not to mention the fact that I couldn't stomach the idea of pretending it were true—made his plan impossible.

Every step we took, she grew stronger, got closer to healing, and walked further into the fable that grew around her.

One of the unintended consequences of Cinder surviving her fall was that the stories of the King's Fighter who would one day be Queen were growing more important to the country than the legend of the Dragon Kings.

I didn't mind. As far as I was concerned, the more the people loved her, the more we had in common.

Finally, we left the palace, and stood atop the stairs into the courtyard.

But even here the people weren't done celebrating her life.

The guards stopped what they were doing, some stepping out from the training area, all of them looking to their soon-to-be queen, standing tall next to me with only my hands on her arm for support, after death came so close to stealing her from us. All of them lifted their hands in a salute they reserved for me, and I smiled as I saluted them in turn.

Cinder, swallowing, took her hand from mine. I tensed, and prepared to catch her should she need it. She returned the salute in perfect form, showing no sign of weakness.

For a moment, she held her stance, as did the guards. Then they shoved their fists into the sky and cheered.

She dropped her hand, grasping tightly to mine, leaning on me a touch more than before. Only then did she smile, and take a deep breath.

"Alright," she said, "let's get down there. I need to move."

"Cinder," I said, helping her as she wanted even though I shook my head, and hoped this wouldn't end up with her in far too much pain tomorrow, "maybe we should take a break before we do this."

"Not you, too," she said, her eyes bright as we made it down the steps, and started across the courtyard.

"I know how much you want to get back to healthy. And how much you need this kind of activity. But you also need to accept that not pushing yourself too hard is part of healing."

She leaned closer to me, resting her head on my shoulder as we kept walking.

"How about," she said as we passed under the arch into the throwing and shooting range, "when the war is over, I will rest."

No matter how hard I tried to remain stern, to press the issue one more time, I failed and laughed instead.

Cinder pulled back from me, grinning, and turned dancing eyes toward the weapons along the wall.

"Do you want to try your archery skills?" I asked, knowing what the answer would be even before she turned a flat, level stare on me.

"Tristan," she said. Even though her voice was tinged with irritation, it was still a beautiful thing to hear her say my name. I reached out to cup her cheek, her flat affect switching immediately to a smile before she pulled back. "Stop it."

"Stop what?" I asked, stepping closer to her again, which only made her narrow her eyes.

"Being cute. You're distracting me, and I have work to do. Now, I don't want to shoot a bow. That's your weapon." She was so serious, so grave. I nodded, and stepped back.

"Fine. But I can't stop being cute." I grinned as she rolled her eyes, and I pulled down some knives for her to throw. "Especially when I love you so much."

"Why did I like that?" she asked, laughing and taking the knives from me, slipping them into the cuff on the arm I still supported. "That was a terrible line."

"You liked it because you love me so much, too." I leaned down, stealing a kiss before she could stop me, feeling the curve of her mouth as she smiled while my lips were on hers.

"Come on," she said, pulling away, the grin still tugging at her mouth. She yanked on my arm so I could help her walk to the target.

I walked with her into place in a line, and took a step back toward the wall to get a bow. Cinder caught hold of my jacket, and tugged me close to her.

Her eyes danced with mischief, and her lips pouted, the corners still turning up just a tad even as she fought it.

"No matter how this practice turns out," she said, "I need to do this again tomorrow."

I didn't follow. Furrowing my brow, I wondered why she wouldn't do this tomorrow. How did she expect this practice to end?

"Alright," I said, and she let me go, finally giving in to the smile that burst onto her face.

She shuffled into her throwing stance. Her independent movements were still more careful, weaker. I made my way to the bow and arrows that I needed for my own practice.

But, even as I made a long production of getting my weapons, I braced myself, watching her.

This was far more than a simple walk around her rooms. This was more than a walk down the stairs. Even the grand staircase was nothing compared to the effort that her body would exert just throwing knives at the target.

More than the work involved, I was concerned that if her injuries—especially the one Jacquetta said she sustained to her brain—meant that her ability to throw was impaired, she wouldn't handle it well.

What would it do to Cinder if she could never fight again?

No matter what, I would love her and want her as my queen. Selfishly, a part of me wanted her to not be able to fight anymore. But it was a tiny piece. The rest of me wanted her to be happy, and doing this made her far too happy for me to truly want her to lose it.

As my heart lodged in my throat, beating an unsteady rhythm, I held my breath, and she lined up her hand with a knife at the ready.

Her other hand was tucked at her back with another knife ready.

Cinder threw, and, with a swift flick of her hand, the knife hit home at the bottom edge of the center of the target. She pivoted, slower than she used to, flicked her other hand, and let her second knife fly.

It struck the top edge of the center of the target.

Another pivot, a grab of another knife from her cuff, and another throw.

She kept moving, her footing sure, her body fluid, even if it wasn't as fast as before. Cinder didn't do all the crouching and twirling that she used to.

Finally, her pattern of knives was complete: a perfect cross on the center of the target with one blade in the middle of it all.

Just as I sucked in greedy breaths, Cinder sagged where she stood, her hands curling into fists.

I dropped the bow and arrows in my hands. They clattered to the ground as I darted to Cinder, grabbing her arms, and holding her up.

"Too much?" I asked, as she dragged in deep breaths, squeezing her eyes shut. "Cinder, if we need to go back—"

"No," she said, her voice strong even as she kept her eyes closed.

"Alright, my Queen." I kissed her forehead, and held on as she regained mastery over her body, despite whatever pain ran rampant through her.

Finally, she sighed and looked up at me.

"Let's get to work," she said with a smile as she squeezed my hands, and pulled hers away.

She said it as if she expected me to practice. Instead, I stepped to the side, and waited until she needed me again. Even if all she ended up needing me for was to carry her back into the palace, my place was here, by her side, as she healed and prepared to keep fighting.

CHAPTER 7

THAT WILL WORK

Cinder

By the time I got to the top of the stairs, every bit of strength in my back and muscles was spent.

I sagged into Tristan's waiting arms.

"Don't worry, Cinder," he said, scooping me up so he had me under my knees and behind my back, tucking me close to his chest, "I've got you."

"Tristan," I said, letting my eyes slip shut, and my body relax.

"How bad does it hurt?"

"No pain." And there wasn't. Not anymore. As soon as I put down the knives, and took his hand, the pain ebbed away. Now there were aches, a lot of aches, but they were only from sore muscles no longer used to moving let alone working. And I was willing to admit I had pushed my body to do more than I should have. "My body is just tired."

"Maybe you should have gone a little easier on yourself today."

As much as I wanted to be frustrated that he was giving me a version of I-told-you-so, I couldn't be. Not when he said it like I was punishing myself for being injured, because he was right about that. And especially not when he said it in that soft voice full of concern for me.

"I love you," I said, leaving the conversation there because there was no point arguing this.

He knew I would push myself too hard tomorrow, too. He also knew I wasn't going to allow anyone to stop me.

"Cinder," he said, my name a caress in his mouth, "I love you."

As soon as he opened the door to my rooms, the peace of being with him in the hallway, and all the relaxation of being in his arms were wrenched away from me.

"Now what did you do to yourself?" Jacquetta said, her voice as hard as his was soft.

"She's just tired," Tristan said, tightening his hold on me.

"Let's get her in a bath," Gus said, her hand on Jacquetta's back.

Jacquetta sighed and nodded while Tristan carried me into the bathroom.

They prepared the bath for me while he continued to hold me, leaning against the counter. I ran a hand along his bearded cheek.

"You can put me down now, my King," I said, my voice low for only his ears.

He turned his head, and kissed my palm.

"But I don't want to let you go," he said, matching my tone, and filling it with more.

As simple as the words were, they meant more to me than he probably thought. They meant that what I was planning was the right thing.

"I'm not in danger like I was." I pulled his face down to mine and kissed him, showing him that I was telling the truth, putting all the strength I had left into the kiss before I pulled back. "Put me down. Jacquetta and Gus will help me into the tub, and you can go take care of all the things I know have piled up while the King has locked himself away with me."

Tristan's smile was a gift that made it easier to stand without flinching as he set me down.

With another kiss, this one promising more when he returned to me, Tristan let go of me and left.

But no matter how much I acted like I was fine, the pain wracked through me again the second I stood on my tired legs. I held my exhausted back straight, and watched him leave.

Still, I held onto his kiss while the tub filled, and used it to hang on long enough to be sure Tristan was out of my rooms before I sagged against the counter behind me, letting out a plaintive, pathetic cry.

"Cinder," Gus yelled, grabbing me before I could drop all the way to the floor.

"I..." a wave of pain swept through me, and I gritted my teeth, "I just need to take a bath and rest."

There. I managed to get it all out that time, and avoided making them worry more.

"Fine," Jacquetta said, beginning to untie my simple dress as Gus pulled off my cuffs, "but we'll see if your bruising and injuries are worse."

She unwrapped the bandages from me, revealing the poultice still coating my back.

Gus helped her wipe away the poultice, the gentle swipes still enough to make me grind my teeth and suppress a cry of pain. My bruises must still have been lurid and terrible.

"Damn it, Cinder," Gus muttered.

"Irresponsible," Jacquetta said, wiping more. "You think nothing's going to hurt you, and I think you're starting to buy your own legend. You believe you'll never die."

"You must be really angry with me," I said, as they helped me walk to the tub and climb over the edge. The hot water and Jacquetta's fragrant additives, her herbs and oils and flowers, always managed to help me in whatever way I needed. They immediately relieved the aches in my legs as I slipped into the water. I let out a sigh.

Once my back was submerged too, the instant easing of my aches and pains was so intense compared to how thoroughly they wracked my body before that it was almost euphoric.

"Why do you think Jacquetta must be so mad at you?" Gus asked, using a pitcher to soak my hair.

"Because she slipped out of her formal pronunciations," I said, smiling to myself at how the most proper of the three of us wasn't the one about to become a queen.

"Do you want me to use only formal speech when it's just the three of us?" Jacquetta asked.

"No," I said, opening my eyes, and looking at her as she crushed more flower petals into the bath. "That's silly."

"Good," she said, offering a small smile, even though it was accompanied by an exasperated huff, "I only speak that way in front of the King. Mother's ghost might come back to haunt me if I didn't."

"Please don't say that," I said, laughing, "because that means she would expect you to act all uptight with me after I become Queen."

"Well," Gus said with a scoff and a wry grin, "I think even Madam Valentin would forgive us for continuing to talk to *you* however we want."

"After all," Jacquetta said, nose in the air with her most superior look stamped on her face—which, for the daughter of Madam Valentin, meant that no royal of any kingdom would be able to top it, "we knew you when you were still Lady Cinder who didn't know how to dance."

I laughed along with them, allowing the soothing heat of the water to soak into me, and all of Jacquetta's remedies to carry the pain away from me before it rooted deeper into my wounds, becoming more than a fleeting, transient thing.

After they washed my hair, I had a dilemma.

"Gus, Jacquetta," I asked, "tonight, the Chamberlain will be coming to have a private meeting with me. After that, I expect Tristan to come to me again."

"Sorry, Cinder," Gus said, and I furrowed my brow, confused as to why she would apologize, "but if you don't know how to handle him in bed after all this time, we can't help you."

"Flower," Jacquetta said, smacking Gus on the hand, and ducking her head while Gus let out an uproarious laugh. I shook my head and grinned.

"No. I'm fine there."

"Oh, good," Jacquetta said, "because she was about to be really embarrassing."

Gus grabbed her wife, kissing her with a loud smack sound on the cheek while I laughed.

Jacquetta shook her head.

"What I want to know is," I said, trying to get back on track, "do we have anything that would be appropriate to meet with the Chamberlain in, while still comfortable enough to lay down in, and easy enough to get off."

"See, Star," Gus said, gesturing to me, "I wasn't stepping out of line. Cinder is as bad as I am."

"You don't know the things I've said to Tristan. I might be worse."

Jacquetta covered her face in her hands, and let out a high-pitched screaming sound while Gus and I lost any composure we had laughing.

Finally, we all recovered enough for Jacquetta to uncover her face, and, even though her skin was too dark to see much of a blush, it was suddenly awfully flushed. I was pretty sure that if she was pale like me, she would have been red.

A day full of accomplishments, then.

"Yes, Cinder," Jacquetta said, shaking her head while Gus wiggled her eyebrows, "I think I have something that will work."

CHAPTER 8

SOMEHOW

Tristan

"Tell me we know where he is," I said, dragging my hands through my hair, more than distracted by the fact that I was away from Cinder for the first time for any significant length since she fell. Even the distance from one side of the palace to the other was enough to fray my nerves.

I needed to get my mind right.

"Unfortunately, we have yet to find him," General Pace said, standing on the other side of my desk in my public office. Rath lounged in a chair next to her, and other people were gathered in little groups around the room, waiting for me to handle their issues as well.

"But we have some idea, correct?" I asked, trying to keep my voice from projecting exactly how much we needed to hear from him.

"Not yet," Rath said, "but we'll find him."

"Rathmoreland seems to think that Shield Elio should be easy to find." General Pace pursed her lips, and I wanted to do the same.

"If a Shield does not want to be found," I said, my voice low so the others in the room wouldn't be alarmed or overhear too much, "then I seriously doubt our ability to hunt him down."

"King, I always find who or what I'm looking for. And a giant, loud-mouthed, bearded Shield should stand out." Rath leaned back in the chair, one leg flung over an arm of it, no sign of concern on his face at all.

"You would think that," I said, slumping back in my chair, wishing I were with Cinder having this conversation. Being with her made everything seem like it would turn out better than I thought. "But the problem with any member of the clergy, including a Shield or someone in the High Sect, is that they can hide themselves away in their little creeks and ponds while people pass by without ever knowing they were there."

At that, Rath's face clouded over. A thoughtfulness descended upon him, stilling his leg where it swung off the arm of the chair.

He played with his fingers in his lap before he looked back to me, "How likely would I be to turn one of the clergy or the High Sect?"

"Turn one of them into a source for you?" General Pace asked. The skepticism in her voice was answer enough.

Rath didn't have a lot of interaction with any of the clergy besides Shield Elio, and the salt singers who lived in the occasional cave near the sea. He didn't know the way the clergy really operated. Although we all knew how they wanted to operate.

"Some of their people travel to other countries, and they're safe there because they never get involved in politics," I said, "just like the Protectorate."

A snort of derision popped out of Rath, and his leg went

back to swinging as I kicked myself for making that unfortunate comparison.

"Well," I said, following up to make my point clearer, "the Protectorate is not *supposed* to get involved, anyway."

"How do the clergy expect to continue to maintain that level of ease going between countries if they become so connected to our government that we're more like Agodona?" Rath looked truly confused, but I just sighed.

"Once they obtain that level of control and power…" I said, wishing I didn't have to tell him this. All it did was bring up the ugly conversation I had with the Vane, the head of the High Sect right after I was coronated, "…I was assured they would be glad to set aside their easy travel. For them, the trade is worth it."

"Exactly how much of the country do they want control over?" Rath asked, because we never really worried about them getting a true foothold on power until now. "The Marshlands are already larger than some duchies."

"Yes, well," I said, choosing not to guess or worry about it. No matter how much they wanted, I wouldn't be able to give any of it to them.

"Maybe," Rath muttered, his eyes narrowed, and his focus far away from this room, "maybe I can talk one into thinking that if they told me things, kept me apprised of the situation, and let me know what the plot was, I could get your ear, get them closer to their goal."

"Be careful," General Pace said, "since we do not know what their true goal is, it might be dangerous to broach the subject, or even try to play that game, to hint that you know."

Rath waved a hand, as if he were dismissing every bit of her warning and concern. I sat forward, and leveled a stare at him.

"It is good advice, Rath," I said, waiting until he sat up straight and paid serious attention to me. "They might already be working with Ash and the Corvids thinking they could benefit if I fall."

His eyes narrowed, and his jaw tightened for a moment before his lips turned into a sharp-edged grin.

"They would find that any attempt to profit off of such a thing would end up being a problem for them." His voice was as weathered and strong as the hull of his ship. I smiled back, knowing that if they took me during that war, at least Rath, his crew, his spies, and anyone else he knew would haunt them until they regretted my loss.

"Great," General Pace said with mock enthusiasm, "except that in that scenario, our King would be dead, we would be hunted as his friends, the traitor would be on the throne, and the country would be lost to a madman's rule."

"We do not actually know if he is mad," I said, hating to say anything that could be construed by anyone as defending Cinder's fucking asshole brother.

"Only a madman would do what he is doing," General Pace added with a nod as if positive she was right no matter what I said. "He must know that the goal now, whether he survives the war or not, is to separate him from his head."

I laughed a burst of humorless air as I curled my hands into tight fists, and imagined giving him as many bruises as he gave Cinder before I killed him.

"There are things you do not know about him," I said, my voice even lower than before. The full truth of Cinder's brother wasn't my story to tell, and I didn't want the other people in the room to have any hint that there was more to her story than what she wished our people to know.

"And those things would be?" Rath asked, his voice leading, more than a little curious.

"Former Duke Ash," I said, my voice barely there at all, forcing Rath and the General to lean even closer across the desk, "is a lot of things...calculating, deluded of his own importance and skill, sadistic, abusive...but I doubt he is mad."

When I said "abusive," Rath's eyebrow flicked, a line

appearing between his brows for a moment only to disappear again, while General Pace's chest expanded in a deep, swift breath.

Even though I didn't want to tell her story, nor would I give away any of her secrets, they needed to know the extent of his evil. They needed to know exactly how badly his depravity demanded he pay for his crimes.

Somehow—even if the clergy turned against me, and I had to fight every one of their watery gods along with the crows, part of Amethyst, and an increasing number of my own nobles—I needed to spill Ash's blood.

Finally, after a long, silent moment lost in our own thoughts, I said, "If it comes to it, I will haunt him from beyond the grave until I drive him to strip himself of each layer of skin before leaping from the roof of the palace."

"Don't," Rath said, his voice a bark and dripping with rage.

"That is not how this will end," General Pace said.

Looking at them both, meeting their eyes one at a time, I saw their resolve as hard and unyielding as the Obsidian of the palace itself.

I took a deep breath, and nodded.

"No," I said, "you are right. It will end with a sword through his heart."

Rath and General Pace both nodded in turn, and I vowed to myself that somehow, whether I remained King or not, Cinder's brother would die.

CHAPTER 9

A FIRST

Cinder

The Chamberlain smiled, bright and happy, as he walked into my room.

I was dressed in a halter top gown of crimson velvet with dragons embroidered in gold thread wrapping down from my waist to the bottom of the skirt where my feet were tucked under the folds of the fabric. It was beautiful, soft, comfortable, and exactly what I asked for.

Gus and Jacquetta were very good at their subtle and unsubtle work on my wardrobe, as was Madam Valentin. My trunks were still mostly full of the choices Madam had made for me.

"Thank you for meeting with me on such short notice," I said, and the Chamberlain nodded.

"It is my honor." With a wide-eyed study of my face, and the long, untied fall of my hair, I wondered what this dignitary would think by the time this meeting was done.

"My Ladies are working on ordering new clothes for me," I said, a seemingly disconnected comment, but I wondered how it would be interpreted.

"Your Ladies always do an exceptional job. When you first came to the palace, I was impressed by their choices."

Nodding, I waited for the Chamberlain to say something else, maybe to allude to how we were pitted against each other, but nothing followed.

"Well," I said, shifting and stifling a gasp when the movement caused a fresh line of pain to travel across my ribs and down my back. I covered with a smile that felt less than convincing, and went on. "The reason I called you here is because I want to marry the King."

"I know, and I am thrilled you will be our queen," the Chamberlain said, sitting forward. "As soon as the war is over, I know there will be royal representatives from every country on the continent."

"That is not what I mean." I tried to steer the conversation back to what I wanted, what I needed the Chamberlain's help with, but my voice was too quiet.

"No pressure to get started right away. As soon as you wish, we can begin planning. In fact, I know General Pace said you wanted the same roses Queen Tanith loved. We can start there." The Chamberlain missed my rising hand, palm out, and instead pulled open a notebook tucked under one arm, making notes in it before I even said anything.

"Yes, I do love them, but there is something else I need to discuss."

"Oh, I am sure there is even more to discuss than you realize."

"Um."

"We have been looking forward to King Tristan finding a queen since he was first crowned. The entire country will rejoice, and celebrate with you. It will be the perfect way to bring the country together again, and celebrate the end of the war."

I shook my head, and opened my mouth while the Chamberlain continued. But it didn't seem to matter how many times I tried to say something, I wasn't fast enough.

"But I have something else I need you to do," I said, finally finding a break long enough to say something without sounding rude.

"The coronation. Yes. I have many ideas for that, too. We can plan that for the day after the wedding, then everyone will be able to call you Queen like we all want to anyway. Did you know half the palace refers to you as Queen in private conversations?"

"I—"

"Well, it will be a wonderful day."

That didn't work. I wasn't sure if the Chamberlain didn't hear me, or was choosing to ignore my repeated attempts to interrupt. And all this detail was starting to be far too daunting. I wasn't ready to plan all of this. I was still healing, and we were still at war.

"Although…maybe we should delay the coronation by a month," Rezan went on with no sign of stopping. "Because if we have it right away, the foreign dignitaries will expect to be invited, and maybe it would be better if it was reserved for the people of Onyx alone."

Did Chamberlain Rezan ever breathe?

"Of course, there are many ways we can do both important celebrations. I have studied all of the past coronations and royal weddings. We can do something that harkens back to those, or something new for you. We have had fierce queens, but never one that was also the King's Fighter. So, this one has more room to be unique. Then agai—"

"Chamberlain Rezan," I yelled, cutting off whatever was going to come out next. To the Chamberlain's credit, nothing about the open expression and interested gaze facing me suggested that my very rude way of finally get my point across was upsetting. "Please, for now, I only want to talk about a small ceremony that I would like you to help me plan."

"A small ceremony for what, Duchess Cinder?" The Chamberlain asked, charcoal poised above the notebook as if everything about to come out of my mouth were enough to set the words into the paper like a magic spell.

No matter how long it took to get here, no matter how much I wanted start this planning, now that it was time, my heart danced in my chest as if re-enacting the moves of the ancestor's pairing.

"When I fell in the last battle," I said, my voice quiet enough to hear the sharp intake of the Chamberlain's breath, "I woke up thinking I did not want to wait to make King Tristan mine in every way."

"Oh," the Chamberlain said, voice soft, more like a sigh someone would give to their newborn child than one usually given to a duchess about a wedding.

That sound, just an exhalation, made the fluttering in my chest speed up to a clamor.

"I know the country deserves to celebrate with us." Although this was my way of keeping this a private moment like I had wished it would be, there were requirements for marrying a king. One of them was that it was a whole-country affair, and, as much as I wished it wasn't, the Chamberlain didn't need to hear me complain. "But I do not want to wait until the war is over, because none of us knows exactly what will happen. And I *will* heal, and return to the fight."

"Everyone knows that King Tristan's Fighter will be on the battlefield again." The Chamberlain's voice now was strong, and offered in such a way that it was as if it were something I could borrow to help me get better, faster.

Smiling, I tipped my head in thanks.

"Before that, though," I said, my smile broadening as my heart danced thinking about the day when what I hoped for became real, "I want to surprise my King with a secret ceremony for just us."

"A secret?"

"Yes. One where the marriage is real, and the only people who know about it are the ones who are there, the ones who must know."

"This is what you want me to plan?"

Nodding, I said, "I do not know who should perform the ceremony, or how to make it happen without the King finding out beforehand. The only thing that matters to me is to be able to call him my husband."

"I can make that happen." The Chamberlain's smile felt like a reflection of the shine I felt every time Tristan was with me.

"One of the things I am also unsure of, is who to have there for the consent." It was one of the largest holes in my plan, and something I thought about often.

"Do you wish for your ladies to be there?"

As soon as the Chamberlain asked, I nodded, biting my lip.

"But I want them to be surprised as well. I will need to get dressed by myself, so they do not suspect what is about to happen."

Gus and Jacquetta would be crying messes, I was sure of it, and I would love watching them. Although part of me wondered if I would even be able to see them when Tristan would be my whole world for those moments.

"This has never been done before," the Chamberlain said, brow furrowed, and a thoughtfulness taking over every feature.

"You did say that a Dragon King has never married his Fighter either. This will just be one more first. And no one needs to know. The country will know our public wedding day as the anniversary, this one will just be for us."

"Once again," the Chamberlain said, smiling again, "I am honored."

CHAPTER 10

LOCKED

Tristan

Finally, I could return to my queen.

It was far later than I wanted it to be, but I took care of so much that hopefully I could be with Cinder alone for a while...

At least long enough to get some sleep.

Exhaustion dragged at me even as I quickened my pace down the hallway to her rooms. No matter how tired I was, I needed to see her, check on her, make sure my Cinder wasn't just suffering, pretending that everything was fine so I could take care of things.

For someone who was so good at killing, and enjoyed it, she was more selfless than many people I knew. It was one of the many things about her that I loved. But it was also one of the things about her that drove me to the brink of screaming.

She didn't put herself first often enough in normal ways.

Instead, she threw herself between people and danger, taking all the risks on herself.

Knocking on the door to her rooms, I couldn't wait for someone to answer. I swung it open, merely using the knock to announce myself.

Augustina and Jacquetta were walking out of Cinder's bedroom.

Jacquetta carried papers, a quill, and an inkwell. She smiled when she saw me, bright and happy in a way that let me breathe easier. She wouldn't have looked like that if Cinder weren't doing well.

While Augustina was carrying a stack of plates with the remains of dinner on them, the smile she gave me had a secretive bend to it that made me falter for a moment.

"How is she?" I asked, slowing enough to hear the answer.

"She is better than I expected," Jacquetta said.

"Go see your queen for yourself, King Tristan," Augustina said, and Jacquetta shushed her with a giggle.

What did that mean? What was Cinder hiding?

I walked into Cinder's room, half expecting to see her standing there in armor, spike out, doing maneuvers.

But she was lying on the bed, much like she had been for days, pillows piled high behind her.

Now, though, her hair was freshly brushed in a shining cascade that hung over one shoulder. And she wasn't under the blankets in a nightgown.

She wore a beautiful dress that showcased the defined muscles in her shoulders and arms while the draping of the fabric around her legs hid within the softness of the velvet just how skilled and dangerous she was.

"Tristan," she said, her voice a sigh that carried a declaration of love within it.

"You're beautiful," I said, moving across the room toward her, my hands already reaching for her. "How are you feeling?"

Lifting her hands to take mine, she smiled and said, "I'm better now that you're here."

I didn't entirely believe that my mere presence was enough to relieve some of her pain. But the second our hands met, she closed her eyes and exhaled, her mouth curving into the softest smile.

"Did you push yourself too hard today?" I asked, bending to kiss her, then lean my forehead to hers.

"No," she said, "it helped me. And I feel accomplished."

"Good," I said, smiling although I still worried that she was trying to paint over any struggles that came along with all those accomplishments so soon after her fall. "But why are you so dressed up?"

She pulled back from me, shaking her head and grinning as if I were an idiot whom she was humoring.

"Tristan," she said, her voice husky. My name on her tongue this time sent a jolt through my cock, "I wore this because I wanted you to look at me like that."

All I could do was lean in again, and press my lips to hers.

My kiss was soft. I held back how much I wanted her, how much I missed being with her in the way her voice suggested. The last thing I wanted to do was hurt her.

She pulled my hands, bringing me closer, running her tongue along my lips, chipping away at my resolve as I opened my mouth and let her in.

Kissing was fine. Kissing wouldn't hurt her.

It was everything else that I couldn't risk giving her right now, no matter how badly I wanted to.

But Cinder was far too good at testing me. She grazed her teeth along my bottom lip, and slipped one of her hands up my arm to tangle in my hair.

"You took the time to shave," she whispered into my jaw as she took her lips from mine, trailing them along my skin toward my neck.

"When all I can do is kiss you," I said, my voice betraying my growing need of her, "I want to feel as much of your skin on mine as I can. Earlier, I couldn't feel your cheek against mine in the same way."

She moved along my neck until she reached my ear, whispering as she teased my earlobe with her teeth and little flicks of her tongue, "Then shut the door and take this dress off me."

I pulled back. Even though the thought of her naked next to me in the bed produced an acute ache in my cock, I couldn't do this.

"No, Cinder." I leaned further back from her. "I'll shut the door, but we can't. I don't want to hurt you."

"Where do you belong?" she asked, which was only slightly worse than if she asked me to tell her what I wanted.

"You know I belong with you." That was not in doubt. Not when she was falling from the sky. Not when she was a broken heap on the ground. Not when I wasn't sure if I would ever have her the same way again. I would still belong with her, even if she was no longer able to be Fighter Cinder. I just didn't want the inherent need in her to fight to prove it to morph into something that would hurt her more.

"Then shut the door, and get in this bed with me," she said, her eyes shining with the same desire that coursed through my body as hot as hellfire water.

I let go of her hands, watching her closely for any sign that she was in pain as she lay back against the pillows.

Even as I shut the door, I wondered if I would be able to see it, if she would be able to mask it from me, because I didn't trust that she'd achieved the level of recovery she tried to sell me.

"Cinder," I said, turning back to look at her, my words stalling in my throat as she unhooked the neck of her dress, and let it fall, exposing her breasts.

"My King," she said, her voice soft and sweet even as she

trailed one hand down, running her fingers through her hair, as the other fondled her breast.

"What are you doing to me?" I asked, trying to remember my own name, or why I was turning down the most beautiful woman I had ever seen.

The muscles in her arm flexed and bunched as she massaged her breast in a display designed to trap me, specifically.

"You know that when you do that, everything I love about you shows in your body, and it ruins me." I still couldn't move. Stuck next to the door, some small part of me screaming that I couldn't do this, while the rest of me, led by the desperation building in my pants, screamed at me to go to her.

She smiled, her eyes giving a slow, languid blink, and I curled my hands into fists to stop myself from jumping on her.

"I need you," she said, and I crumpled. The small, screaming part of me was finally drowned out by my need answering hers in a tidal wave of fire that swept through me.

How I made my way to her without falling, I didn't know. But I got to her side, close enough for her to reach out and tug at the laces in my pants.

"Let me see you," she said, and king or not, I was powerless to deny her anything, least of all this.

Never in my life had I taken off my clothes faster. The moment I stood up from pulling down my pants, her eyes went to my cock where it stood for her.

She moved her hand from her hair, and stroked me with a feather light touch of fingertips along my length before she wrapped her hand around the shaft, giving me a small pull, drawing me to her.

With a groan of wanting her, I bent and claimed her mouth. Bracing myself on the bed with one hand, I reached out and joined my other hand with hers in massaging her breast.

Cinder moaned into my mouth, and broke away from the

kiss, making me release a plaintive whine as words fled from me.

But she didn't speak. She just grinned, and raised a brow.

"Tell me what you want," I said, my throat half-closed, my voice low and rough. If she didn't tell me to get in bed with her soon, I was going to lose my ability to speak at all.

"Get this dress off me," she said.

I smiled and climbed to kneel on the bed, straddling her legs, looking at her as I did, half expecting her to tell me not to, or tell me the jostling hurt her.

When she didn't, I leaned in and kissed her. I wanted her mouth on mine more than I wanted air.

Still kissing her, I slipped one hand along her back, careful not to press too hard along her bruised spine and ribs, until I tucked my hand under her dress, grabbing her ass while my forearm braced her back. I lifted her from the bed ever so slightly.

As she made a gasp in my mouth around my tongue, I used my other hand to tug her dress out from under her, then halfway down her thighs.

Once I had it that far, I groaned, broke the kiss, and sat back to pull her dress down the rest of her body, trailing kisses down her legs as I did.

Finally, crouched at the foot of the bed with her body free of the dress, I took in the beautiful vision in front of me.

"*My* Queen," I said, the words coming out as a growling claim more than the declaration of love they normally were. I didn't try to change my tone. She was mine, and I was hers.

"*My* King," she said, turning the claim back on me, her voice every bit as fierce. Her answer nearly turned the words into a spell. I swear I heard something locking us together, tighter than ever before. And I didn't think that was possible.

I crawled up the bed, and slammed my lips onto hers. She let out a mewl, grasping at my shoulders.

That noise never failed to make me want to drown in her.

CHAPTER 11

CAREFUL

Cinder

"Please tell me if I hurt you," Tristan said. His voice was only slightly softer, but still at odds with the words and the sincerity in his eyes as he peppered me with kisses in the middle of the short sentence.

"You won't hurt me," I said, running a hand along his cheek, staring into those shining, golden eyes.

His mouth crashed into mine even as his hands remained gentle on my body, the fingers of one hand trailing down my stomach, slipping along the outside of my sex.

A growl, low in his throat, rumbled through him into me. I moaned as he ran his fingers along the edge of my center.

"Did you lay in this bed imagining this while I was gone today?" he asked, smiling against my mouth, his fingers continuing to tease in a way that made me tilt my hips to follow his hand, seeking more of his touch. "You're wet, my Queen."

"No," I said, smiling as he pulled back to pout. I wrapped

both my arms around his neck, my fingers playing with the soft hair along his nape. "I imagined it every minute since I woke up."

Tristan sighed, his pout morphing into a self-satisfied grin as he kissed me, moving one hand to my cheek, caressing my scar, now little more than a thin white line, with his thumb.

"As did I," he said, and the warmth of his voice moved through me, forcing my want of him to grow more urgent.

His other hand traced the edge of my center again, his thumb flicking in a teasingly soft touch against my clit, making me gasp and arch my back.

But the movement paired with the noise made him still and pull back, studying my face, the gold in his eyes rimmed in bright green.

"Cinder," he said, just my name, but hiding within it was all the worry and the fear that plagued him since I fell.

"I'm fine. It's fine. You didn't hurt me." I grabbed his face, my palms on his smooth cheeks, and pressed my lips to his. But there wasn't the same answering fire and passion from him.

His kiss was melancholy, and tasted like unshed tears.

"Tristan," I said against his lips, trying to pour every piece of reassurance I could into my voice, trying to make him drink it down until he was filled with it, trying to push out everything else.

But I failed.

Instead, he let out a sigh that echoed his distress, and stepped off the bed, pulling his body away from mine, making me ache for him.

He kept his face close to mine, one hand on my cheek, until he was standing next to the bed.

As soon as he pulled his hand away from me, his fear of hurting me manifested itself in aches all over my body. I reached for him, grasping at air. Not letting me fall too far down into the pain of his absence, he slipped his hands under me, one at my back, and one under my knees like he had so many times since I fell.

Squeezing my eyes shut, I pressed my head to his chest, my hand over the steady beating of his heart, and allowed myself a moment to mourn my plan for tonight, at least relishing this closeness.

Moving me around, he pulled down the blankets and climbed into the bed, his knees on the mattress, before he laid me down on my side.

Watching him over my shoulder, I tried to catch his eyes as he laid down behind me, but his gaze was focused on my back.

"Your bruises aren't as dark," he said, his voice low, his fingers trailing along my skin, tracing my bones with the scorching heat of his touch, releasing all the aches from the day into the air to burn on the wind like paper lanterns.

"Because I *am* getting better," I said, my voice low.

His eyes finally met mine, bright green and burning with faint lines of gold running out from his dark pupil.

"Tristan," I said, reaching behind me and threading our fingers together when his hand met mine. "Please. Don't worry anymore. I'm going to heal completely."

Wrapping his arm around me, our linked hands just under my breast, he put his forehead to mine, and held me tight.

"And your pain?" he whispered, his body still taught, held just beyond touching my back, as if he were a bow string about to snap.

"Fine. I'm fine." I pushed my hips back into him, pressing my ass against the lowest portion of his abdomen. "But I want you."

Sliding his other arm underneath my neck, he ran his hand along my cheek, and let out a groan filled with longing as his lips crashed against mine.

I grabbed onto his arm, deepening the kiss, not wanting him to separate from me again.

He shifted and slid the length of his cock between my legs,

brushing the soft skin against the outside of the center of my own need.

Pressing my back flush against his chest, the heat of his skin almost shocking after going so long without layers of fabric between us, my body turned molten in his arms.

Just kissing him and feeling him rub slow, languid brushes of his cock against my wet center, sliding easily, was enough for my mind to empty of anything beside pleading for more.

"Tristan," I moaned into his mouth, and he answered with a low growl, unclasping my hand to run his fingers down my stomach until he reached my clit.

In the same teasing brush of skin, he rubbed at the peak of my greedy center, creating waves of pleasure that crashed against my bones like the sea against the shore, relentless and wild.

After being contained for so long, barely moving, assaulted by pain and the inability to stay alert, I was remade, reanimated by his hands, mouth, and body.

He took his fingers away from me, and I whimpered a plaintive, desperate question I couldn't quite form the words to. It poured from my mouth to his. But a second later, he used his hand to press his cock to my clit, wrapping it flush against me from behind, and a shudder ran down my legs.

Pulling his mouth from mine, letting me moan and cry out, he nipped along my neck as the pressure between my legs drove me over the edge.

My hands clenched around his arm that still supported my head, my short nails digging into his skin as my body shattered and reformed again and again.

Tristan rode out my breaking with his mouth on my neck, his teeth marking me the same way my nails marked his arm.

When it ended, and I was left gasping for breath, turning my head to put his finger in my mouth, desperate for something on my tongue, he groaned into my skin and shifted again.

His cock stroked against me, back and forth, and his fingers, now slick with my need of him, lightly caressed my clit.

I wanted him. Now. If he didn't do it soon, I was going to make him. I wanted him inside me, moving with me, as close to being a part of me as he could be.

"Please," I managed to say around his finger, my tongue lapping at his skin.

"Cinder," he said, "my Queen."

Pulling his hand from my mouth, he pressed it to my face, and tilted my head in his direction as his lips left my neck.

Looking into his golden, shining eyes, I still saw worry. But it was eclipsed by hunger now, as urgent as mine, before he sucked in a breath and slammed his mouth down on mine.

CHAPTER 12

SLEEP WELL

Tristan

"I love you, my King," she said against my lips, and my entire body lit on fire, the heat scorching through my veins in a low, roiling wave of energy that made every part of my skin a point of pleasure where it touched hers.

"I love you," I said, wanting to tell her more, wanting to make her understand how much she meant to me.

But I didn't give her what she asked for, even though she meant so much. She asked for so little when she deserved the world.

Moving against her, rubbing my cock along the wet lips of her pussy, playing my fingers in circles along her clit, I wanted her to cum again. I wanted to feel her shake against me. I wanted to hear her moan my name again.

With the threats all around us, I couldn't give her the world she so deserved. I couldn't even give her the country she loved, that she would rule beside me. But I could give her body this small thing, this release.

She made that whimper noise I loved. I never wanted her to stop. I took my mouth from hers, and kissed along her neck and ear, relishing the sounds she made, the way she rocked back against me as I pushed against her.

But, fuck, I wanted to feel her as she came. I wanted to feel the way she clamped down, fluttering against me.

"Tristan," she moaned, my name like a shudder in her mouth that made my cock throb for want of her.

"Not yet, my Flame." My voice was little more than a guttural growl, rumbling against the soft skin where her neck met her shoulder.

Cinder made a plaintive whine, and it drove me almost past the point of restraint. But my Queen needed me to be gentle as much as she wanted me not to be.

I shifted, my hand reaching further down until I plunged my finger into her wet pussy. Cinder gasped, forcing a groan from me in answer.

Her hips rocked as I rubbed the heel of my palm hard against her clit, curling my finger inside her just a touch.

She cried out, her nails digging into my arm again.

Before, she would have been writhing beneath me. But I barely had to press against her to keep her still as her walls clamped down on my finger, throbbing against my hand.

While her cries crescendoed, I moaned. My teeth dug into that soft spot in the crook of her neck.

Keeping up with her moans, I trained my attention on her pussy while she rode through her body's tremors again.

Her sound, so close to begging, one I knew no one would ever hear but me, almost made me follow her off the cliff we built together. But I wanted to be inside her, I needed to.

"Tell me what you want," she said, her voice breathless and

needy. That was my undoing. I couldn't hold back any longer, couldn't let my finger be inside her one second more when my cock ached so hard to feel her around me that my skin felt too tight.

I pulled my hand out, sliding it up her body to rub at her clit with my soaked fingers, and tilted my hips.

She rocked hers, her back arching just enough to create the right angle to drive my cock inside her warm, wet center.

We both moaned each other's names, calling out to one another as our bodies met in a way that let me feel exactly how alive she still was, to know that my Flame still burned even after cheating death falling from the sky.

Our mouths met, soft and tender kisses long since giving way to frantic explorations of lips, teeth, and tongue as I moved inside her in slow, deliberate thrusts.

I was hers. And she was mine.

After everything, that was still true, and it always would be.

Lost in her, in the way she felt against me, around me, inside my mouth, deep in my soul, I moved slowly, carefully to avoid hurting her, even as our mouths came together with all the fury that our bodies couldn't.

My Queen was ravenous, and I was no less hungry for her. Both of our appetites were only barely constrained, and I couldn't let myself answer the growing pressure in my body to make love to her with any more force than I was already using.

But, damn it, with every thrust, every kiss, every moan from her lips and desperate whine as she grasped frantically at my arm, she wore down my resolve, making it nearly impossible to hold back.

While she moaned and mewled into my mouth, I groaned in response, my kisses growing wild, frantic. The walls of her pussy clamped down around my cock.

She pulled her mouth from mine to scream my name, and I watched as her head fell back against my arm, her hand reaching up to tangle her fingers in my hair.

I kept moving, just a fraction harder and swifter inside her, spurred on by the flutter of the outside of her pussy against my fingers, around the base of my cock.

My fingers picked up their pace, their pressure against her clit driving her harder toward yet another cliff.

Her eyes darted back and forth under their lids, the movement wilder with every thrust I made. My blood ran hotter, my own body singing in response.

Everything she did, every noise and movement echoed through me, making me want her more.

She came down from her high, breathy moans still escaping her mouth, the walls of her pussy still clenching around me, throbbing against me, and then releasing again.

I pressed her face to mine, my lips on hers, closed my eyes, and lost myself to the desire and sensations rolling through me.

Cinder was everything to me.

And even as we slowed our movements, even as my heart exploded with my love for her, even as tenderness swept through me for this woman whom I feared I had lost, she whispered my name into my mouth, and a desperate shiver ran over my skin.

"Tristan, my King." My name formed a moan of need deeper than this physical connection we shared.

She wrapped her hands around mine on her cheek, and I felt her scar under my thumb.

My Queen was as fierce as any Dragon of any legend. And yet, here, in my arms, it wasn't that side of her gripping my hands, and kissing me as if it were the only way to show she loved me.

Between us, in the tiny space that kept us still two different beings when our hearts were this bare and this close, lay the truth of this moment.

I broke the kiss, brushing my lips against hers as she

moaned, and I pressed as deep into her as I could, watching and waiting until she opened her eyes.

When she did, her body and mine both shook as we held ourselves back. Desperation built for both of us. Her eyes were full of nothing, save for a love so deep that I wished to drown in it.

"Cinder," I said, pressing my hand against the lower part of her abdomen, pushing deeper within her still, just a fraction. She sucked in a gasping breath, and a tremor ran through her whole body.

"I love you, Tristan. We belong together. You are mine."

That was all I could handle. I moved again, soft and slow, as deep as I could inside her. Our eyes remained locked. Her moans built. Louder. And louder.

"And you are mine," I said, my voice a groan as I held myself from the edge only by want of pleasing her again. And then her walls clamped tight on me.

No throbbing that time, her entire body tightened down, every muscle flexed hard, her strength showing everywhere from her hands around mine, to her hard ass pressing against me, to her pussy almost too tight around my cock.

It was impossible not to follow her into that undoing, for us not to fall apart together, and be remade, even more tethered to each other than before.

As soon as she shuddered around me, her walls loosening, I pressed my mouth to hers and drank up her kisses, her love, everything I could.

"Do you have any idea how much I love you, truly?" I asked, unwilling to stop kissing her between each word.

She shifted, allowing my cock to fall out of her, then she settled back, tighter against my chest, running her hand along my jaw as I kissed her shoulder.

"Enough to marry me?" she asked, smiling even as sleep tugged at her eyelids, her hand falling limply around mine.

"Yes," I said, my heart soaring on a gust of wind as hot as the sun as I watched my Queen sleep.

"When you wake up..." I whispered, unwrapping myself from her enough to grab the blankets and pull them over us. She frowned in her sleep until I had her tucked tightly against my chest again, "...I'm going to remind you that you asked."

And then I was going to marry the love of my life.

CHAPTER 13

DAWN

Cinder

Waking up to Tristan's soft, hot fingers brushing hair away from my face, and tucking it behind my ear made me sigh in satisfaction.

"Cinder," he whispered, placing a kiss like a caress on my shoulder, the heat of his mouth sending a shiver through me as I thought about the night before. The want in me rose as if saying my name were a command, and I were a loyal soldier.

"Don't stop there," I said, my voice as low as his, although mine probably sounded like I was smiling because I couldn't keep the grin from forming on my face even if I tried. And I didn't want to hide it.

He laughed a low, rumbling sound that shook through his chest and into my back, acting like a massage on the tender flesh there.

"Before you get us both in trouble for neglecting our duties," he said, kissing my shoulder even as he denied me with words, "I have to ask…"

At that, I opened my eyes, and looked at my King. His hair was sleep-mussed and sex-disheveled in a way that ached for me to tangle my fingers in it above a soft, adoring smile, and eyes of shining gold.

"Have to ask me what?" I reached up and touched that hair, loving the feel of it on my skin, like silk against my calloused fingertips.

I expected him to ask me what I wanted. My stomach tightened in anticipation.

Instead, he said, "Do you remember what you said right before you fell asleep?"

For a minute, I didn't. I ran through the words of the night before, and all I could clearly remember were the feelings.

My hand still played with his hair, and I shifted to lay more fully on my back.

With him beside me, the work yesterday, and the latent relaxation in every part of my body, it didn't hurt to lay on my back. I even smiled as I tried to delve through my memory for detail.

"That I love you?" I asked, going for something I knew I said, and wanted to say again and again forever.

"I love you, too," he said, claiming my mouth in a languid kiss, allowing us time to linger with our lips and tongues, delighting in a pain-free morning.

But eventually, he pulled back, placing one last peck on my lips, then hovered over me, smiling.

"Not what I meant, though, my Flame." He had himself braced with an arm near my shoulder, and his thumb rubbed along the top ridge of that shoulder, trailing warmth that traveled down my arm to tingle in my fingers.

Finally, it came to me, the last thing I said before sleep stole me from the world before he could answer.

Even though I knew the answer—with the morning rays shining through the windows to light on his hair and paint it gold, not even the sun as dazzling as his eyes—my stomach flipped, and my heartbeat picked up its pace.

I nodded and waited for him to realize what that meant.

He swallowed, and his eyes widened.

"Will you help me sit up?" I asked, my voice even less substantial than before.

Tristan didn't hesitate. He sat up himself, and scooped his hands under my back, one under my neck, the other under my lower back to support all of me as he lifted me to a seated position, leaning me back against the pile of pillows.

"Are you alright?" he asked, gaze sweeping over me as if checking for himself.

"More than alright," I said, taking both his hands in mine, rubbing my thumbs over the backs of his hands, and losing myself in the depths of his mercurial eyes that shifted from solid gold to gold with green painted along the outside edges as I looked at him.

"You know you're perfect, right?" I asked, unable to see him like this and not comment.

"I'm not perfect," he said, laughter in his voice, "but you make me want to be better."

"Perfect for me."

He lifted our linked hands, and kissed the back of mine, looking at me from under his lashes.

"Just as you're perfect for me. Do you know you're beautiful?" He smiled at me as he sat up again, squeezing my hands on the word "beautiful."

What I knew was that he thought I was beautiful, and he knew I wasn't perfect. But he still thought I was perfect for him.

"At no time in my life," I said, wanting to do this right this time, "did I ever expect to have someone love me, least of all someone to love me as well as you do."

He pulled one hand from mine to cup my cheek, a touch of sadness playing at the corners of his eyes even as his soft smile stayed in place.

"The last thing I expected was to meet someone as fundamentally good as you, someone whom I know I will fight to deserve every day for the rest of my life, and still fall short. And for that someone to ever love me."

Closing his eyes, he shifted so he was sitting right beside me. But his torso twisted so his chest touched mine, and his forehead leaned against mine, our hands still clasped between us.

"No matter what brought us together," I said, and he blinked, his eyes on mine, "there was no other option but for me to fall in love with you so desperately that I no longer have a heart. It may beat in my chest, but when I thought I lost you, it tried to break me open from the inside so it could return to you. Because it's yours now. I'm yours."

As if he couldn't help it, his lips found mine in a hard kiss, and I sighed into his mouth, his kiss enough to let me relax again, loosening the knot in my stomach.

Pulling away from me, he kept silent, but with his kiss he told me what I already knew to be true. He was mine.

"Will you make me yours forever?" I asked, my voice giving away how much this meant to me, tender and more vulnerable than I had ever been, my voice shook on the last word. "Will you marry me?"

"Yes. Always, Cinder. Forever, yes." He wrapped me in his arms, and pressed his lips to mine again. This time it was sweet and pure, even as he shuddered while I wrapped my own arms around his back, and sighed in relief against him.

"I didn't want to push you to talk about it," he said, moving so my head was in his neck, and his was bent to lay in mine. "But it was killing me not to ask you, and not to plan our wedding. I can't wait to tell everyone on that day how much I love you."

"How about…" I said, swallowing, because this next part was the hardest part to ask him for. It was the one thing I wasn't reasonably sure I already knew the answer to, "…we have a private ceremony?"

The look on his face as he pulled back from me almost made me laugh. He looked so innocent and confused, as if I asked him to run naked through the streets with me. And he wanted to make me happy. But wasn't sure how to do that, and be King at the same time.

"Cinder," he said, my name more careful in his mouth than I had ever heard it.

"Listen," I said, leaning in to kiss him, sweet and soft before I went on, "we'll have the ridiculous royal wedding we share with everyone once the war is over, but I want to marry you now. I don't need a crown. I don't need fanfare. I need you."

Every bit of tension and confusion in him melted in the bright shine of his smile as he wrapped me in his arms again, and pressed his lips hard to mine, claiming more than any crown could.

A knock at the door reminded me we still had life to live, healing to do, and more work than either one of us could imagine because it all piled on top of itself in times like these.

Tristan let out a low growling sound of frustration that I loved as he broke the kiss and looked at me, his golden eyes seeing only me and somehow still shining as if that was enough.

"Was that a 'yes?'" I asked, basking in the heat radiating from him.

"Yes. Forever yes."

My King said yes.

CHAPTER 14

PROTECTION

Tristan

She was going to marry me.

Throughout the day—the first entire day I spent separated from Cinder since she fell—the thought would hit me.

In the middle of a conversation where it shouldn't.

"Even with the nets and other ways the caravans of goods are being protected from the Corvids," one of the merchants from Bridgeton said, "the number of thieves taking advantage of the otherwise deserted roads to attack and steal our shipments is growing."

And there it was, the image of Cinder as my wife and my queen, unbidden and not appropriate filling my mind.

Nodding and forcing my face to remain concerned and focused only grew more difficult as the day went on.

"Unfortunately," I said, clearing my throat after my silence went on a beat too long, "the guards of every duchy have their hands full at the moment."

"We all understand that, King Tristan," the merchant, Coranis, said, but the pursing of his lips suggested he wasn't at all understanding. "But these goods are not just integral to our profits."

Some of the other merchants that were crowded into my office nodded along to that. None of it made me more likely to believe their concerns weren't focused on their money.

However, I knew there was a problem with thieves. And it was only getting worse. I also knew that some of the goods were probably needed by the duchies they were traveling to, but it still didn't offer an easy solution.

Since the start of the war, nothing offered easy solutions.

"Do you have room in your profit margins to hire some of the locals?" I asked, grasping at any possible chance to breathe while I traveled to the training grounds in the city to check with General Pace, which was my next, and last, stop for the day.

The merchants shifted where they stood, shooting furtive glances between themselves.

Before they could come up with an excuse not to try my idea, I went on, "Because I am positive there are locals skilled enough with a bow to offer some protection, and those who need the goods would be the most invested in making sure they arrived where they were heading."

I omitted the fact that the locals could probably use the funds they would earn. Work was becoming a challenge for some people since the war slowed or shut down so much around the country.

Of course, I already suspended taxes, and ordered all the Dukes and Duchesses to do so as well. The Crown had already paid for supplies of food, but there was so much more that needed to be done.

Soon, it would be spring, and the war would ruin the planting, growing, and harvesting seasons. After the disaster at the end of last years', one caused by this same war, it was not something that would go well for anyone in the country. And Onyx was a big country. As much as I wanted to be able to know everyone's needs and meet them, I couldn't. Not from here, and not from the battlefield. But if I could do this, if I could arrange for this partnership between the merchants and the locals in the areas they traveled through, I might be able to accomplish some good.

Finally, they seemed to realize that this was my suggestion, and I was not about to pull Guard troops from their posts in a time of war to be paid for from the already-stressed public funds when they had the coin to handle this on their own.

No one became one of the leading merchants in Bridgeton without having more funds than most nobles, and the nobles had responsibilities attached to how they spent their coin. These well-dressed, heavily-jeweled merchants before me had no such responsibilities beyond whatever they wanted to buy next.

Again, at that inopportune moment, the image of Cinder as the most beautiful bride in the world popped into my head.

One of the merchants at the back of the group made a "hmph" noise, and I schooled my features before raising a brow in question.

It was bold of them to act so outwardly perturbed with their king.

The guards flanking my back bristled, and I kept my body as relaxed as possible lest they react further. I didn't want a dead merchant in my office.

"Go on," I said, "you have an opinion about this?"

"Well," the merchant, Yassa, said, "I would have thought that your soon-to-be queen would be providing more coin to the war effort. Everyone knows Lehar has more than enough, and that she needs to earn the people's trust back given what her brother is doing."

Yassa should have been more worried about what I would do instead of the guards behind me, who each took a step forward while she made her accusatory comment.

As soon as the words escaped her mouth, I shot to my feet, my hands flat on my desk.

"Let me be clear," I said as all the merchants flinched from me, "you can all afford to do your part for this kingdom. I suggest you start."

I stalked around the desk, wanting to scream.

These people, and others in the country I was sure, questioned Cinder's loyalty because of her abusive fucking piece of human filth brother.

"Duchess Cinder," I said, stopping as I stood to the side of the gathered merchants, my hands in fists at my sides, my eyes cutting their way while my face stayed aimed at the door, "has done more for this country than all of you."

Most of them averted their eyes, or shook with fear.

The guards posted at the corners reinforced my point. But I wasn't done.

If all I could do right then was speak, then they needed to know I wasn't going to bother trying to talk about it again.

"Next time you think it is a good idea to diminish your *hero* and soon-to-be queen," I said, my voice harsh, even to my own ears, "I suggest you think about how many in the Guard owe their lives to her, and keep your mouth shut. If you do not, I will let them toss you out like the trash from which you drew your opinion."

Moving again toward the door, one of the guards behind me, echoed by the sound of their swords pulling halfway from their scabbards, said, "You will all wait until the King has left before you move at all."

Taking in a deep breath as I made it into the hallway, I

couldn't have been more grateful that the entire palace knew I was going to meet General Pace, and no one was waiting for me to deal with anything else.

Except, I needed to do something before I left for the training grounds.

No matter that I wasn't supposed to be here right now, people still stopped as I passed them on the stairs, opening their mouths as if they were going to take the opportunity to ask me something.

At least, they did until they saw my face, and realized that was a terrible idea.

Finally, I made it to Cinder's door, and knocked, attempting and failing to relax.

Jacquetta opened the door, and smiled an understanding smile, although I was hoping she would never hear what I just did.

"She is at the range," she said, her voice thick like she had been crying. "I tried to talk her and Gus out of it, but they did not listen."

"Are you alright?" I asked, hoping I was wrong, and nothing made Jacquetta cry.

"Yes," she said, waving a hand, "I am fine. Go. Check on them, please."

I nodded and waved as I turned around to find my Queen.

Maybe I should have stayed and talked to Jacquetta, made sure she was actually fine, and not just trying to reassure me. But when she asked me to check on them, it felt like she was aware of a threat to them in a way I wasn't.

After the conversation with the merchants, it made me even more enraged. If someone was threatening Cinder, I would make them regret it before Cinder even had to raise her sword.

She was more than capable of protecting herself, but I didn't want her to need to. Not here. Not in her home. And not when I could do something about it.

People still looked my way and then changed their directions as I marched through the grand foyer, and down the front stairs of the palace. Even as I crossed the courtyard, the guard shot me looks, then went back to their perusal of the sky, making no attempt to even salute me.

Good choice. They all made very good choices.

Finally, I moved under the arches to the range where Cinder and Augustina were side by side, throwing knives.

I took a deep breath, and waited while they finished their set of throws.

Cinder was already much closer to moving like she did before, even if for her it probably felt like a long way off as she favored her back.

Augustina was much improved from the last time I saw her throw a knife. Every one of her knives, bristling from the target, was in the ring just outside the center. On her last throw, she hit the target dead center and whooped, jumping in celebration.

My Flame laughed, grinning at her friend, and threw her last knife, completing her tight grouping as she always did.

The second the knife plunged home in the target, I darted forward and wrapped Cinder in my arms, burying my face in the soft place where her neck met her shoulder, and breathing her in. She smelled of flowers and Jacquetta's cures, and, even though I missed the scent of just her, having her in my arms was like going home.

"Hello, my King," she whispered, running her hands along my back, and fitting her body to mine, giving in a way she never was except when we were touching.

"I love you," I said, my voice muffled by her skin.

"And I love you," she said, bunching my jacket in her hands.

Being with her after what that fucking merchant said made my blood temperature rise even higher than it already was. Now, though, instead of that heat wanting to burn the world down around me, I just wanted to keep her warm and protected.

"What happened, Tristan?" she asked, her voice so low I wouldn't have heard it if she wasn't almost speaking into my ear.

Sighing, I pulled back, and looked at her.

Cinder was concerned, that was clear, but she was happy, too. Being out here, finally able to train again even in small ways, made her look like she even felt better.

"Lady Jacquetta was worried about both of you," I said, choosing not to tell her about the meeting in my office. If Cinder knew about what the merchant said, she might have a crisis of faith in her ability to be a queen again. And I didn't want that.

Her focus shifted to Augustina whose chin jutted out as she set her jaw.

"My wife is having a hard time with us leaving the palace, even just to come out here," Augustina said, her voice hard and lacking empathy for Jacquetta. "She thinks the same thing will happen to us that happened to Madam Valentin."

Oh. Suddenly, I understood both Jacquetta's worry, and Augustina and Cinder's refusal to abide by it all the time.

"She knows we're being careful," Cinder said, as if reminding Augustina more than me.

"Do you want me to reassure her I'll do everything in my power to keep you both safe?" I asked, holding Cinder tighter.

"No," Cinder said, running a hand along my cheek, "this is something she needs to work through. She knows that we're all doing everything we can."

I leaned down and kissed my soon-to-be wife, imagining her standing next to me as the consent was given and we were announced.

Cinder pulled away with a wicked grin on her face, mischief

in her laugh, and a promise in her eyes that made me look forward to tonight even more.

"What are you doing now?" she asked, running her nails along the nape of my neck, sending a shiver through my skin as if she could read my mind.

Putting my forehead to hers, I groaned in frustration. I hated telling her no, making her wait.

"I'm going to the training grounds to check in with General Pace," I said, and her eyes widened.

"Really?" she asked, stepping back from me and taking both my hands. "Can I come?"

So far, few people knew for sure that she was as recovered as she was, let alone alive. Part of me wanted to keep it that way. To play into the question mark around her ability that still existed outside the walls of the palace, and the minds of the visitors who saw her. But the guards training at the old tournament grounds would appreciate seeing their Fighter out of bed.

"Of course, but wouldn't you rather stay here and train?"

She looked to Augustina who just smiled, and waved her off before getting back into her stance with a knife in her fingers.

"No. I'm fine for right now. Let's go."

Following Cinder out from under the arches, I held her hand in mine, and marveled at my soon-to-be Queen. In seconds with her, I went from rage at what the merchant said, to wholly comfortable again.

Because it didn't matter what that idiot thought. Cinder was my queen, and would be the best queen I could imagine for Onyx.

"You know," I said, as we reached the carriage and I kissed the back of her hand in mine, "we still have a lot of planning to do."

CHAPTER 15

KINGS AND QUEENS

Cinder

Before the carriage door closed all the way, I rucked up my skirts, and flung a leg over Tristan's climbing onto his lap.

"Cinder," he said, his voice low and rumbling in warning even as he grinned at me, "there isn't time."

"There won't be if you keep talking," I said, crashing my mouth into his, pressing myself against him.

Moaning into my mouth, he dropped his hands to my ass, gripping it tight, moving me against his hardening cock.

The heat radiating off of him collected low in my core, ready to ignite with his touch.

I let him do the work of moving my body back and forth against him so I could hold my back still, but I wanted to tear his clothes off and take him. I wanted to move at my pace, drive us closer, faster, harder together. I wanted. And I burned with the wanting.

My hands dragged down his chest between us, fumbling until I reached under my skirts, and started to untie his pants.

He broke away from my kisses, shaking his head with a groan.

"No, Cinder," he said, panting, "we can't. I have to meet with the General. She'll be waiting to open the door."

"But I want you," I said, dipping my head to kiss his neck right by his ear.

"Oh, fuck," he said, moving his hands to pull mine away from his ties, holding them out to the sides so far away from my goal.

"Yes," I said. That's what I wanted, what I needed. My whole body ached for him since before I allowed myself to recognize it, and now that my body was coming back to me, every piece of me needed him more.

"Cinder," he said my name like he forgot all the other words, his hands tight on my wrists where he held me back even as I yanked against his hold.

My lingering injuries made my attempts to press myself against his cock clumsy and mostly unsuccessful. Tristan used his chest to push me away, and the arch of his own back to pull his hips away from mine.

No matter my attempts, I couldn't reach his neck anymore, either. Instead, I sat on his knees, arms wide, staring at him while frustration built in place of the fire in my core.

"Tristan," I said, ready to argue, read to be angry with him, but the way he looked at me, adoring and concerned, made me pause. "What's wrong?"

He let go of my wrists, tied himself up again, and then wrapped his arms around me, holding me close. There was passion in the embrace, but not the kind that would lead to either of us naked. It was close and careful and full of a worry I thought we were passed.

"My King," I said, running my hands down his back, "tell me."

"Nothing," he sighed against my skin and pulled away, tucking a piece of my hair behind my ear. "But, as much as I hate it, we need to be more careful in public until the whole country knows we're married."

The carriage rolled to a stop, jostling us, before I could respond.

And I was going to respond. This wasn't him. This wasn't what he wanted. He was the one who made it clear how public he wished for us to be. So…what happened?

"When we finish up here," I said, as the door to the carriage swung open and he set me on the seat beside him, "we're going to talk about this."

"Of course, my Queen," he gave me a weak smile full of an apology he had yet to say for something I didn't understand, and kissed the back of my hand before he stepped out.

At least he agreed, but as much as I would normally look forward to a trip to the training grounds, now I was distracted and frustrated as I stepped out of the carriage.

General Pace nodded to me as Tristan took my hand, both speaking about the latest group of guards being trained.

I looked around at the training apparatuses and techniques I put into place. The small number of palace guards that would stay with Tristan, or with the palace itself, really were under a different routine.

Part of me expected the guards here would go back to the same old way they always did things, the same way things were done in the palace. But they were still working with the kinds of weapons I suggested and nothing else, and they were still broken into the same groups I had set up as far as I could tell.

Most surprising was that they were still using the rope hanging from the ceiling to fly around and attack each other while they were blind folded.

Only now, there were three different ropes flying people around.

"Look," Tristan said, leaning toward me, and gesturing to the new rope set ups, "they won't let anyone go to the battlefield unless they get a death when they're blindfolded now."

"Really?" I asked, turning and grinning at the General.

"Yes," she said, offering me a small smile, "it has become their favorite part of training."

Tristan squeezed my hand, and pride swelled within me.

When I trained them, set this up for them, I wondered if it would matter, if it would get across to them what I wanted it to. Now I knew.

Maybe it still didn't fully prepare them for fighting the Corvids. What could really make someone ready to fight giant, shapeshifting crows?

But I had to believe that if they enjoyed it, then they must have found something in it that would help them. I had to believe I did some good here.

"I'm surprised by how many are still training," I said, looking around at the full grounds.

"At this point," General Pace said, heading toward the flying areas, "we have doubled the number of the Guard in the country from what we had at the start of the war. And that is after we take into consideration the lost and injured."

Tristan merely nodded as if he were well aware of this, but it was news to me. And news enough to force my eyebrows to shoot up.

"No matter how many slaves Ash bought," I said, "how can he compete with that?"

General Pace coughed into her hand, her mouth in a grim line. Any joy she displayed when we arrived or when she told me about the flying rings was long forgotten. And my wild inclination to wrap myself into one of the ropes, and show these guard troops how it was done while I hurt my back all over again was gone with her smile.

"Unfortunately," she said, "I have news on that front."

Making eye contact with Tristan, I swallowed.

Did he already know part of this? Was this why he was so insistent in the carriage that we had to stop at kissing?

He gestured for her to head toward the black tent that he stayed in while we were there.

Near his tent, the one that Jacquetta, Gus, and I stayed in was still standing, too. But the door flap was held back, and guards filed in and out.

Whatever they were using it for now, it was a long way from the place where I realized I loved my King.

But as we ducked under the door flap to Tristan's tent, it looked just the same.

The massive table was still in there. Was the one in Breakwater a permanent feature there, or was this one was just hauled around as the King needed.

Standing here, looking down at the table where Tristan and I kissed, in the same arena we first really became something, it brought me back to where my mind was at the time.

I wanted to die then. I thought that if I did, he would find a better queen.

Placing a hand on the table, my other held in his, I looked up into his hazel eyes and saw only love there—a love I almost lost.

"General?" Tristan asked, looking away from me and toward where she was staring down at the map on the table showing the Marshlands.

"We do not know how, or why," she said, still staring at the map as if it would give her answers, "but there are troops in the Marshlands. And they are not ours."

My jaw dropped open.

"Since when do the clergy let any troops in there?" I asked, my voice low and still full of confused rage. If this meant that the clergy, the High Sect, and maybe even Shield Elio had all turned against us, how many regular people would follow?

Almost no one in Lehar was devout or even believed, not

since the ashes began to fall from the sky. No amount of blessed spring water was enough to fix the ashes, or even extinguish the fire in the mine. But I wasn't deluded into thinking there was the same lack of belief in the rest of the country.

Yes. This was very bad.

Tristan let out a long breath, and hung his head, his hand going limp in mine.

I squeezed his hand, and he looked back up at me before giving my hand a squeeze back.

"No matter what is happening in the Marshlands," I said, my eyes focused solely on his, "we will win this war."

His smile was more of a flicker of his mouth than anything close to a real smile. But he let go of my hand, and wrapped his arm around me, kissing my forehead before he looked back at the General with less fear of failure radiating off of him.

"When do we leave?" he asked, his voice low.

Even though he asked quietly, he may as well have screamed it for what it did to me.

"As soon as we hear back from the messenger, I will have a more concrete date for you," General Pace said. "But I suspect you need to be ready to head south in a few days."

"But why are you going personally?" I asked, unable to stay silent, wanting to grab him, to force him to explain to me how he could leave before we were married. For some reason, dread built in my stomach at the thought that we would be delayed, as if somehow the wait would mean forever.

"If I'm going to have any hope of repairing whatever rift the High Sect and the clergy have imagined between us, then I need to be the one to meet with them. Especially if they believe it be so wide as to invite troops in."

"How do you know the troops were invited? Maybe the crows and the troops forced their way in. Maybe the High Sect is in trouble, and they haven't contacted you because silence is the only way they have been able to keep their people safe."

General Pace just shook her head, looking sad more than anything else.

"According to our scouts," she said, "that is not likely."

"Then I'm going with you," I said, but both General Pace and Tristan shook their heads.

"Cinder," Tristan said, turning me so we were facing each other, "that isn't a good idea."

"Why not? Since when do you not want me to watch your back?"

"Since the High Sect does not approve of your relationship," General Pace said, and Tristan winced.

"Excuse me?" My voice was nothing more than a horrified whisper. "Part of the reason there's disagreement with the clergy is because of me?"

"No," Tristan said, grasping my shoulders, and fixing me with a hard stare, "they have problems because of things they want. It is *not* your fault."

"But they don't want me. That's their problem?" Here we were again. Just like the last time we were in this place together, the fact that he would be better off without me slapped me in the face.

He bit his lip, and wrapped me in his arms. Only then did I realize I was shaking, and grabbed onto him.

"Are you sure?" I asked, my voice muffled in his jacket, but he went still and stiff.

"Yes," he said, his voice hard and unflinching. "I don't care what they wanted for my wife. You are my Queen."

"Duchess," General Pace said. I peeked out from his jacket without letting go of him, feeling trapped by my own fears made reality. "The High Sect has been trying to get their way with the monarchy since before you were born. You are just their latest excuse, and they are using the war to press their best chance at causing a problem."

Pulling back from Tristan, I scanned his face, looking for any hint that he was afraid of going to them. All I saw was anger at them, and worry over how I would take this.

"Should I be scared that you won't come back?" I asked, my voice cracking on "back."

He leaned down, and touched his lips to mine before resting our foreheads together.

"I'll be fine. General Pace and a whole compliment of guards will be with me." His voice was soft, his hands on me gentle and strong, but I didn't know if I believed him.

"Maybe…" I pulled back, looking back and forth between him and the General while I tried to find a way around this short of sneaking off after him. That would only infuriate him once he found out. I shook my head, and searched for something that would quell this terrible feeling growing in me. "Maybe I could just stay in the carriage. Not let them know I was there."

"We can't bring carriages into the Marshlands."

"Fuck."

"Cinder." He cupped my cheek, and I sucked in a breath, realizing I wasn't breathing at a normal pace, "I'll be fine. I will always come home to you. Why are you so worried?"

"I…" I didn't know.

Tristan and I had been apart before, even while we faced dangers. It didn't make sense for panic to be setting into my limbs, making me shake. None of the wild and ridiculous scenarios of his doom should have been running through my head. But they were.

Visions of him as my brother's bound captive, or the Corvids dropping him from the sky, or being forced at the point of a sword to sign some kind of joint rule decree that would give the clergy far more power ran through my head.

Shaking my head, I pulled him to me again, tucking my head into his shoulder.

"It's fine," I said, lying and doing a shit job of it based on the way he held me tighter.

Whatever was going on that sent my mind down these paranoid paths, I needed to stop it. Because I was in love with a king, and I needed to learn to act like a queen.

CHAPTER 16

JUST LIKE YOU

Tristan

"Cinder," I said, as soon as the door to the carriage shut, and we were heading back to the palace for a late dinner, "please tell me what's wrong."

She sat next to me, her eyes cast down at the seat across from us, her hand held tight in mine, a frown on her face. Her mind seemed to be so far away.

I waited for her to respond, trying to understand why she seemed so afraid. This wasn't like her. The only time I could remember her getting so upset that she wasn't able to set aside her feelings was when we were on the ship, and I was fighting the crows. That time Second Prince Nevan physically restrained her from helping me. No one held her still now. I didn't understand it.

"You're the King," she said, her voice as far away as her mind seemed.

"And you're my Queen," I said, lifting her hand, and kissing the back of it.

The second I pressed my lips to her skin, she came back from wherever she had been, and looked at me. But there was a desperation in her eyes that didn't make me feel any better.

"No," she said, a quiver in her voice, "I mean, this is going to keep happening."

"I hope we won't keep getting stuck in the middle of wars with traitors popping up, and the clergy trying to gain control." I tried to smile, as if what I said was a joke, although it was completely true.

She ran a hand along my jaw.

"Tristan," she said, her smile melancholy, "you're the King. For the rest of our lives, I have to share you with the country, and your responsibilities. Which I knew. But I wasn't prepared for the way it would feel for you to go into a dangerous situation, and leave me behind. Protecting you is my job."

Grabbing her, I sat her on my lap, her legs draped over the side of me, and pressed my lips to hers.

Our kiss was subdued, her worry seeping into it, but I didn't know what else to do.

What she said was true. This was our life.

Maybe if the Dragon power were real, something far greater than just feeling warm to Cinder's touch, then she wouldn't worry the same way. But, then again, if the Dragon power were half the fabled might that everyone spoke of, then I could have crushed the war before it started.

All of that was wishful thinking. I didn't have the Dragon power to fall back on. The only things I had were my bow and my sword, the guards and the General at my back.

And Cinder. Normally, I had Cinder right behind me, next to me, an incredible power all by herself.

Pulling back from her, I ran a hand along her hairline like she liked, and she leaned into my touch, closing her eyes.

"I know you want to protect me," I said, my voice low, "and I know it will drive you to distraction while I'm gone that you can't. But your job isn't over while I'm away."

Her brow furrowed, a line appearing in the middle, and I rubbed my thumb over it until it went away.

"What am I supposed to do while you're in the Marshlands?" She didn't ask it as if whining, but as if genuinely curious as to what I meant. She asked as if she was Fighter Cinder awaiting an order from her king on the battlefield.

"You're protecting the whole country now, not just me." I smiled as she ran through the idea in her head.

"But protecting you is protecting the whole country."

"Cinder, that isn't true." How could I make her understand this? "I know everyone thinks that way, but this country is more than the Dragon King lineage. We both know that doesn't mean anything anymore."

"We don't know that." She shook her head, her hold on my jacket tightening.

"There may be something to the stories, but it has been so long, no one puts much stock in them anymore. If they did, we wouldn't be having this war."

She just shook her head, denying what I knew she already understood.

No matter how much I didn't want to bring it up, no matter how much I never wanted to think about it again, I had to. There was no other way to make her accept that this was the way it had to be.

"For someone who was willing to kill me not that long ago," I whispered, smiling and trying to make my voice as soft as possible to alleviate some of the pain it would bring her, "you seem more concerned with the end of the Dragon King line than I thought you would be."

Her eyes widened, and her mouth fell open. Her hands

dropped off my jacket, landing in her lap before her entire face hardened.

"That is not funny," she said, her voice as hard as it got when she was fighting.

Damn it. This was what I was afraid of.

"I'm not trying to be funny," I took one of her hands only for her to yank it back. So, I settled on having one hand on her back, and the other resting empty on the seat next to me. "I need you to understand and be okay with this. This will be your life if you agree to be the queen."

Cinder's face didn't change from her look of half shock and half fury, but she didn't climb off my lap, force my hand away from her back, or attack me. So that was positive.

"When the country needs us, even if it risks our lives, we have to answer."

"That is exactly why you have me," she said, her voice still sharp. "But you're leaving me behind."

"No," I said, trying to take her hand again, and this time she let me, her grasp as strong as mine, "I have you because I love you, and I want to spend the rest of our lives together. The reason I have the Guard is to protect me when I take risks."

Her face fell, a shiver running through her that made me wonder if it hurt her back before she leaned against me, crumpling.

"Please explain to me how I'm supposed to handle this, knowing something could happen to you, and I am too far away to do anything to stop it."

I smiled, holding her close, and kissing the top of her head. There was only one way I knew to explain it.

"The same way I handle myself every time you race into a battle."

She sat up and looked at me, eyes full of fear before she squeezed them shut for a moment.

"You..." she trailed off before she opened her eyes and

cupped my cheek, scanning my face as if she was memorizing it. "Every time I fight?"

Just thinking about the last time that we were in battle, watching her plummet to the ground on the back of that fucking crow made everything in me scream. My body felt like it was on fire.

"Every single time." I wrapped her up, and she melded into me, holding on just as tight as the carriage stopped outside the palace.

The door opened a moment later, but neither of us moved.

I didn't care how upset the clergy was about Cinder becoming queen. Not right now.

Maybe we should have been more concerned about what people would think as we clutched each other tightly, delaying our exit from the carriage. But this was my home. And this was the woman I loved. And we were already putting up with enough.

Finally, she leaned back, and scooted off me to leave the carriage. But before we separated even that small distance, she took my hand.

Holding each other's hands, we made our way up the stairs and into the palace, each of us quiet, each of us thinking more about our conversation than either of us were ready to admit. Especially since we weren't alone.

The number of people in the palace since the war started had increased so much that it was uncomfortable to walk through the halls.

Once we got to where the stairs split, I paused. She followed suit, turning a questioning look my way.

"Do you...um..." How was I supposed to ask this? If I did and she wanted to, she might get angry at me for even thinking otherwise. But if I didn't ask, she could feel forced to hold her opinion so she didn't upset the king.

"My King," she said, her eyes soft as I swallowed, "I don't want to let you go until I have to."

Letting out a breath, my shoulders relaxed, and I smiled.

"Which room should we go to?" I wanted her to go to my room, but she looked down the hallway toward her own, and bit her lip.

"If we go to yours, we should at least tell Jacquetta and Gus that I'm fine."

Her smile as I nodded and lifted her hand to my lips was enough to make me want to pick her up and carry her off no matter what people thought.

But instead, like nine times out of ten in my life, I did what was expected of me in public. I followed after her as if thoughts of burying myself in her, and making her forget that I was going to leave soon weren't running through my head.

"You keep doing that," she said, as we reached her door.

"Keep doing what?"

Cinder looked at me from under lashes, her tongue darting out to wet her bottom lip before she pinched that lip with her teeth.

She stepped closer to me, tilting her head to whisper into my ear.

"Most people probably think you're sighing like a lovesick dope."

I almost laughed because I didn't realize I had sighed at all. Yet it didn't surprise me in the least. It did make me wonder how successful I was at keeping those sounds from happening while thinking about her during meetings.

"But I know," Cinder said, her voice as seductive as she was when she was sparring, moving as fluid as a river, and as fast as a hummingbird with all the strength her well-built muscles afforded her, "that when you make that sound, you're picturing us, naked, with your cock deep inside me."

"Fuck," my voice was a strangled croak, too quiet for anyone other than her to hear, but the way the blood in my body flooded downward had me looking around us in case anyone noticed what was going on.

With a wicked grin flashing on her face before it settled back into the same careful expression of before, she leaned back and looked at me again.

"Don't worry, my King," she said, in her normal voice, "I plan on having you stay that way as much as possible until you need to leave."

"You told me once that you don't know how to flirt. You lied." Any sting from my accusation was stolen by the breathlessness of my voice.

She smiled.

"I still don't know how to flirt. That was just telling the truth."

CHAPTER 17

WARNINGS

Cinder

"I must see your back before you go," Jacquetta said, her hands on her hips, once we were inside my rooms and standing before her, asking if I could have a night in my King's bed. As if I were a child asking to play late with a friend outside the nursery.

"You sound like my parents," I said, smiling despite how ridiculous it was.

"Good," Jacquetta said, "someone needs to keep you in line. King Tristan is far too besotted to think clearly."

"Lady Jacquetta," Tristan complained. I laughed both at the fact that he didn't argue, and at the look on Gus's face which clearly showed that she agreed with her wife.

"Fine," I said, "let's get this over with."

Making my way to my room, I pulled Tristan along with me. Once we were all in there, he helped me undo my dress, exposing my back. Something about the whole process sapped away the heat of the comment I made to him in the hallway.

Jacquetta and Gus hovered behind me. But it wasn't until Tristan stepped beside me to look for himself, keeping a hand in mine, that I bothered to say something.

"What?" I asked, bracing myself for more bad news, that I had somehow worsened over the course of the day.

"Your bruises are already less swollen, and turning green at the edges," Jacquetta said.

"That's a good sign, right?" I knew bruises. They turned green before they healed completely.

"It is good," Gus said, sounding odd.

"Just very fast," Jacquetta said, sounding just as strange as Gus did.

"Well," I said, lifting my dress back into place, and beginning to tie the front, "your baths and poultices are like magic."

"Do you want to bring things with you?" Tristan asked, coming back to face me, relief in his eyes.

"Yes, but..." I did need different clothes for tomorrow, but what would the servants do? Would the palace get to talking? Would it get back to the clergy? Would this plan make everything worse for Tristan? More dangerous?

"Cinder," he said, squeezing my hand, "this is your home. No one here should cause too much of a problem. We can control the spread of information some from here."

I nodded and went to my trunks.

With Gus and Jacquetta's help, we set aside a small pile of things we thought I would need.

Looking to Tristan, I was in awe of the fact that we were here now, after everything.

No matter what happened next, no matter how long he had to be away from me, I was going to share his space in a much more real way than we had before.

And he looked so happy.

Grin on his face, eyes bright, he ran a hand along the soft fabric of one of the dresses on the bed.

"Why don't we just move your trunks up to my room?" he asked, voice quiet and soft as he swallowed, turning to meet my gaze.

"Because you haven't married yet," Gus said, raising her brows, and smirking like it was a challenge.

"Then, soon," Tristan said, making his way to me, pulling me close to his chest, his eyes shifting as I watched, the hazel gaining more gold in a moment.

When he said it, it was a wish for more than just me as his wife. He said it as a wish for the end of the war, and the safety of both of us.

"Yes," I said, "soon."

If I had my way, it would be sooner than he thought. No matter how hard it was to share him with the kingdom, to have him risk his life for every person in the kingdom just as I risked mine for him and the people I loved, it would never stop me marrying him.

Not now. Not anymore.

"Alright," Gus said, giving him a shove on the arm that made me laugh, "get out of here before you both get too far to leave. I don't really want to hear you again."

"Gus," I said, burying my face in his chest, feeling it shake against my face as he silently laughed.

"Gus," Jacquetta said, "he is the King."

"Who is our friend, and fucking our other friend. I don't see the problem." Gus looked so proud of herself that I had to lean on Tristan to stay upright because I was laughing so hard. Meanwhile, Jacquetta looked scandalized.

After knowing Madam Valentin, I could only imagine how hard it was for Jacquetta to accept this level of breach in formality.

"She's right," I said, "no matter the titles, we're all friends."

"I...I do not know if I can stop acting like you are the King." Jacquetta seemed apologetic, wringing her hands together as she looked back at him.

"You have before," I said, "but don't worry, Jacquetta. It will get easier for you to yell at him."

"What? Why would she yell at me?" Tristan looked back and forth between me and Jacquetta, but Gus and I just laughed as I patted his arm.

"No reason," I said. "Let's go."

Turning to them, these women who brought me here, and made it possible for me to have my King in the first place, it suddenly felt like spending more nights in his room meant something for our friendship that I wasn't entirely sure I was ready for.

"See you soon," Gus said, her smile softening as she wrapped an arm around Jacquetta who leaned into her.

"Goodnight," I said, following after Tristan toward the royal private wing of the palace.

As soon as we were out in the hall, Tristan slipped his hand from mine and placed it on the small of my back in a comforting touch.

"What are you thinking for dinner?" he asked, as if he wasn't aware of how loaded the last moments were with my Ladies.

I smiled at him, more thankful for him right now than usual. And I was always thankful for him.

"Do you have anything specific in mind?" I asked, deciding to play along.

After all the emotions running through me from the news at the training grounds, I wasn't sure I could handle the thought of leaving my rooms. I wasn't sure I could handle anything other than pretending everything was alright, and that the largest decision in my world at the moment was picking dinner.

"Cake," he said, with a grin.

"You want to eat cake for dinner? Since when are you the

child sovereign kind of king? That's not a proper dinner." I shook my head and tried not to laugh at the false shock on his face.

"Child sovereign? Are you calling me spoiled, Duchess Cinder?"

"Oh, you're ridiculous. Of course, you're spoiled, Dragon King Tristan, who has never known a time when he isn't supposed to be the most powerful person in the kingdom."

"Since when are you my mother?" He barely kept it together on that one, his chest lurching as he held in his laughter.

I waited as a servant passed us, probably headed to gather my things, biting my lip to hold in my comment.

We crossed the stairs, finally alone in the private, royal wing of the palace, and I said, "Well, if I'm your mother now, does that mean I get to punish you if you're a bad boy?"

"Cinder," he said, his tone changing to one of serious reprimand that only made me smile wider, "if you keep saying things like that, I will never believe you haven't been pretending this whole time that you don't know exactly how to flirt, and haven't been playing with my mind."

"Actually," I said, enjoying this power a little too much, not willing to feel bad about it as we took the first few steps up the stairs towards his room, "I just think that I'm only good at flirting with you because you like fucking me so much."

Tristan made a growling noise under his breath, turned, pressed me up against the curved exterior wall of the stairwell, pinning my arms against the stone, and shaking his head as he stared at me.

"You have no idea how much I love fucking you. If I really were spoiled and could have whatever I wanted, whenever I wanted..." He bent down and kissed my neck, his teeth pressing into my tender skin, his tongue caressing.

My body responded in a second, every need in me to have him, to hear him moan, to see his eyes devour me made me wet, made my legs tremble as the heat of him soaked into my muscles, rendering them almost useless.

He moved up from my neck to my ear, biting on it before he whispered, "You and I would do little else other than fucking. I would watch you train, spar with you, marvel at the way your body moves and the strength of you, then fuck you until you screamed my name, and were reduced to a weak, wet, quivering body, too relaxed to even move."

"Do it," I said, my voice thin as my breathing picked up.

That growling sound from deep in his chest rumbled through him, shaking me as he continued to nibble on my ear and my neck.

With my arms trapped by his hands, I was at his mercy. What started as something I loved, grew into something I was starting to hate because it made me want him so much. Right now.

"You make that noise…" he said. I didn't realize I was making a noise, but I was about to moan as his hot breath ran over the wet spot on my neck from his mouth, sending a shiver through me. "If I had my way, you would never stop."

"Then…oh." I could barely talk as he bit into my neck, and pressed his body against mine.

And then I heard it, the plaintive whining moan that came from me. It was like begging without words. I desperately wanted him to drag me up the stairs and show me what he wanted.

"Oh, what, my Queen?" he asked, smiling against my skin as he moved his mouth down my neck toward my breasts.

"Bring me upstairs," I said before he shifted, rubbing his hard length against me. Even through his pants and my skirts, I wondered if he could feel how wet I was.

"For dinner?" His laugh against the top of my breast made me want to shove him against the wall, and have my way with him. But before I could try it, he shifted, lifted me up, and carried me up the stairs in swift movements.

I wrapped my arms around his neck and tried to kiss him.

"No," he said, pulling his face away and grinning at me, "we need to eat dinner."

"There are other things we can do with our mouths," I said, trying not to beg, but close to it.

"King Tristan," a servant said behind him, carrying a tray and looking more than a little shocked at finding us walking up the stairs. "Forgive me. Should I come back when you and Duchess Cinder are ready for your dinner?"

"You ordered when we were in my rooms, didn't you?" I whispered, staring at him, more than a little frustrated about the delay and the game he was playing.

His smile was radiant, and I shook my head.

"Of course not, Silvain. Come on up."

Fine. We could eat dinner, but I was going to get my way tonight. Preferably more than once. I was done with being thwarted. And if he thought everything about tonight was going to go his way, he was very wrong.

CHAPTER 18

SWEET

Tristan

Cinder was so frustrated that it made the ache in my cock worth it.

Her eyes bored into mine the whole time I carried her up the stairs, and it was an effort not to laugh at the scowl on her face.

I meant it when I suggested cake. Although it was only part of the dinner I ordered while she picked out clothes with Jacquetta and Augustina.

Finally, we made it into my room, Silvain following behind us.

Part of me thought about just keeping her in my arms, just to make her even more frustrated. I wondered at what point she would start yelling at me. But I didn't want to find out exactly how angry she could get, so I set her on her feet.

She stepped away from me, her arms crossed under her

breasts—all of which did nothing to deter the heat collecting in my cock.

Adjusting my jacket to cover up the evidence of our few moments in the stairwell, I walked over to Silvain to help him lay out our dinner on the table.

While I helped him, another servant arrived with Cinder's things, and she finally uncrossed her arms to help him with them.

I stole a look her way as I put the last dish on the table to find that most of the tension had seeped out of her. As she found space on a vanity for her things, the way she looked around the room made me think she was deciding where her trunks and other things would go, where she would move things, how she would make the room hers.

The same place in my chest that ached thinking about her when we were on the trip to the valley to get the kids ached in a wholly different way now.

Silvain waited at the door until the other servant joined him, both bowing as I nodded my thanks and Cinder gave hers.

As soon as they were gone, I turned to Cinder, who continued staring at her things on the vanity in front of her, playing with a hairbrush.

"I love you," I said, my throat tight. "Will you please move your things in here?"

Having Cinder share a space with me was in some ways more important than a wedding. She couldn't understand it, and part of me didn't either.

My heartbeat was loud in my ears as she turned to look at me.

Even after everything, I didn't understand the flat look on her face. I couldn't guess what it meant. And not knowing what she was thinking about this was enough to make it hard for me to breathe.

She took a deep breath, and made her way across the room

to stand in front of me, looking into my eyes as if searching for an answer to a question I hadn't heard. But I so desperately wanted to give her the right answer.

"Why do you have to be so wonderful when I want to be irritated with you?" she finally asked. I wrapped her up in my arms, breathing her in, basking in the way her mere presence made my heart ache for the best possible reasons.

"Does that mean you'll bring your things in here? Does that mean you're ready to share a room with me?"

Her hands ran up and down my back, her hair tickling my face.

"Of course, I will," she said, her voice quiet, which made me think she understood exactly how much it meant to me.

"But only," she said, pausing for a long moment as she pulled away from me, her face still with the same unreadable expression, "if you marry me."

"Cinder," I said, smiling and shaking my head, "for a queen, you're a terrible negotiator. I asked you first."

She bit her lip, stepping back, taking my hands, and tugging me over to the chairs next to us around the table full of food.

"No," she said, "I mean will you marry me before you leave for the Marshlands?"

"I...really?" The space between my eyebrows hurt from furrowing them so hard. "Don't you at least want a gold dress? A special dinner? A dance? Anything?"

"Tristan," she said, my name like a promise on her lips that made me want her in my lap so I could hold her, "all I want is you. I want to know that, while you're in the Marshlands, and I have to wait here, that..."

She shook her head, looking away and then back at me. And I waited, more than confused by what she was trying to get at.

"You'll probably think I'm being silly, or stupid, or just not making any sense in my worry. But it feels like our vows will connect us."

I surged up off the chair and pressed my lips to hers in a kiss with more force than was strictly necessary, and she probably wasn't expecting it based on the little sound of surprise that popped out of her.

Pulling back a second later, perching myself on the edge of my seat, I put a hand to her face, running my thumb along the scar on her cheek.

"Whatever that feeling is," I said, "it's not silly or stupid. With or without the vows, I'll feel my connection to you no matter how far away you are. But if you think that will make it stronger, I'm not going to argue with you. And I love you even more for wanting that with me."

"Tristan, I love you, too." She smiled, and I leaned forward to kiss her again. But she wouldn't let me deepen the kiss, pulling away a moment later. "But we need to have some of this cake."

Laughing, I sat back down, and looked at the dinner laid out before us. Picking up one of the tiny cakes, I turned back to Cinder, holding it between my thumb and forefinger.

"I had this idea we could pick a flavor for our wedding cake today, as a happy thing for the day." I grinned and took a small bite out of the little cake before holding it out to Cinder.

Her smile was radiant, and her laughter soft as she opened her mouth, and took the rest of the cake from me.

We both ate our pieces, but I was so lost in looking at the beautiful woman in front of me that it was an effort to focus on the chocolate flavor as it filled my mouth.

The dress she wore was a simple one with a leather panel that laced together in the front, holding it all on her.

But the best part of the dress wasn't that the leather panel hugged her waist, and pressed her breasts up and out, the tops of them clear and full above the neckline.

No, the best part was that the sleeves had long slits in them so that, at times, like right then as she leaned one arm on the table, I got a glimpse of the muscles in her arms as they flexed, showing off their perfect shape and sheer size.

I wasn't lying when I told her that watching her train was one of my favorite things. Her arms were part of the reason why.

She worried for me while I was gone, and I would worry for her, too. But there was something about knowing just how capable she was at fighting, just how strong, and just how much she had already survived that gave me a measure of peace. More peace than I thought I would ever get in loving a hero.

And that said nothing about how much it made me want to pin her to the wall again.

"Tristan," she said, "you're staring."

"Yes, I am." My smile was wide as she shook her head and reached out to take another cake.

This time, she took a bite and fed me the rest.

Strawberry with chocolate frosting.

"I like this one better than the first," I said once I was done. She made a face, her mouth going to one side.

"First one," she said, taking another off the table before I could.

Cinder fed me a bite first, and something like vanilla ran over my tongue.

My reaction was just a nod side to side, and Cinder made a face that made me think she agreed with me on this one at least.

Before she had a chance to take another, I did it for her, holding the little cake out to her for a bite.

She took her bite, her eyes widened, and a grin formed on her still chewing lips.

"That good?" I asked, popping the bite into my mouth.

It was some kind of play on the flavor of the musa fruit, a long, yellow fruit that we rarely got because it only grew in the Southern countries on the continent.

"You want this one?" I asked, enjoying it, but wondering if it wasn't too strange. The flavor was so different from other things we ate, I couldn't even decide if I liked it.

"Out of what we've had so far, this is my favorite."

We had yet to get to the cake I thought she would like the best. I was sure it would be my favorite, but I nodded anyway.

"Here," she said, picking up a cake and letting me take a bite.

Finally, this was the one I wanted, the one I thought she would love.

It was a cake version of the rolls popular throughout the country that we all ate in the morning, sweet and spicy at the same time. The smell was heavenly, and even reminded me of Cinder, the way her hair and skin smelled when she wasn't doused in Jacquetta's cures.

But when Cinder put it in her mouth, her face fell, her eyes downcast, staring at her own hands.

"Cinder?" I leaned forward and put a hand on hers, more than worried now that the fun was over, and she was trapped again in her concern over me leaving her for the Marshlands soon.

"No," she shook her head and met my eyes, turning her hands to wrap them around mine, "I'm fine. Just…" She licked her lips, and tried again, "This cake tastes like the air in Lehar smells. It made me wish that the war was over so I could try Duchess Inara's machine. Maybe if we cleared the air, we could actually eat the rolls there again. No one does now. I didn't used to either. But now…"

She turned to the side, her eyes softening and her mouth quirking up at the corner.

"Did it make you miss Lehar?" I asked, rubbing a thumb over the back of her hand.

"Yes and no." She smiled, and, even though there was still a shadow hanging over her, making her eyes not match the open and full curve of her lips, I knew she wasn't as upset as I thought.

"What does that mean?" I hoped she wasn't about to tell me she wanted to return to Lehar for a while. I hoped she wouldn't tell me this wasn't her home.

My heart beat harder in my chest, and the heat spread through my body with every thump.

"Before it happened, Lehar didn't smell like hellfire water all the time. It used to smell that way close to the mines, but everywhere else it was the roses that floated by on the breeze more often than anything else."

"The Valentin roses?"

She sighed and looked over at the roses growing in my room, tracking the vine as it wrapped into the rafters.

"Can we do the musa and the morning roll cakes?" she asked, turning back to look at me.

"You could tell the morning roll one was my favorite?"

"Tristan," she said, cupping my cheek and grinning at me, a wicked glint in her eyes now, "I'm pretty good at knowing what you want."

CHAPTER 19

NUMB

Cinder

I grinned as Tristan got that look in his eye, the one that said he wanted me as much as I wanted him.

He leaned forward, tugging me toward him. But just over his shoulder, outside the large windows, dark shapes swooped in front of the glow of the moon, blocking out the light.

Surging to my feet, I darted around him toward the window as he asked, "Cinder? What's wrong?"

But I didn't need to answer, another shape blocked out the moon, and over my shoulder I heard him suck in a breath before his feet pounded along the floor.

"Tristan," I yelled, whirling around only to see his back as he flung open the door and looked over his shoulder at me.

"Please, stay here," he said, and then he ran down the stairs.

"Fuck," I picked up my skirts, running after him.

Maybe I needed to look at his back as he left me to go to the

Marshlands. Maybe he needed to go down to the courtyard, and see what was happening now. But I sure as fuck didn't need to sit here and wait while he did it. Not right now. Not yet.

Running down the stairs, my healing back flared up in a rage that made pain radiate down my legs, numbing my toes.

But I just kept running.

This was the last thing Jacquetta would have suggested I do while the bruises and deeper injuries still bothered me. No matter what Tristan said about my position as soon-to-be queen, this was, and always would be, my first priority. Protecting my King.

My numb toes made it hard to land my feet properly on the steps. I wasn't going fast enough.

Pressing myself to increase my speed, I caught a toe on a step, and careened forward.

Unable to do much more than fling my arms out before me, and position my head so it didn't crash into the outside wall of the curving staircase, I slammed into it with my back.

Shoulder blades first, my body hit the unforgiving wall followed by the rest of my back. I stretched to catch myself on my hands and my knees on the stairs before I continued the fall.

Even that little movement made me cry out as every bone in my back became as obvious as my hands in front of my face.

I couldn't be sure if I skinned my hands and knees, or not. The only thing I could really feel were the bones in my back as they wailed, making themselves my tormentors instead of just my skeleton.

On shaking arms and legs, I tried to shove myself up, tried to continue down the stairs to the courtyard and Tristan.

But I couldn't get much further than sitting upright, my breath heaving, still not getting enough oxygen into my body.

Leaning against the interior wall of the stairwell, I looked down toward where the curve led too far away for me to see. I thought of Tristan.

He would be out in the middle of the battle if it really was a Corvid attack.

No doubt about that.

My King.

Pressing my side against the interior wall, which was little more than a thick post of stone, I used my leg muscles, shallow breaths, a back as stiff as the wall I was touching, all the muscle mass I built up over the course of years of training, and the image of my King needing me to get myself up to standing.

Once I was up, I took desperate breaths while I waited a moment to prepare to move again.

"Go, Cinder," I muttered. My voice was strained, yet as hard as the obsidian the palace was made of.

The long days spent bandaged, cut, bleeding, and immobile served as powerful motivation to take one shaking step.

But now my toes weren't numb as I set them down on the step below me, and then the next.

With each step I found that place, the one right next to the cold place in my mind that was as warm as my skin after being in the baths under the manor in Lehar. That place was as comfortable as Tristan's hand in mine, and as perfect as his eyes.

Waiting for me in that place were all the people I loved. And the future I wanted. And they all told me to keep going, to feel the pain later, to save Tristan.

Making my way to the bottom of the steps, I picked up speed, not running, not jogging, but moving fast and sure, the screaming in my back drowned out by the voices of the love-filled place in my mind.

Even here, though, deep within the place in my mind that allowed me peace, the sounds of war reached me.

Someone was yelling, the voice harsh, barking out orders loud enough to get to me as I stepped out of the royal wing of the palace.

The last time I stood in this spot when the palace was under attack, I was too late.

I couldn't be this time.

Here, I could grab the railing, using my arms to help me as I hurried down another fucking flight of stairs, this one with servants and others hurrying past on their way to do whatever their job was during this moment.

At least that was something—here in the palace everyone knew what to do.

When Lehar was attacked during the last war, the manor was left with so few who had any idea what to do at all, let alone what was the right choice.

Back then, I didn't know either.

Past protecting the people flooding into the manor for refuge, I had no idea. That much was still true. At least this time, I had a better chance at success, injury or not.

That's what I took with me as I stalked out of the massive doors that stood wide open at the front of the palace and onto the steps.

I expected carnage, destruction, desperation, fear, and a terrible chasm of sadness yawning open to swallow us all whole.

Bracing myself for the impact, I was left standing as dumbfounded as Tristan was at the bottom of the stairs, bow in hand, an arrow nocked, aimed at a whole formation of Corvids.

They beat their oversized wings, every one of them facing my King, holding scraps of white fabric in their massive talons, seemingly paying no attention to the guards positioned all over the courtyard and on the balconies, also aiming at them.

What were they waiting for?

Making my way down the stairs towards Tristan's side, General Pace flanking him on the other, I passed one of Tristan's personal guards, and grabbed a sword out of the scabbard that lay across his back.

He barely let his eyes dart my way before he focused again on the threat, his own bow and arrow ready.

Finally, I ducked under Tristan's bow, stepping in front of him, lifting the sword. Ignoring the pain shooting through my back, I focused on the giant bird above us.

The Corvid at the head of the group let out that terrible, not quite human laugh.

As it did, a commotion happening on the other side of the courtyard caught my eye for a moment before the Corvid's voice, crackling in that mix between a bird's call and human's speech came to life.

"So," the bird said, "the rumors are true. I did not believe it."

Narrowing my eyes, I stayed silent, although I was sure it was talking about me being alive.

Behind me, Tristan sucked in a breath, and I wondered if they had kept my condition a secret, hoping the news wouldn't get back to Ash.

Did that mean that me coming out here would be a problem? Did I make a mistake?

"You made your delivery," Tristan said, his voice harsh, "now leave before we take the opportunity."

The fucking bird laughed that twisted laugh, making the hairs along my arms stand on end.

"And we thought there were rules of war," the bird said.

"What rules were you following when you helped my brother torture and murder a child?" My voice was a hiss of fury. I didn't care if they knew how much I wanted them all dead for what they had been a part of.

One of the birds in the back shifted, dropping down into the courtyard, making everyone brace themselves for whatever was about to come next.

But the bird ducked its head, feathers along its extended wings shaking as it shifted between one breath and the next into a human woman with floor-length, black hair and a skin-tight black gown, her tan skin flawless along her exposed, outstretched arms.

"The few Corvids involved in the death of the child were stripped of their wings," the woman said, keeping her arms out, palms forward, the white cloth draped over one hand.

After the funeral for Princess Fiachra, I didn't question the odd position of this woman's arms as they clearly communicated by arm and hand gestures often. But I did question whether slave holders cared enough about a single child to punish her murderers.

"Is this your apology?" Tristan asked behind me as I scoffed.

"Yes," the woman said, "consider this return an exchange, a life for a life, for the child."

"No matter what you say," I said, my jaw clenched tight, my back aching, although I wouldn't let the Corvids see any weakness in me, "as long as you are still working with my brother, you are all fools."

"Fools?" The Corvid woman snarled in my direction, but I just shifted to be more menacing to her than to the bird at the head of the formation still flying above us.

"Ash wants to take over Onyx, Amethyst, and then Corvid before he marches on the rest of the continent."

She laughed loud and long, throwing her head back. The sound echoed by the other birds, their not-fully-human voices adding a note of nightmare to her cackling.

"Oh," she said, her voice slicing and derisive, even as it was almost a purr, "you really are a deluded little girl who thinks she is a sword."

Everything in me wanted to attack her, to dash forward, heedless of the threat of the birds above, and whatever trap this was. Because I didn't think for a second it wasn't a trap. But I held back, tightening my grip on the sword before I allowed my hands to return to the proper hold.

Her mouth split into a grin, her chin dropping as she stared at me as if her eyes alone could do damage.

I grinned back, putting every bit of the woman who enjoyed having a death mask for a face into that expression, and basking in the way she lifted her chin while her smile vanished.

"Someday," she said, "you will understand that there are ways to twist other people's goals to your own while never intending for them to get their wish."

"Like right now," I said. "What exactly are you trying to accomplish with this show right now?"

"Ah," she said, "well, that is the question, is it not?"

Between one second and the next, I knew she was going to shift her hands, and signal to the all the birds whatever she wanted to.

Instead of letting her, I screamed as I darted forward, ready to strike her down.

With a burst of dark light, she shifted, launching herself into the air before I reached her, cawing as she went.

The second she joined the other Corvids, they all made their squawking bird cries, and flew off into the night.

My own ability to push through my pain flew away on the backs of the crows, taking with it the ability to keep fighting, keep attacking, and be strong.

By the time I reached the place in the courtyard where she was standing moments before, I dropped the sword, the sound of it clanging to the stones echoing in the silence. My legs gave out, and I crumpled to the ground, unable to do anything as my body shutdown.

"Cinder," Tristan called out behind me as my hands hit the stones, and I tried to stop the world from spinning around me.

CHAPTER 20
MASKING

Tristan

"Damn it," I said, my voice little more than a growl under my breath as I made it to Cinder's side, my bow and quiver long forgotten by the base of the stairs.

I scooped her up, one arm under her knees, another behind her back in a position that was becoming all too familiar.

She whimpered and curled forward away from my arm, so I shifted, my hand bracing her side more than resting on her back, leaning her tighter against me.

"What happened?" I asked. Turning, I headed straight for Jacquetta. It was the only thing I knew to do when she was in pain, which made the fact that I couldn't do anything other than this an acute ache in my heart.

"Fell," she said, her voice thin and breathing shallow like she was back to not being able to fully use her lungs, "on the stairs."

By the time she was done speaking just those three words in a row, her voice gave out, trailing off into nothing.

"Damn it. Fuck." I shouldn't have left her. I shouldn't have run out of the room without making sure she made it down the stairs in one piece.

I knew she was too tired, her body too worn out from pushing herself too hard today.

"King Tristan," General Pace said, stopping me by the large main doors, her hand on my arm, "you need to see to him, too. Find out what happened with the Corvids."

"Bring him to the physick," I said, continuing into the palace, "I'll be there shortly. I need to get Cinder to Jacquetta."

"Someone can do that," General Pace said. "His information—"

"No." I cut her off. I was more than done with her suggestion. "His information can wait. No one else will touch her."

Hurrying up the grand staircase, turning toward her room again where we had started this night with hopes that she would never have to stay anywhere but in our room again, made that ache in my heart worse.

"Who?" Cinder asked, her voice a strangled sound that made me walk faster down the hallway.

"What do you mean, my Flame?" I asked, desperate for her to start sounding like that fierce, undying flame she was again.

"Needs…physick…who?" she asked, with a breath between every word.

"Are you asking who needs to see the physick? Who I need to talk to?"

Finally, we were close to her door, and as much as I wanted to explain, the way she spoke made me worry it was making her worse. I called out before I even got there.

"Lady Jacquetta," I yelled, "Lady Augustina."

One of them had to hear me. I needed one of them to hear me.

"Help," I yelled again, even louder this time.

Right before I got to the door to her rooms, it creaked open, and a very confused looking Augustina stepped out, her eyes widening as she saw us.

"Get her inside," she leaned back in the room and yelled. "Star, Cinder's hurt."

With a wave for me to follow, I ducked into the room as she held the door open, Jacquetta darting over to me and looking over Cinder, her face like a thundercloud aiming lightning at both of us.

"You were supposed to be careful," she said.

"She fell running down the stairs because Corvids were in the courtyard, and I ran to meet them. This is my fault." The last thing I wanted was for Jacquetta to be angry with Cinder.

After everything else, if her friendships began to suffer, I wasn't sure I could forgive myself for my role in it.

"No," Cinder muttered. But she didn't go on. As much as I knew I was right, that it was my fault, I wasn't going to argue with her right now.

"Bring her in the bathroom," Jacquetta said, shaking her head. "I need to see her. I need to understand how bad this is."

I followed after them, more than worried about how bad this was myself, and still not wanting to let go of her for Jacquetta to do what she needed to.

Augustina started a bath, holding pots out to Jacquetta, but Jacquetta shook her head.

"We have to find out what we need first," Jacquetta said, motioning for me to set Cinder down.

The last thing I wanted was to put her down, to risk her feeling any additional pain, but I still needed to see the General, and take part in the questioning, too.

Holding back a few select curse words, I shifted, carefully setting Cinder down near the tub, keeping my hands tight on her and supporting her so that she wasn't relying on her own power.

Cinder groaned, but her eyes opened wide, her focus singular, her jaw clenched in a look I knew well. She was preparing herself not to show her pain.

"Don't do that," I said, keeping my voice and anger contained to my eyes, not wanting to yell at my Queen when she was hurting, no matter how much I thought she needed to hear what I had to say.

"Don't do…what?" she asked, still holding onto my arms as she continued morphing into the picture of unbothered stone I knew to be a lie.

"Pretend you're not in pain." My voice was low, barely more than a whisper.

"I'm going to be fine…nothing Jacquetta can't heal…and you have work to do. Go."

Her face betrayed nothing, and I ground my teeth, torn between forcing the issue and leaving to question him.

"King Tristan," Jacquetta said, "this is war. Go, take care of it so you can get back here."

Augustina came to Cinder's side, taking her arm, supporting her with a nod to me.

They were a unified front against me, and damn it if they weren't right. After looking for him all this time, the fucking crows dropped him into the courtyard, a very battered gift I hoped could tell us something to win this war.

But I didn't want to leave her.

Everything in me rebelled at the idea of walking out the door when she needed me.

"Fuck," I said, my voice harsh in my throat, causing a physical pain to match what was raging in me as the blood in my veins grew even hotter.

"Go," Cinder said, her entire body still wearing that damn mask to make me feel better, "I love you."

I stepped in close to her, putting a hand on her back as gently as possible, and pressed my lips to hers, careful not to hurt her.

She made a sighing sound deep in her throat, and I pulled back to look into the eyes of my Queen.

Words failed me. I wanted to tell her I would be back soon. I wanted to tell her we would make this right, she would get better, not to push herself too hard.

There were a thousand things I wanted to say, but nothing made its way past my throat except, "I love you."

And I ran from the room. I would sprint until I could get back to her, and he better be ready to answer my questions.

CHAPTER 21

RUNNING OUT

Cinder

As soon as I was sure Tristan was through the door and into the hallway, I sagged against Gus, the last of my strength sapped by the effort to hold myself up without alarming him.

"Cinder," Gus said, her voice half sigh and half admonishment, "he was right."

"He...needed...to go." My voice was a sad impersonation of the one I spoke to him with, and the few words left me gasping, my back screaming, and not enough air in the room.

"And now you need to take off this dress," Jacquetta said, leaning over and turning off the bath that was strangely empty of anything other than water.

"But..." I wanted to ask why nothing was in the steaming tub yet, but Jacquetta shot me a look that stopped the words in my mouth.

"We already had to wait until your growling dragon left.

Come on," Jacquetta said, her voice sharp as she and Gus proceeded to undress me in moves more careful than their voices, with hands that managed to help me stay upright while they did it.

"How bad is it?" I asked once I stood before them nude, Gus and Jacquetta each supporting an arm and staring at my back.

"Not as bad as I expected," Jacquetta said, "except…"

She touched a spot on my back, close to my spine by my shoulder blade, and a line of pain shot out from the point of contact to trace my rib cage, under my shoulder blade.

I gasped, and my legs gave out.

The only thing that kept me standing was the support of my friends behind me as the whole bathroom swam in front of me. The water in the tub and steam coming off of it turned my vision into a maelstrom.

"Broken," Jacquetta said, her voice making its way into my mind even as it whirled with the information. "That's what I was afraid of."

"Hnngh," I muttered, wanting to ask what she meant, but unable to manage when I was so tired.

After so long in bed, such a long recovery from my fall, would a trip down the stairs really set me back so much?

"Get her in the bath," Jacquetta said.

Their hands shifted, and Gus helped me step over the side of the tub into the near-boiling water.

Jacquetta moved to the counter full of her cures, but even the heat of the water was enough to let me breathe easier. I floated in it, releasing all the pressure of standing from my body.

"When you fell," Gus said, holding my head in such a way as to allow me to float even more freely, "Star thought you broke bones in your back and your ribs. But the King wouldn't get away from you long enough for us to check."

"Here," Jacquetta said, coming to my side with a pot she

dumped into the water and a vial she held to my lips, "tip her head, Flower."

With the three of us working together, the contents of the vial, tasting somehow of honey and cloves, made its way into my mouth without dripping, and I drank it down.

Although the cool wash of the drink spread through my body, relieving me of the worst of the pain, sleep pulled at me harder, tracing panic through my limbs.

"I don't want to sleep," I said, my voice slow, words slurred.

"Just let the medicine work," Jacquetta said. "Whether you sleep or not. This is called boneknit. It's made specifically to aid in broken bones."

"Star," Gus whispered, ducking her head as if I wouldn't hear what she said if I couldn't see her say the words, "boneknit can be painful."

"That's what the bath is for."

Like Jacquetta's words were a cue, that same place in my back, and the rest of the rib it was connected to were suddenly replaced by a bar of metal hot from the forge and my body was the quench.

A scream built in my chest, and I arched up, splashing water that made Gus and Jacquetta both exclaim. They grabbed hold of me at the same moment.

With their support, and their insistent hands keeping me submerged in the water, the scream died in my throat as the rod of furious agony in my back ebbed into a steady wave of pain that my body was finally able to shove to some other part of my mind.

Broken bones.

Jacquetta thought I suffered more than one when I plummeted from the sky, and the thought surfaced, as I floated through the sea inside my body that mimicked the water in the tub now, if that was why I couldn't stay awake.

Maybe it was the brain injury. Maybe it was my body's way

of escaping the pain of the broken bones. Either way, I didn't want to be in that state again.

Tristan needed me awake. The country needed me functioning. The war needed me fighting. And my dreams needed me to find a new place in my mind.

All my dreams so close at hand—marrying Tristan, being able to call him mine no matter what the clergy thought, and being able to finally end this war—would be easier to reach if I found a way to get past my own body.

"Used to be fine," I mumbled, my voice still a garbled mess.

"What used to be fine?" Gus whispered, although I wasn't sure why she was so quiet.

Oh.

Maybe she wasn't.

Maybe my ears were under the water, distorting her voice.

But she asked me something. And, even though it was hard to remain focused and not fall asleep, answering was something to distract me.

"Ash."

Saying my brother's name made them shift, lifting my ears clear of the water. I heard Gus curse, and Jacquetta suck in a breath.

"He hurt me, and I used to be fine. Hid. Cold place, next to it. Why not now?"

Looking for either of the places in my mind that I went to for escape left me just twirling in circles with nothing to hold onto, nothing to help me out of this mess.

"Did she say 'cold place?'" Jacquetta asked.

"I think she found a way to ignore her pain back then, and can't find it now." Gus' words weren't a question, but her voice was.

"Cinder," Jacquetta said, and I peeled my eyes open, wondering when I closed them, trying to find her face, "you don't have to pretend anymore."

"Yes. I do."

Finally, my eyes met and held hers without losing her again in the spinning room.

Did she not understand? My friends needed to understand. They had to help me find that place again.

"No, you don't." Jacquetta's face looked funny.

Tears that didn't make any sense to me dribbled down her cheeks as she looked at me.

"My King, Onyx, need me. Killer me."

"Onyx, the King, all of us," Gus said, her voice harder than Jacquetta's, not sounding like tears were anywhere near her eyes, "we need our queen. Not the killer. And we'll get both back as soon as you heal. Just be patient."

Good advice, if there were time.

It was easy for them to pretend we had time, Jacquetta kept them locked inside and they were already starting their married life together.

But I knew better, as deep in my body as the ache and the hidden cold place, was a certainty that I was running out of minutes.

Patience was a luxury this queen couldn't afford.

Somehow, I needed to put her aside, and focus on the killer, before the clock hit midnight.

CHAPTER 22

SHIELDS

Tristan

Darting through the palace after the fucking Corvids were just there wasn't wise. In fact, it was unbelievably stupid. Judging by the sudden intake of breath from and the terrified looks on the faces of the people I passed, I would need the Chamberlain to offer some explanation for my wild dash through the halls.

Finally, I reached the area of the Guard meeting room.

Most of their facilities were in the building just outside the palace itself on the bridge side of the island in the river the palace was on, but they did have a meeting room near the tunnel.

Here, the guards simply stepped to the side as I careened by. They had to know where I had been, and where I was going.

The rest of the palace inhabitants probably didn't see Cinder collapse in the courtyard, nor did they know who it was that the Corvids dropped off when they showed up.

But these guards did, and even if they didn't, General Pace trained the Guard to maintain their composure even in the face of a King losing his mind.

And my mind was all the way inside the palace, in Cinder's room, with her.

Guards stood watch outside one of the doors inside the meeting room, and I made my way to them, finally slowing so I didn't break down the door. Although part of me wanted to. Maybe it would help me focus.

Opening it, the groan of pain from the cot along the wall was enough to make me curl my free hand into a fist.

If Cinder was making a similar noise now that I was out of the room…I ground my teeth, and stepped forward to General Pace's side.

The physick bent over Shield Elio, her focus singular on the wounds along Elio's shoulders and chest.

Elio's face glistened in the too-bright hellfire lamps from the sweat that dotted his skin.

"What happened?" I asked, keeping my voice low and directed at General Pace.

"Crows," Elio said, his voice a strangled moan of pain.

"The Corvids pierced him with their talons," General Pace added, and I looked closer at the deep puncture wounds seeping blood just under the ridge of Elio's shoulders.

"But they are in league with the High Sect," I whispered, turning to speak almost into the General's ear, hoping he didn't hear me, "why would they target a Shield?"

"High Sect has no more need for me," Elio said, hearing me again, making me think I shouldn't say anything in his presence. Maybe he had enhanced hearing somehow. Shields were mostly a mystery. I still didn't know what he did to earn the title. "And I refused to be their little crow worm."

Elio's voice on "worm" was closer to his normal, boisterous presence than anything else from him, but it wasn't fueled by the carefree quality it usually had. This time his voice dripped with fury.

"Nothing about you is little," General Pace said, and I suppressed a snide grin.

Although, looking at him closer, he was diminished somehow. He was still a large man, but his edges seemed sharper. It was possible he lost weight.

"Smaller than I was," he said, sucking in a hissing breath.

"My apologies, but hold still," the physick muttered, getting back to work on the wounds.

"Can you tell us more about what is going on?" I asked, trying to contain the frustration in me that this wasn't moving faster, that he was so hurt, that Cinder needed me.

"Those birds have taken over the Marshlands," Elio said, holding eerily still now, and staring right at me, "invited in by the new Vane of the High Sect. Apparently they made some promises to him."

"Promises," I said, turning to look at General Pace, stretching my hands out so I didn't cut into my palms with my short nails from clenching my fists too hard.

"You know what they want," he said.

I nodded and he relaxed a fraction before freezing again as the physick applied some kind of salve to one of his wounds.

"Do they have a similar deal with Ash?" General Pace asked, her voice as hard as mine. Maybe she was thinking about the trip to the Marshlands, if it were a trap.

"Not that I know of," he said, "But they are not going to trust me with their plans since I stood up in the last council, and told them they were all making a mistake."

"How long have you been there?" The General asked, her voice low and careful in a way that made me dart a look her direction.

"They locked me up right after the council meeting."

She nodded, but my mouth dropped open.

"You are the Shield," I said. It didn't make any sense. Shields were so rare and so important. More than anything else, the stories of the Shields and the miracles of magic some of them had performed in the past were why people continued to believe at all and give to the clergy.

Elio sighed, a long, deep sound that sounded like it was full of an untold sadness before he said, "King Tristan, there is a new Shield now."

"What?" I asked. Based on the way General Pace's brow furrowed and her mouth fell open for a second, she was as shocked as I was. "There has not been a Shield other than you in more than a generation."

"There has, but not in Onyx," Elio said, his voice thinning.

"Soon, I will need to end this conversation," the physick said, not looking at any of us as she went about her work on his wounds.

"But why would having another Shield matter?" the general asked, leaning forward.

"Shield Reol has purple hair."

"Fuck," I said, running a hand roughly through my hair. "Where the fuck did an Amethyst Shield come from, and why would Reol come to the Marshlands?"

"As far as I can tell, this new Shield is not loyal to Amethyst." Elio met my eyes, his heavy with meaning.

"This new Shield is loyal to Ash," I said, the news making my heart slow, and fall into my feet as I shook my head.

Elio didn't argue. The General let out a quiet groan.

"I am willing to bet," the General said, crossing her arms behind her back and looking at me, her jaw tight, "Ash heard about the mutterings in the clergy, and used it to his advantage. Reol may not even be a true Shield."

"Reol is *not* a true Shield," Elio said, his voice as strong as it used to be even as it shook. "Of all the things I do not understand about what is happening right now, I do know that."

"Every fucking time," I said, dragging my hands down my face, wondering what was going to happen next that would make this war even more complicated, "Ash is ahead of us every time we think we know what his next step will be."

"No, he is not," Elio said, trying to sit up before he sucked in a breath and collapsed back to the cot, the physick placing a hand on his chest.

"Stay still," the physick reminded him.

"How is he not ahead of us right now?" I shook my head, more than furious that I didn't see how to handle this.

"Because the Corvids told the High Sect they were taking me to be a slave."

I blinked. Staring at Elio, no further explanation seemed to be forthcoming. Looking to General Pace, I was still confused. The line between her brows told me she didn't understand what the plan was for them either.

"Why would they do that?" The General muttered as if talking to herself.

My mind spun, trying to look at it from the angle of the damned crows, knowing I was missing something.

"No one can possibly guess why they do whatever nonsense they do," Shield Elio said, staring up at the ceiling, his voice barely there.

"Could they really be concerned about Angeline?" General Pace said under her breath.

"I cannot imagine they care about a single child," I said. An idea was forming in my mind, only half there and a bit disjointed, and I hated myself for thinking like them. But I needed to know if I had any chance of being correct. "Shield Elio, do the clergy have any presence in Corvid?"

At that, the General focused on me, as did Elio, and even the physick shot a look in my direction.

"No," Elio said, slowly as if he were running through the idea in his head as well, "they have no clergy at all in their country."

"So, the Corvids want to keep it that way," General Pace said, and I nodded.

"That seems like the only explanation," I said. "They do not want the clergy in Corvid at all, and they must think that telling me will make me more likely to destroy the clergy for them without angering their partner, Ash. Maybe they think Ash is not attempting to take over more than Onyx, and maybe they want to have a country full of people they can drag back to Corvid with them."

"It is a story that is so unbelievable, I must trust it."

"Except that Duchess Cinder told them the truth," General Pace said.

"And the crows acted as if they already knew…" I stared at the wall, replaying in my mind what the Corvid woman said.

"Can we get the Corvids to back out of this war?" I asked, not allowing the thought to become a real hope, no matter how much I wanted it to be true.

"They want revenge," General Pace said.

"What are they waiting for, then?" I was still thinking aloud, running through the possibilities, trying to find a way to end this damn war by understanding my enemy.

"Revenge for the death of their princess," Elio said, and when I looked at him, his eyes bored into mine.

"You seem to think that has more meaning than I am seeing," I said, trying to follow his reasoning, yet coming up empty. I was still stuck on the fact that Corvid was playing a tune they expected us to dance to when it came to the clergy, and I didn't see a way to ignore the sound.

"If they wanted to get revenge by killing someone in our kingdom," Elio said, and the General took a deep breath, eyes closed like she understood while I still didn't, "who in Onyx would be the equivalent?"

"Me," I said, shaking my head. That was obvious. They already tried to kill me. They tried every time we faced them except tonight and that was only because if they attempted anything tonight, all of them would have been slaughtered.

"And when you make Duchess Cinder queen?" General Pace asked, her words slamming against me like a physical blow.

"I need you both to let me work…" the physick said, but I didn't hear whatever else was said in the room because I was running again.

This time I was racing back to Cinder, and I wasn't going to leave her again.

CHAPTER 23
PROTECTORATE TRAINING

Cinder

Gus and Jacquetta helped me into a nightgown, a soft garment I could only feel along my ass because bandages were wrapped tightly around my chest. Again.

I smelled. That poultice was far worse than the one I had before.

"Are you sure I don't need the same poultice as before?" I asked, my breathing thin even though much of my pain had ebbed away, washed down the drain of the tub. The rest was reduced to a low throb by the medicine she gave me.

"Stop complaining," Jacquetta said, shaking her head as she held my arm, and Gus supported me with a hand on my lower back and one on my stomach. All three of us shuffled across the floor toward the bed.

"But this one stinks," I muttered, curling my nose at the pungent odor wafting up from my bandages.

"And it will help," Gus said, looking up at me from her bent position. "Now quit whining."

"I'm not whining." Well, a little bit. But at some point, Tristan would come back to me, and I didn't want him to associate the stink with me being hurt, or he might get even more irritating about not risking myself.

"You *are* whining, and no one cares about the smell." Jacquetta was as close to yelling at me as she had been since I fell. I tried to focus on moving smoothly instead of making her angrier.

The medicine was becoming a problem because I couldn't keep my words inside my head. No one wanted my unfiltered thoughts.

"Tristan might care," I said, and bit my lip to stop talking.

"Oh, Gods and Goddesses, stop," Gus said, turning a baleful eye my way. "He will not care. After everything, you think he's that shallow?"

"No," that wasn't it, and now I didn't even try to stop myself, "but he already worries. He might use this as another reason for me to not fight."

"That's a stupid excuse," Jacquetta said with a scoff, causing me to miss a step. "We all know that the reason you're really worried about it is because you've never thought you're good enough for him. Stop pretending your own shallow thoughts are his."

Well, fuck.

I stopped walking, lost in my own head. Was Jacquetta right? Did I shove all my own worries over what a queen was supposed to be onto Tristan?

"Come on," Gus said, pressing on my back to get me moving again.

Finally, we shuffled our way to the side of the bed, and I bent over to press my hands to the mattress in an attempt to climb in.

Pain ricocheted from the ribs on the side Jacquetta said were broken and down that arm.

Yanking that hand back with a cry, I balanced on the other, trying to breathe slowly to get enough air.

The door to the hallway in the parlor slammed open, and feet came thundering into the room.

"Cinder," Tristan said, at my side in a second, his hand replacing Gus' on my back. "Let me get you into bed."

He managed to lift me without hurting me in a motion that he'd had far too much practice executing since the battle in the Kaleidoscope Fields.

"My King," I said, my pain ebbing away as he laid me down, and crawled in behind me, letting every part of my body relax into him just like before.

"What are her injuries?" he asked.

Jacquetta sighed, giving me a look I couldn't decipher.

"She broke at least two ribs. I think they were already broken, and were just beginning to heal." Her voice was resigned, and I wondered if this was my new reality. Would I just keep re-breaking my bones as I slammed my own body against Ash and his forces?

"Damn it, Cinder," Tristan muttered and held me closer, kissing my head.

"I'll be fine," I said, but the medicine mixed with his presence and my relief was pulling me under faster than I wanted it to.

"You will be if you stop pushing as if you need to win the war all by yourself," Jacquetta said, but Gus turned to her wife with a shake of her head and her mouth a grim line.

"Who else do you expect to kill my brother?" I asked, mumbling the words because I didn't actually want to have this conversation.

They all thought I was wrong. I thought they were wrong. And there was no chance we were going to agree on what my place was, or what responsibility went along with that.

But they all needed to stop trying to pretend I would just be a different person because I got hurt, then didn't heal all the way before I needed to try and fight again.

"A whole army is out there," Jacquetta yelled, pointing to the balcony. "An army of guards *you* trained are fighting this war. Let *them* kill your brother."

"Cinder," Tristan said. His voice was low and soft, but I knew he was going to agree with Jacquetta.

Everyone was agreeing with Jacquetta lately. Based on the way Gus looked at the floor instead of at me, she probably did, too.

"No," I said, my voice strong as my own anger bypassed the medicine yanking at my mind, "no one knows him the way I do. No one understands what Jocelyn is capable of. We could throw every single guard in Onyx at Ash at once, and I'm sure Ash would still manage to get away while Jocelyn bought him time."

"Jocelyn can't be that powerful," Tristan said, holding me tight even as his voice lost that soft quality while he argued with me.

"Let me be clear," I said, turning my head to slowly make eye contact with everyone in the room one by one, even waiting for Gus to lift her eyes to mine, "every single thing I learned about killing, fighting, surviving, I learned from Jocelyn. She trained me. And I still can't beat her alone, head on."

"You don't have to," Tristan said, his voice an angry rumble in his chest that shook through my back, making me hurt less somehow.

"I might be the only person on our side who has any chance of getting to Ash without Jocelyn being there. They trained me for things like this. And no one has ever deserved a visit from my spike more than he does."

None of them said a word to that. They had to know I was right.

Finally, I sagged against Tristan behind me—the fight, for

the moment, seeping out of me along with the last of my pain.

Sleep clawed at me like a starving animal, as if I were the only food it was capable of eating, and it intended to swallow its fill.

But still I resisted the urge to give in, not trusting they wouldn't try to talk about me while my mind was far away. What I expected them to say, I wasn't sure, but I half thought these people who loved me would try to devise a way for me to sit out all the upcoming fights.

'That will never happen,' I vowed to myself.

"How long do you think it will take for her to fully heal?" Tristan asked, all the simmering rage gone from his voice. He just sounded as tired as I felt.

"I have no idea," Jacquetta said.

"She healed from a worse fall way too quickly already," Gus said, sounding confused even though I didn't understand why.

Jacquetta already explained that I healed faster than other people. It wasn't a mystery. It was just something that was probably a happy accident from years of being trained by a Protectorate witch.

Ash didn't care about whether I was hurt, or not. When I was training or out on a kill, I was expected not to allow it to impact my ability to do what needed to be done. He didn't even want it to slow me down.

One of the things Jocelyn taught me was how to keep going.

That's all this was. Another thing for me to keep going through.

No matter what they worried about, or how hurt I currently was, if the Corvids showed up in the courtyard again, I would get out there. Sword first.

And as soon as I was able-bodied and could get some information on Ash, I intended to end this war. Not just that, though. I wanted to end the threat of my brother.

I meant what I told them. I was the only one who could.

CHAPTER 24

CHRYSALIS

Tristan

"How is he?" I asked, keeping my voice low so I didn't wake Cinder.

General Pace paused, dragging in a deep breath. She looked exhausted, and I couldn't blame her.

"Shield Elio is awake, and feeling much better than he was last night," she said.

"By that," Rath said, leaning against the wall with his arms crossed and a wry grin on his face, "she means that our friend, the Shield, is being very loud about his need for more wine to drown his pain."

"Ah," I wasn't sure what I could do about that. The man had been impaled by the crows. If I were in his position, I might have been asking for the same thing.

I looked down at Cinder in my arms and smiled. No, I wouldn't be asking for a drink. I would be asking for her.

"How's Flame?" Rath asked, his voice even more a whisper

than a moment ago.

Fighting the urge to tighten my arms around her, I looked back up at Rath and sighed.

"Cinder is too damn strong for her own good. She thinks she's the only one that can get to her brother."

"What if she's right?" Rath whispered, and I squeezed my eyes shut, letting out a long breath so I didn't yell.

"Then we may as well say we're losing this war," General Pace said, her voice hard.

A sigh left Cinder's lips as she shifted in my grasp. We all froze, waiting to see if she would wake.

Holding too still to be comfortable, I waited a long moment before relaxing again, and looking back to Rath.

"Ending this is not going to fall on her shoulders alone." I may as well have been issuing a royal decree, my voice was as hard as it was for me to stay quiet. "I refuse to let her be the one risking the most throughout this war. I am the King. The responsibility lies with me."

"Short of tying her to the bed," Rath said, looking down his nose at me as he lounged against the wall, head tilted back, his position belying the stiffness of his back and how tight his fists were, "what do you plan to do to keep her away from the field? You know her well enough to know that ordering her to do anything won't do you any good."

"No," I said, my voice a groan, as I rubbed a hand over my eyes, "you're right. She won't stay out of it entirely. But I don't want any information making its way to her about Mariposa, or where her brother is exactly."

"That should not be a problem," the General said with a nod, slipping back into formal speech. "We do not know where he is within the duchy right now. He could be in Imago or Instar. We do not have enough eyes on the area anymore."

"Honestly," I said, studying the way Cinder's hair fell across her face and wishing we were other people for just a day, that we were the kind of people who didn't have to worry about this, "I think even telling her that much will make her believe she needs to break in just to find out."

"Duke Asshole is in the Chrysalis Tower," Rath said, nothing about his voice or his posture suggesting he just managed to rip the bed out from under me, and leave me holding Cinder as we plummeted to the floor.

"Rathmoreland," General Pace said, her gaze hard on his through narrowed eyes, "how do you know that, and why have you been keeping information from me?"

"Because I know a lot of things. Until I know they're something we need, or something that might help, I keep them to myself."

"None of that explains why you would avoid telling us where her brother is, especially while you knew we thought he was in one of the cities, and were wildly wrong." The General—for as quiet as she was—still managed to make me feel like a recruit in the training grounds. "We could have sent guards in to end this."

"Suicide," Rath said with a laugh and a shake of his head. "Have you been to the Chrysalis Tower, General?"

"It's impenetrable," I said, not bothering to let them continue arguing about it.

"The towers in Instar and Imago can be taken," the General said.

Running a hand roughly through my hair, I wondered how to explain it to her military mind.

"Yes," I said, "they can. But even if we do, his army will fall back to the Chrysalis Tower if they aren't already grouped around it. Once they do that, we would be in a siege that could last far longer than we can afford in possibly hostile territory. We don't know which twin the people of Mariposa sided with. Are they loyal to Onyx, or Ash?"

"How could they withstand a prolonged siege?" she asked, staring out toward the balcony as if trying to imagine it.

"Few people are ever allowed to see the Tower from the outside," Rath said. "Even fewer are allowed inside it."

"So, we do not actually know if it can be breached." The General turned back to look at Rath, her gaze hard, her mouth pressed tight.

"I've been inside. Between the grove's water source and the sap, they can stay inside forever," I said, rubbing a pain shooting into my brain through a spot above my eyebrow. "Besides, the only creature getting inside uninvited is a squirrel or a bird."

"We cannot tell the Duchess that," General Pace said, heavy emphasis on cannot.

And, looking down at my Queen, the heat in my veins rising as high as the Chrysalis Tower was in the canopy of the winged tree grove in Mariposa, I couldn't agree more.

"Flame would just hitch a ride on a Corvid, and fly up there," Rath said, laughter in his voice.

Trying to keep my voice down, I managed not to scream about how not funny that was. But I did growl in his direction.

"Calm down, King," Rath said, shaking his head and only managing to make me angrier, "I'm not going to say anything to her."

Finally, I could breathe.

Cinder made a low moaning sound, and shifted in her sleep, the movement making me realize that I was holding her too tight.

My own fear for her almost made everything much, much worse.

Looking at her, I swept aside the piece of her hair draped over her face so I could see her clearly, careful not to touch her skin for fear of waking her with the heat of my hand like I often did.

"Remind me," I said, not caring which one of them would remember to do as I asked, "when this is all over, and we finally beat Ash on the battlefield, to apologize to her for not telling her."

"Are you kidding?" General Pace asked, her voice seemingly full of honest curiosity.

"No." The General didn't understand what it was to be in love with Cinder.

She knew what it was to love Madam Valentin. She knew what it was to keep herself apart from the one she loved to protect them both from the depth of their feelings, and the risks of her position. How could she ever understand what it was to love someone who was even more likely to be in danger than she herself was?

"General," I said, my voice low and sad as I turned to look at her, suppressing the urge to tighten my hold on Cinder again, "what do you think it took for Madam Valentin to love you, and accept you going into battle?"

The General opened and closed her mouth, her eyes widening before she swallowed and shook her head.

"Cinder and I can't avoid talking about it. We can't pretend for even a moment that we are not the biggest targets of this war. We also can't stay away from the battlefield, and live with ourselves as others die in our stead while we do nothing."

Rath cleared his throat, straightened from his leaning position, and dropped all pretense of relaxation, his arms falling to his sides.

"I told her I wouldn't keep her from fighting, from doing what she can do that no one else can. And I meant that."

They both looked at me, lines forming between their brows as I was sure a lack of understanding fell over them.

"But she might see me keeping this from her as exactly that, when it's not."

"Forgive me," the General said, her voice a reedy whisper, "but how is it not?"

"A battle where both sides meet, and know the parameters of

the fight leaves nothing hidden. But we don't know enough about Ash's people, the people in the duchy, or even what his plans are. We can't do anything with the information of his location. All I know is that, if Cinder thinks she can get in, she will try. And she won't come out."

CHAPTER 25

CONNECTIONS

Cinder

He didn't know I heard him.

None of them knew I heard every word of their conversation.

I had to keep reminding myself that they didn't know, and couldn't know, as I continued to spend far too much time in bed under Jacquetta's care as she worked on healing me.

Whatever they expected me to do or not do with the information, I was not in a position to make any real moves.

Not yet.

"Cinder," Jacquetta said, "you need to focus."

"Fine," I said, closing my eyes, trying to be there in the moment instead of back in Tristan's arms listening as they gave me hints I could use to get to my brother.

"Just tell me when something hurts," she said from behind me.

Gus squeezed my elbows where she supported me, and I

squeezed hers back as Jacquetta began poking and prodding along my ribs and my back.

Every time she poked me, I felt it. But even when it was sore, even when I might describe it as pain, nothing shot down through the entire bone she touched like it did before. So, I stayed silent.

Her touch was firm, sure, yet not harsh or uncaring.

"Are you pretending?" Jacquetta finally asked after touching some spots in my back for the third time.

I opened my eyes, and looked over my shoulder at her standing behind and to the side, her hands on her hips.

"No, I'm not pretending. What would the point be?" They were still going to keep me away from anything that might slow my healing for as long as they possibly could.

She made a humming noise low in her throat.

"Well," she said, with a shake of her head and a long exhalation, her hands dropping from her hips as she stepped to Gus' side, "I don't know how you're not responding to touching right along where I'm sure your ribs were broken, but you didn't."

Gus raised her brows and looked at me, studying my face as if searching for something.

"I didn't lie," I said, trying to keep from sounding irritated that they didn't seem to believe me.

Yes, I lied to them in the past, but I didn't make a habit of it. And they knew everything now.

"Cinder," Jacquetta sighed, deflating completely, wringing her hands together, "I just don't know how…"

"How, what?"

"Anyone else who fell from the sky the way you did would be broken forever," Jacquetta said, her face wilting as if imagining me that way, "if not dead."

"The Corvid broke my fall," I said, but the conviction was missing from my voice, even to me.

My entire life, when I got hurt in some way, I slipped into

the water under the manor, and allowed the pools to help me heal. Yes, I healed fast. That was always true. Why it was suddenly somehow a problem, I didn't know, but it made me feel even more like I didn't belong the way everyone else did.

"Healing isn't a bad thing," Gus said, nudging her wife with her shoulder.

Jacquetta took a deep breath, and walked behind me. Both of them helped me put my clothes back on.

"If I'm so much better," I asked as they sat me back on my bed, and I waited for lunch to be delivered, "does that mean I can go back to some regular activities?"

"Let's give it a little while longer before you return to training," Jacquetta said, giving a sideways glance to Gus.

"Can I go back to staying with Tristan?" I wanted to start my life with him. Now.

"Maybe we should not yet risk those stairs," Tristan said, coming into my bedroom, followed by servants with lunch.

He smiled, kneeled in front of me, and leaned in to give me a kiss.

"You don't want me to share your room anymore?" I whispered, smiling back as he wrapped his arms around me to lay gentle hands along my back.

"I always want to share everything with you." His eyes closed as he leaned in to kiss me again, and all I could think about was how that was a lie.

But I couldn't be angry with him.

Frustrated, yes.

Maybe disappointed that he didn't think I would be successful.

But not angry. If I didn't think he would survive something, I might make the same decision. And he planned to ask forgiveness whenever this was over.

Without meaning to, my hands grasped at his shirt, pulling

him into me as I kissed him with growing desperation, because there *was* something I was worried about him not surviving. And every day it got closer, even if I didn't know when exactly it would happen.

Tristan broke the kiss, just like he always did since this latest round of injuries, and rested his forehead against mine.

"How long will I have you?" I asked, pouring more than I intended into the question.

"Until hellfire water goes cold," he said, and I smiled, closing my eyes to revel in it, even if I knew it was another lie.

Death would claim both of us. Eventually.

My job was to make sure it didn't take him before he became an old man.

"What about right now?" I asked, keeping my eyes squeezed shut as movement continued all around us. "Are you staying for lunch?"

"I wish I were," he said, and my eyes popped open. "We finally have word back from our message to the Marshlands."

"And you're leaving?" I could barely get the words out of my closed-up throat.

"Cinder," he said, leaning back to look at me better, apologies all over his face, "I don't want to go, but I need to find out if there's anything I can do to stop the High Sect from making things worse."

"Yes," I said, "but you can't risk going into their place, it's too likely to be a trap."

"We're meeting them on the border, with a full contingent of guards. General Pace will be with me. I promise, I'm doing everything to come back to you." He ran his hands along my back in gentle strokes, but it didn't calm me.

It did the opposite.

My hands cramped as I clutched at his jacket, not wanting to let him go.

"Stay with me," I said, knowing he wouldn't, but unable to stop myself from begging.

He shut his eyes, and buried his face in my neck, holding me tighter, folding me into him.

"Cinder, my Queen," he whispered into my skin, the heat of his breath making the words pour into my veins, "I love you."

"Tristan," my voice was a whisper as I pulled back, looking into his weary eyes, seeing every bit of the weight of the crown and whole of Onyx as it hung on him, "marry me."

A smile tugged at the corners of his mouth even while his brow twitched in confusion.

"Before you go," I said, rushing through my quiet words, "I don't want to risk it never happening. I need to know you're coming home to me. Let me help you carry it all while you're gone."

Everything about him softened, as if he were melting into me, one hand leaving my back to run along the side of my face until he cupped my cheek with a thumb trailing along my scar.

"There isn't time to even get you a gold dress," he said, looking as if he wished he could say yes.

"I know I have something that will work. Please." Part of me thought I shouldn't need to beg him for this, but I was past caring.

My panic rose within me. If he asked me why I was so persistent, I knew I wouldn't be able to explain it.

But after having time to get used to the idea of him leaving for the Marshlands, a fresh wave of the same old terror rampaged through me at the thought of him leaving without being mine in a more lasting way than just my own feelings. Thinking about him leaving while our vows connected us was bad enough, without that connection…my entire body shook every time I thought about it.

He leaned in and kissed me, one that calmed all my nerves

while it lit me on fire from the inside, and made me almost as warm as he was.

"Do we have time to do it tonight?" he whispered against my mouth.

CHAPTER 26

NOTICE

Tristan

My knee bounced up and down under the table even though I pressed down on it with my hand to keep it to a minimum. Hopefully, no one else noticed.

They would probably think I was worried about the mission, but I just wanted to get our damn meeting over with as fast as possible so I could get back to Cinder.

I needed to be with Cinder.

"Your personal guards are all going," General Pace said.

"General," I said, shaking my head, "I thought I was clear, some of them need to remain at the palace for Duchess Cinder."

"King Tristan," she pronounced my name carefully as if she thought that was the only way to get me to understand what she was saying, "They are your personal guard. Rathmoreland and the rest of the palace guards have everything here taken care of."

"Besides, King," Rath said from his place lounging in a chair on my other side. The table was surrounded, with little space left, but the General and Rath were closest to me, "she's plenty deadly on her own, even with wounds."

"And…" Shield Elio said from the end of the table opposite me. His eyes were red at the edges from the sheer amount of wine he consumed. He refused to take any other medicine at the risk of blurring his focus. "…your not-yet-queen will be safe inside the palace walls. While we…are going to need all the help we can get if this goes wrong."

"Shield," I said, looking at his unkempt hair and dirty robes, "are you sure that wine is better for you right now than medicine?"

"Yes," he sighed, nodding his head and taking another drink with a wince before he set his glass down, looking me in the eye, "you and I will both need my shield for the trip, and I had no connection to it when I was on that medicine. It remains less than it was before."

His shield? He made it sound like he was talking about something physical that could be measured like the kind of shield some guards fought with, or even like his loss of stamina.

But he *was* the Shield.

Part of me wondered if I shouldn't know more about the clergy and their Shields. No one else asked what he meant by that, and none of them seemed confused.

"Are you sure you want to come with me?" I asked again, still not sure if he would be able to handle the trip, let alone whatever happened once we got there.

With a grin that made him look more like his normal, boisterous, happy self, he leaned back in his chair and said, "You need me to be there, King Tristan."

I nodded, even though a feeling of impending threat, as heavy as the weight of the crown itself, dropped onto my shoulders at the words.

"Now," General Pace said, "we need to talk about the Mariposa problem."

The only thing I could offer to that was another nod.

Every person around the table, from the Chamberlain's assistant who was busy taking notes for the absent Chamberlain, to the General and Shield Elio, we were all dedicating our lives and energy to this war. And I wasn't sure it was enough.

"So far," General Pace said, "stationing the guards around the border to Mariposa has meant that our battles with him have been limited to the occasional skirmish with a small number of his troops testing our lines. There have also been two more large scale battles in the Kaleidoscope Fields."

"After all of this," I said, sadness at the unnecessary scars this war was inflicting on the country seeping into me further, "the beauty of the fields may never recover."

"It will, King," Rath said, a grim smile on his face, "the Gods and Goddesses of nature always make small work of recovering from the things humans do."

"That is true," Shield Elio said, nodding to Rath.

Maybe they took some comfort in that. And maybe I should have, too. Our acts were only temporary as far as the Gods and Goddesses were concerned. Instead, it made the entire war more frustrating, more futile, and more tragic.

So many lives lost, so many changed forever, and all for something that didn't register enough to the Gods and Goddesses for them to even notice.

"What have we heard of the goings on inside Mariposa?" I asked, trying to move on to the things I could control, things more than important enough for me to notice no matter what the Gods and Goddesses thought.

"No new information," Rath said, quirking an eyebrow, and making it clear to me, even if no one else around the table except the General understood, that as far as he knew, Ash was still in the Chrysalis Tower.

Discussion turned to the strategies for convincing the High Sect away from supporting Ash by leaning heavily on the fact that he was planning to double-cross his existing partners. Why wouldn't he do the same to the clergy?

"Ash really thinks this country will be in a position to fight Amethyst next, and then go directly after Corvid?" Senior Wayson, the one in charge of supply lines asked.

"It would seem so," General Pace said, and I curled my hand into a fist thinking of his seemingly unquenchable thirst for power.

"He does not care about logistics the way we do," I said, drawing their attention. "Why would he worry about working the people into the ground by forcing them to grow the food, transport the food, cook the food, do all the other support chores, and maintain the weapons, all in an effort to support the Guard while the Guard's numbers swell to fight a war?

He bought slaves. He is making them fight for him already. I have no doubt that if he gained the crown, he would treat the entire kingdom as if they were also his slaves."

Rath made a snort of derision, and shook his head, leaning on a fist propped up by the arm of the chair he was draped over.

"Duke Asshole," Rath said, "will pillage and destroy as he goes, then enslave all the people he comes across. He's just like Corvid. He'll fit right in there when he goes to take them over, too."

"Ash," I muttered, "the false king of the ashes left behind in the trail of his destructive dreams. His parents named him well."

"Speaking of dreams," General Pace said, getting to her feet, and looking around at the assembled group, "we all have a lot of work to do, and all of us need to get some sleep tonight so we might come up with a war-ending idea tomorrow."

"Good plan," Elio said, standing up next, albeit gingerly.

"Will you bring a message to Chamberlain Rezan?" General Pace asked as the Chamberlain's assistant stood up. "Please tell the Chamberlain that he and I need to speak about getting the machines from Breakwater to Lehar as soon as the war is over, and the roads are clear."

The Chamberlain's assistant nodded and scribbled a note on her papers before tucking them under her arm, and getting ready to leave.

"Oh," the General said, drawing the assistant up short, "also, tell the Chamberlain I will be there."

A shy grin split the assistant's face before she scurried away, and I looked closer at the peaceful smile on General Pace's face.

"General," I asked, making my own way toward the door and dropping my voice, "where will you be?"

"Just something the Chamberlain and I need to handle," she said, tipping her head, and leaving before I could puzzle out the mischievous twinkle in her eye.

Normally, I would let them plan whatever they wanted without worry. I trusted them both. But right now? I no longer looked forward to any surprises even something as innocuous as a fancy dinner for the guards before we left for the Marshlands.

With that question hanging in my mind, I had so much to do and not a lot of time.

Thinking about it, about her, made me pick up my pace, and hurry toward my room.

Whether the Gods and Goddesses cared enough to notice what we were about to do, I didn't care. Because for me, the entire world would change tonight when I touched my own star again.

CHAPTER 27

READY OR NOT

Cinder

"How do you want your hair done?" Jacquetta asked, a soft smile on her face, her voice dreamy as if she were talking to Gus about how much she loved her.

"I'm not sure," I said, enjoying the way the water sluiced down my back as Gus poured it over my tipped back head. Even though I wanted this to be a surprise to everyone, I was happy that they were in on the secret, that they could be part of helping me. I wanted no one else to do it. "You've seen the dress. What do you think would look right?"

"Well," Gus said, setting down the pitcher and coming to my side to help me climb out, "I have an idea. And I know the King will love it."

She wiggled her eyebrows up and down, and I laughed. The movement of my back and ribs tightened to the point of aching as I maneuvered to a standing position.

Even now, when no one could say I wasn't healing, I remained uncomfortable in my own body. More than the pain and the forced stillness, feeling like I wasn't in full control over my physical self was the most difficult part of this.

Maybe I was uniquely bad at being hurt.

Although, I already knew that.

"I should probably just let you do it for me, then," I said, finally getting all the way upright, taking a few moments before I climbed out.

With Gus and Jacquetta helping me, drying me, and leading me, we got out to the bedroom where the dress lay across the blankets on the bed, shimmering in the light.

"Cinder," Jacquetta said, her voice low as she rubbed a hand along my arm, "pick out what you want for tonight. This one is for you. The next one won't be, so you should enjoy this."

"The next one…" I took a huge breath, the fluttering in my stomach worse than the ache caused by that much expansion of my still-healing ribs.

"Don't worry about that," Gus said, her voice like a scoff put to words.

"But how can I not?" What was she thinking?

Fine. Everyone thought I was some kind of magic because I was good at killing, because killing usually didn't bother me at all. But that didn't mean I managed to avoid feeling anything at all.

Especially not since I came to the palace.

"You won't," Gus said, nodding as if issuing the rules of a sparring match, "because you and I both know that when it comes. Not only will you look at it just like you do a battle, like it's a mission to finish. You'll attack it the same way."

Maybe.

It was good advice, and I would use it to help me. But this was a lot bigger than a ball or a dinner or any of the other things I had done with Tristan. The entire country would be there for the next one. With every last person looking at me, expecting things from me.

"But…" I wasn't sure how to explain this pressure weighing down on me. It probably didn't make sense—and maybe it was just the ghosts of my doubts that I would be a good queen—but it was there all the same, and I couldn't get it to leave me alone.

"No buts," Gus said.

"And," Jacquetta said, making me whip my head to the other side of me where she stood, "tonight, and the next time, you will be able to see him the whole time."

She looked across me to Gus on my other side, her smile back to an expression so full of love it made me want to give them time alone.

But I knew what she was thinking. She had to be thinking exactly what I was. She spoke from experience.

"Were you nervous?" I asked, my voice a croak.

Gus laughed, and Jacquetta nodded with wide eyes.

"You can't imagine how nervous," Jacquetta said.

"As great as it was," Gus said, "the King himself presided over it, and a lot of the people there were part of the palace. Never thought either would happen to me."

"None of us had any idea anything was wrong," I said, looking back and forth between them, marveling at how well they managed to pull off being under all that pressure, and just after we lost Madam, too.

"Well," Gus said, looking past me to her wife, her eyes so full of admiration, I understood why she called Jacquetta her Star, "it was easy as soon as I could see her."

"Once I saw her, it was the easiest thing I have ever done," Jacquetta said.

Dragging in another long breath, I stared at the beautiful gown on the bed, and I thought of Tristan, with the support of my friends on either side of me.

I thought of his ever-shifting eyes, of the heat of his touch, of the way he said my name, and the gentle way he loved me.

"Let's get me ready, then," I said, smiling, the nerves slipping away from me the same way they came, at first like a punch, and then slowly, a bit at a time, the way a bruise healed.

"Good," Jacquetta said while Gus made a whooping sound.

I laughed as they sat me on the little stool in front of the vanity.

They helped me into my panties, and wrapped a robe around me while they did my hair.

Gus didn't tell me what her idea was, but it was easy to figure it out once they got started.

"Are you sure?" I asked when the thin, braided piece was nestled into the curls like a crown. The curled hair, pulled back into a high ponytail that hung down my back with little loose, curled tendrils framing my face was lovely, but the braid was…a lot.

"Cinder," Gus said, shaking her head as she pulled out shining things from one of the drawers in the vanity, "one day, you're going to have to accept that you will sometimes need to look like the queen you are."

"But tonight isn't supposed to be about that. It's just supposed to be about us—him and me." I shook my head, and leaned away from her searching hands, knowing that it would normally be fine. But I was right.

"Maybe she's right about this one," Jacquetta said, unpinning the little braid, instead wrapping it around the long ponytail before she fixed the curls to lay properly on my head again.

Gus sighed, but she did pin a few of the delicate little bursts of light that those gems were into the braid around my ponytail. Then she managed to make the ponytail look bigger, longer, curlier than before while Jacquetta put on the last touches of makeup.

Finally, it was time for them to help me into the dress.

The gown was a simple, form-fitting dress with lines that acted like a bustier, all in a shimmering gold so pale it was almost white. But that was only the underdress.

Over top of that laid a complicated array of what looked like part interlinked necklaces, part gems, and part dragon scales like pieces of armor, all of it in gold.

It draped down along the low neckline of the under dress with a large link of gems that connected to more delicate, necklace-like chains that followed the cups of my breasts. More chains and gems wrapped around my waist, and trailed down in a line between my legs in the front. All the gems and chains in the back hung, draping down in the middle at regular intervals all the way down my back to drag along the floor.

My favorite gems though were the dragon scale along the ridges of my shoulders with more lines of chains draping down my upper arms with little gems that looked like tiny diamond stars. They were just like the ones that adorned the dress I wore when Tristan and I danced in my apartment so long ago.

The gems in my ponytail managed to match the overdress perfectly, and I smiled at my own reflection thinking about how much I looked like the human version of an intricate, Damascus steel sword.

"Final touch," Gus said, picking up my mother's shoes from where they sat on one of my trunks.

Biting my lip, I nodded, touching the supple fabric and the embroidery on them, more than shocked that I was actually able to wear them again.

Gus and Jacquetta helped me step into them, and we all turned to take in the image of the duchess they made me into.

"You look beautiful," Jacquetta said.

"Amazing, Cinder," Gus said.

"I feel beautiful," I said, touching my hands to my hips and taking a deep breath as I met their eyes in the mirror. "Are both of you ready?"

"Us?" Jacquetta said, smiling and cocking her head to the side.

"We're just watching," Gus said, shaking her head, her brow furrowed.

"No," I said, turning around and taking each of their hands in mine, looking into the eyes of my best friends. My real family. "I want you both to walk with us, and give the consent."

"Cinder?" Jacquetta said, her voice thin and too high. She blinked rapidly, looking up at the ceiling.

Gus just smiled wide, and swept both of us up into a hug.

"She would have been thrilled to do it," Gus said, knowing without me needing to say that I was originally planning on having Madam do the honors for me.

"And…" Jacquetta trailed off as she sucked in desperate breaths.

We both gave her time to get her emotions under control so she could finish her thought. Gus and I understood how hard this was for her.

"And I'm honored to stand where she would have stood," Jacquetta said.

I squeezed my eyes shut, taking steady breaths so the tears building behind my lashes didn't fall.

Finally, I pulled back and smiled at my friends as they wiped their eyes, grinning back.

"Go," I said, "get ready."

"Yes, my Queen," Gus said with a laugh as she and Jacquetta ran from the room.

CHAPTER 28

CRIMSON ROSES

Tristan

I breathed in a deep breath, filling my lungs until it hurt, willing the air making its way through my body to cool the heat in my blood. I held the breath for a long moment, imagining everything going right, until I let it out slowly.

When all the air was gone, I finally opened my eyes, more ready for what came next.

I opened the door to my private office. It was the best place to carry this off without alerting everyone in the palace to what was going on, even if it meant so many things would be different than tradition dictated.

But, then again, nothing about this was traditional. I wasn't even wearing heels because my soon-to-be wife knew me well enough to know I hated them. Although, I was in formals with gold lace because Cinder and the Chamberlain thought of everything.

They thought of everything except the way this would wreak havoc on my mind.

Not that I realized it either.

Reaching for the door to my office, my hand stilled, and another wave of the same fear that plagued me all day slammed into me, almost knocking me off course.

If we did this, would we be condemning ourselves to failure? Were we tempting fate? Were we mocking the Gods and Goddesses that we had the hubris to think we would both make it out of this war alive?

"King Tristan," General Pace said, making me jump and drop my hand back to my side. Her only reaction was to raise a brow and smile at me. "Are you coming inside now, or waiting for Duchess Cinder?"

Duchess Cinder…just imagining her there with me made it easier to reach out and open the door for us both to step inside.

The office was transformed, the Chamberlain making sure everything dripped in golden fabric, golden weapons, and the crimson roses with the hellfire green stems that Cinder and I loved.

No matter how the worries thrashed through me, I smiled as I looked around at the little office that was now our private place to celebrate together.

She was right about this. Even if it angered the Gods and Goddesses, it might turn out to be worth it to have this private moment with my Queen instead of a public spectacle.

But she wasn't here yet, and her lack of presence made it impossible to hold onto the positive thoughts.

Instead, I stood next to the General by the windows worrying my hands together while the lights of Bridgeton painted a twinkling mirror of the stars in the night sky. The hellfire lamps inside burned low, flickering off the gold fabric, making the crimson roses an even deeper color.

"King Tristan," General Pace said, her voice low and gentle, "relax. It will be fine."

Nodding, I swallowed as the door clicked, announcing an arrival.

The temperature of my blood shot higher even as my entire body froze.

Was she there?

A second later, Jacquetta entered, wearing a gown colored the bright green of hellfire water, and my breath quickened, my chest heaving.

Augustina followed her wife, also in bright green, honoring Lehar.

Neither of their expressions suggested any kind of problem. But where was...

"Cinder," I said, my voice little more than a breath as she walked into the room.

Her gown was the palest gold, the metal overlay—also light gold—was like an homage to her deadliness in a delicate way that made me want to fight for her on a battlefield.

She paused at the end of the room, her eyes on the floor, focused on her slippers sticking out from beneath the hem of her dress.

My breath left me. All I wanted was for her to meet my eyes.

Fear rippled through me in a shiver. Was she changing her mind? Was she about to turn and flee from this room? From me?

But she sucked in a breath, and lifted her eyes to meet mine.

"Tristan," she mouthed, her voice too quiet for me to hear it over the pounding of my heart.

Her mouth turned up at the corners, all the tension left her eyes, and her shoulders relaxed.

I could breathe again.

Lifting my hands, I held them out toward her. She did the same, coming toward me.

None of this was traditional, and I no longer cared.

Jacquetta and Augustina followed her to stand just behind us as Cinder's fingers threaded into mine, General Pace on the other side of us.

Even if the Gods and Goddesses had a problem with us straying from tradition, they couldn't enact a retribution more powerful than the way my heart suddenly exploded when I looked into Cinder's eyes.

General Pace asked Jacquetta and Augustina for consent, and, before they could answer, the door slammed open.

No, deities couldn't pull my focus away from Cinder, but Rath managed to as he burst into the room, a wide grin on his face, sending the slamming door bouncing off the wall.

He was every bit the pirate, slightly disheveled as if he ran here, dirt on his boots, and a sword in the scabbard at his side.

"Did you really think you could get married without me?" he asked, coming to wedge himself between Jacquetta and Augustina, wrapping his arms around their shoulders as they smiled, and shook their heads.

"Rath," I said, but Cinder threw her head back and laughed before I could admonish him. And I couldn't pull my eyes from her again.

"Please, General," Cinder said when she finished laughing, her smile radiant as the General took her cue to return to the consent process.

This time, Jacquetta, Augustina, and Rath all offered their version of the consent with Rath saying, "Yes, please marry them before we all die from secondhand pining. And then we can eat."

General Pace pressed her lips together, yet didn't fully succeed in stifling her laughter.

"We're being teased," I whispered to Cinder, which just set off more laughter among our friends.

She leaned into me, causing Jacquetta to make a shocked

sound, but Cinder just put her lips to my earlobe, and whispered, "Not yet, you're not."

"Duchess Cinder," General Pace said as Cinder pulled back from me, a wicked grin on her face that didn't match her beautiful wedding dress at all.

A different kind of heat built within me. I kept her closer than I should have, wanting to be married to her already.

In another break from tradition, we each held the other's rings instead of Augustina or Jacquetta. When we exchanged them, the simple act of sliding hers onto her finger made everything so real.

When she slipped mine on my finger, everything felt right within this world we created inside this room, regardless of what was happening beyond the palace.

"Tristan," she said when it was time, skipping past every title to make her vows to me as a man, not a king, "I vow to be your partner, protecting when you need it, supporting when you want it, and as devoted to you as the stars are to shining."

A pressure built at the backs of my eyes, one I wouldn't give in to even as I sent up a prayer that my mother witnessed this from wherever she was in the afterlife.

General Pace led Cinder through the traditional vows, and when Cinder said, "I do," I couldn't stop the single tear that leaked out from between my lashes, trailing down my cheek.

She let go of my hand to gently wipe the tear from my face, and grabbed my hand again.

"Cinder," I said when it was my cue, choking for a moment on how much she meant to me, "I vow to be as much to you as I am capable, as you are everything to me."

I hoped she understood that this wasn't something I could say in the public wedding. It wasn't something I should have said ever. I was a king. My country should have come first. But, since meeting her, falling for her, feeling her love me more than the crown, every bit of passion I put into protecting the kingdom was as much for her as it was for the people.

"And I vow to love you with all the heat of the hellfire source, to protect you when you let me, and even when you don't, to be your partner in all things, and to be as devoted to you as the moon is to the water. I love you."

Her mouth wavered as she nodded, her eyes filling with tears.

Now it was my turn to wipe away the few that broke free of her lashes as I said, "I do," after General Pace read the traditional vows.

"You may start your path as a married couple with a kiss," General Pace said, and I pulled her to me, her mouth slammed into mine with the power of all the relief in my body, and all the love between us.

I cradled her face in my hands as our kiss deepened, and Rath whooped loudly next to us.

She pulled back, her tears flowing freely now, but her smile brilliant as our friends fell on us with hugs, more tears, and laughter.

No matter what happened now, Cinder was my wife, my Queen, and now we were as tied together as two people could be in this life. No matter what anyone said or did, our bond could never be denied again as we faced our future together.

"You were what I was waiting for," I whispered in her ear, surer of that than of anything else.

CHAPTER 29

GODDESS

CINDER

After being bombarded with congratulations and hugs, even a smack of a kiss on my cheek from Rath, Tristan picked me up, and carried me out of the office, our friends trailing after us, laughing and full of joy.

Other people in the palace looked confused as we passed. They all probably assumed I had hurt myself again, just in a funnier way this time.

Looking up at Tristan, I ran my hand along the hard lines of his jaw with the soft gold lace surrounding it. The fact that our marriage was a secret, held only by those people who loved us, filled me with something close to peace.

Because he was mine. And I was his.

"I love you," I said, drawing his eyes to mine as he smiled down at me with those full lips that I got to kiss for the rest of my life.

He leaned down and kissed me. It was too short, and made me clutch at the lace around his neck, because he needed to watch where we were going, but I didn't care.

"Cinder," he said, my name like a vow in his mouth, "I love you, too."

Our smiles were mirrors of each other just like our rings were—just like our fates were.

No matter what happened next, we were connected, tied together by more than our love for each other.

For some reason, feeling the ring on my finger, being able to run his vows through my mind again, it all made the idea of our connection more real, more tangible.

Before he ever proposed to me, I was forever connected to him. All of my previous interactions with men were either transactional, terrible, or tragic. Usually, none of them involved any feelings at all. They often didn't even include conversation. Most of the time, we didn't know each other's names.

Tristan was different. I fell in love with him before it ever dawned on me that I could wear his ring or say those vows.

And now, I had both.

He opened the door to my apartment, sweeping us inside, carrying me right to my bedroom where the lights were turned down as low as they could go, casting a glow throughout the room that took my breath away.

"Did you do this?" I asked, looking back at him.

Gently, he laid me down on the bed, pressing his lips to mine.

I took his face in my hands, deepening the kiss, never wanting it to stop.

"You are everything to me," I whispered to his lips, hoping he would swallow the words, and keep them in his heart as long as it continued to beat.

Tristan made a noise close to a moan, but sounded like he was equal parts agreeing with me and fighting back tears. In either case, he was unwilling to stop kissing me. But he said against my lips, "We belong together."

Even though none of us wanted to think about it, there was a chance that this wedding would be one of the last things I did in this life because of this war. And the same was true for Tristan.

For the first time since the Corvids attacked, I knew that the connection between us would live on whether we did or not.

No one, no matter how powerful they were or how much they hated us, could ever take away what we were to each other.

Secret or not, General Pace and the Chamberlain already put us under royal seal as a married couple.

"Come here," I whispered into Tristan's mouth while he kept kissing me, my hands tugging at him.

"First," he said, pulling back from me and going to the door, shutting it in Rath's smiling face.

"Hey. King." Rath yelled from the other side.

"Rath," everyone else in the apartment yelled at him as I laughed. Tristan threw the lock on the door, turning to grin at me.

Whatever our friends were going to spend the night doing, I didn't know and didn't care. Whatever else they said on the other side of the door was lost as my entire world narrowed to my new husband, and the unwanted distance between us.

Tristan's grin turned soft while his eyes trailed along my body, shifting to deep gold as he took me in.

I took the chance to fully appreciate how beautiful he looked in his formals. The weight of what we were about to do, and then his eyes, were too much for me to do it to my satisfaction while we were in his office.

Gold lace in a pattern of delicate flames framed his face and his striking eyes in a way that made him seem like a Sun King instead of a Dragon King. The jacket was white leather with gold stitching that may as well have been painted across his strong chest, and every muscle in his arms.

But while everything on top was gorgeous with an ethereal touch, the pants were almost obscene.

Licking my bottom lip, snagging it between my teeth, I made no attempt to hide my study of the way the buttery, gold fabric of them showed off the tone of his thighs or the size of his cock

—which looked like as if it were about to break free of their hold.

Meeting his eyes again, he looked as hungry as I felt. My breath sped up, warmth flowing through me, resting low in my belly.

"You know," I said, my voice as dimmed as the lights around us, "I really like you in that."

He grinned, a lascivious lift to his brow and his hooded eyes.

"Nothing surpasses you in that gown," he said, his voice low and rough as it ran over me, raising every last tiny hair on my body.

"Come here, my King." I poured every bit of my want into my words, so they dripped from me before biting my lip again.

I watched a shiver run through him as he walked to my side, slipping his arms under me, pushing me to the middle of the bed to give himself room to lay beside me.

Tristan didn't kiss me. He didn't undress me. He stared into my eyes, running his hot fingers along my cheek.

"My wife," he said, his voice that of a god addressing a goddess.

"My husband," I whispered back, the title making me touch my ring with my thumb, and clutch at the lace around his neck with the other hand, wanting him to hold me closer.

But he just kept running his fingers along my skin, trailing blazing heat down my neck, across my shoulder, continuing down my arm.

"Are you sure you're better?" he asked as he folded his hand around mine, staring down at where they were joined together.

"Not entirely," I said, swallowing as I admitted it, and hoped my own healing wouldn't keep him from me tonight, "but I'm better enough."

"Enough?" He grinned and leaned forward, his breath brushing across my lips, tingling along the tender skin, the promise of a kiss that raced through my whole body to send me aching for his touch everywhere. The smile fell from his mouth as his eyes trapped mine and his breath hitched. "I don't want to hurt you."

"I don't care." I lifted a leg to slide my calf along his, my leg hooking around his as much as the confines of my dress would allow. "Break me, and when I put the pieces back together, they'll be full of you. Maybe then I'll be sated."

He drew in a swift breath, leaving my lips cold before the burning heat of his mouth met mine. The soft skin of his lips pressed hard to mine, his tongue dancing along my own in my mouth to the tune of our beating hearts.

Tristan pulled away and kissed my neck, his mouth hot on my skin, sending that warmth through me. I realized that even then it wouldn't be enough.

"You're already part of me," he said, his words pouring into my veins, traveling down my limbs, forcing my toes to curl and grip on him to tighten. "Everything in me, my heart, my spirit, my mind is filled with you."

"Because you are mine," I whispered into his ear, running my teeth along the shell of it, thrilling at the shudder it caused in him.

"And you are mine," he said, pulling back and looking me in the eye, his gaze a challenge.

I nodded, "We belong together."

There was no more need for words. They were all laid out between us. The ones we just said, and the ones we vowed in front of our friends, they bound us together in a way that was outside ourselves. But he was right.

Long before he gave me his ring the first time, we already belonged to each other as much as we belonged with each other.

He sat up, pulling me up with him, and shifted down on the bed.

My eyebrow quirked in question, but he just smiled at me, took the trailing end of the metal overlay of my gown that hung past my feet, and started to lift it up past my ankles.

"Are you taking it off?" I asked, trying to sound innocent, although my thoughts were not.

"Well," he said, wrapping the chain around his hand and sliding my mother's slippers off with his other, "that was the plan, yes."

"How about we leave it," I said, unable to suppress my smirk, especially as he looked up at me so confused, "and take off the dress under it instead."

"Cinder," he said, his voice rough and strangled.

"Don't hold back, husband." I swept my feet to the side, and sat up, kneeling, pulling the straps of the underdress down my shoulders. "Don't be gentle. Not tonight."

Growling low in his throat, he surged toward me, claiming my mouth with his, hands rough as he pressed me to him.

"Oh," I moaned into his mouth, desperate to feel normal again after being treated like I was so fragile for so long.

"Stand up," he said between kisses, voice still harsh, barely contained.

I wasn't sure if he meant to stand there on the bed, or to crawl off and stand on the floor. But I didn't want to waste a single second, so I gripped his shoulders as I shoved myself up to stand right there on the blankets.

Looking down my body at the King on his knees before me, I smiled and thought about our first night together.

"Are you bowing to me tonight?" I asked, running a hand through his hair as he started to move to my back.

He gave me a hungry grin and laughed.

"No," he said. My smile almost fell, but he said, "Tonight, I worship."

My eyes closed as he ran a hand up between my legs, and maneuvered to stand behind me, his fingers leaving my skin before he reached my core where I already grew wet for want of him.

Fingers on my back, slipping between the jeweled chains to undo my dress, he whispered in my ear, "Keep making that whimpering sound, my Queen."

His mouth fell on my neck, teeth skimming my skin, and a plaintive noise slipped out of my mouth. One I was aware of this time.

Rumbling something that sounded like, "Yes," into my neck, he slipped the straps of the underdress down my arms, the front of it falling free of my body since he undid the fasteners in the back.

With deft hands, he managed to push it down until it fell from me, pooling at my feet. Only then did he release my neck, and step back from me, the bed shifting.

"If others saw you like this," he said, running a hand along my ass, pressing the chain into my skin, the chill of it compared to the heat of his palm enough to make me suck in a breath, "Onyx would worship a warrior Goddess above all other deities."

Tristan stepped in front of me again, his eyes devouring the way the jewels and chains fell along my breasts and waist, tracing all the way down to the one that dangled between my legs.

My skin tingled under his gaze as if it were a physical thing. I held my hands out to him.

"Nevermind," he said, voice a rasp of feeling as his hands met mine and his eyes returned to burn their gold fire into me, "I'm jealous in my devotions of this deity."

With a step that shifted the bed under my feet, he forced the foundations of my heart to shift in such a way that more of my love for him poured through me, blazing hot, as he closed the distance between us.

"Only I get to worship here," he said, and crashed his mouth to mine.

182

CHAPTER 30

DEVOUT

Tristan

Cinder's mouth on mine was like hellfire water on an already raging inferno.

She burrowed so deep inside my heart that she burned me up from the inside out.

Her hands quickly shoved their way between us, undoing my jacket, and pushing it off my shoulders.

I didn't want to let her go to get rid of it, but I didn't want these damned, too-tight formals blocking me from feeling her skin.

With a grunt, I pulled back from her, and yanked my jacket off, throwing it to the other side of the room while she went to work untying my pants.

Bending down to peel them off me, I trapped her pert nipple in my mouth, and she moaned, her hands tangling in my hair.

Gods and Goddesses, that sound. Every quick inhale, every

moan, every scream, and every cry, thrummed hard in my cock, building my need of her into an acute frenzy.

Finally, I ripped my pants free of my feet, throwing them out of the way.

Only then could I do what I had wanted to since I knelt in front of her before. I dropped down to the bed and grabbed her hips, leading her to stand over me as I reclined amongst the pile of pillows.

"Come here," I said, my voice rougher than normal. It made me wish I could be softer for her right now, but then she grinned.

She dropped down slowly until she knelt just above my chest. My hands still gripped her hips, my fingers pressed into her hard ass muscles that flexed as she moved.

I shook my head, even as the word "yes" screamed through me, a smile on my own face.

"No, Cinder," I commanded. Letting go of her with one hand, I pointed to my lips as I pulled at her hip with my other hand. "Come here. I want you right here."

With a wicked grin, she grabbed my hair roughly, and bent to press her mouth to mine.

This kiss was lingering and gentle, the opposite of her grip in my hair, and my grip on her ass. It only served to make me want her more.

Finally, I couldn't wait to taste her. A groan left me as I broke the kiss, shoving her hips closer to my face. This time Cinder did as I wanted, her pussy directly over my face.

Her chain, that delicate hint of armor, trailed down to drape over my chin and onto my neck.

Surging up, pressing down on her with my hands at the same time, I clamped my mouth on her pussy, the chain cold between the heat of my tongue and the warmth of her clit.

Cinder shivered, her fingers tangling in my hair again, a moan escaping her lips.

Licking and sucking at her, from her entrance to her perfect little clit—the wet of it making me groan, sending a throb through my cock—was a prayer I was more than willing to commit to making for the rest of my life.

If the High Sect, the clergy, and the Shields worshipped her, worshipped this, instead of the various little deities that they swore lived in their shrines, I would understand their devotion far more.

"Tristan," she moaned as she rocked against my mouth, the muscles of her ass and legs quivering as the perfect taste flooded my mouth. I moaned in response.

Moving one hand, I slipped a finger into her pussy even as it clamped down all over again. Her shaking gave way to full body tremors.

We rode out her pleasure with my mouth still on her, the chain tangled between us, my finger pumping inside her.

"Please," she whined, the sound going straight to my cock.

Oh, but I was not done yet.

I shook my head, not taking my mouth from her, and she let out a warring cry, her legs weakening on either side of my head.

Grazing my teeth along her clit, I slipped in another finger. She shook, her cries getting louder and closer together, her breath shallowing and speeding up.

Clamping my mouth down on her clit, sucking it hard against my teeth as I teased it with my tongue, I moved my fingers in and out of her throbbing pussy, and she broke again.

She was so wet now. Her cries grew wild as her legs lost all ability to hold her up. I wrapped one arm around her, that hand pressing her ass to shove her against my face as I kept working my fingers and tongue.

Waves of pleasure crashed over her, each one building, her orgasms enough to make me cum, too, if I let them.

"Tristan," she screamed my name, and I moaned into her hot,

wet center, unsure if I would be able to leave her in the morning for the Marshlands.

All I wanted now was to make her scream my name again.

Her body rocked and bucked against me, my attentions unrelenting as she flooded my mouth again and again, both her hands in my hair, her grip punishing.

"Please," she whined. I moaned even as I shook my head again.

But it was that, the shaking of my head that made her throw hers back so I could no longer look up at her, her voice raw as she screamed my name again.

Slowing down, easing the pressure, I lifted her off my face a little as we both rode out the last of her orgasm.

Finally, I let her hips lower. She bent to meet my mouth, soaked in her, with her own lips.

Her tongue on mine, she moaned into my mouth, and I moaned back even as I wrapped my hands around her hips, and pressed her further down my body.

"You like your taste?" I asked. "Because I fucking love it."

All she could manage was a whimper, but I smiled and kissed her harder.

She shifted, her legs still shaking, as she moved her hips further down. When my cock brushed against her wet pussy, she cried out into my mouth.

Maybe my Queen was a little overly sensitive now.

"Fuck," I said, breathless as her reaction made it harder for me not to flip her onto her back, and take her with abandon.

But I didn't want to hurt her, and this was the best way to avoid too much pressure on her wounds.

Instead, I moved her hips, pressing that throbbing pussy against my hard cock, thrilling to the shivers that ran through her, forcing a plaintive noise from deep within her.

Cinder didn't whine again. She didn't beg. She didn't let me continue playing with her. No, she took what she wanted.

Reaching down between us, she grabbed my cock, eliciting a moan from me, and she positioned the tip at the entrance to her pussy.

I let go of one of her hips to cup her cheek, pulling back so I could look at her beautiful face, into those eyes that I got lost in.

"My wife," I said, voice hushed, "I love you."

"My husband," she said, her voice shaking as she lowered herself onto me, making me suck in a breath as she did, "I love you."

With the hand still on her hip, I pressed against her, and pushed myself into her.

She shook around me, her walls wet and welcoming even as they stretched and tightened down around me again.

But after closing her eyes, she began to move with me.

Cinder was slow and torturous, allowing me to feel every single sensation along my body as she moved up and down, then ground forward and back while I was as deep as I could be.

I moaned as she moved, and, with another thrust off my hips, her hands pressed harder into my shoulders, her eyes going wide.

No matter how gentle I wanted to be, no matter how much I didn't want to hurt her, I couldn't hold back. Not when it was clear I hit that spot in her, the one she enjoyed the most.

Grabbing onto her hips with both hands, I slammed into her. She cried out, her nails digging into the skin of my shoulders.

"Tristan," she moaned, but I wanted to hear her louder. I wanted her to remember this while I was away.

With a wild cry I managed to keep my own undoing at bay as our bodies slammed together, again and again. She shattered around me, screaming out as her walls tightened, making me see stars.

But it wasn't my name.

Scrambling my hands against her hips, I wrapped them up

into the chains around her body, and pressed the cold metal into the hot flesh of her ass.

Yanking on the chains, she sat up, her hands leaving my shoulders.

From that position, her shuddering grew worse, her cries louder, her head thrashed from side to side.

I used my hands, tangled in the cold chains to move her body against mine, slamming again and again, deep inside her, grinding her against me.

Still, she didn't say it. The withholding was enough to drive anything else from my mind.

My wife, my Queen, my Cinder, I wanted her to say it. I needed her to say it in the same way I needed air.

Loosening the chains from one hand enough to move it to her front, I ran my thumb along her clit in the way she loved, losing myself in the movement of our hips against each other.

Even with her back, her shaking legs, she responded, slamming against me harder and harder as I met each of her movements.

This time, her cries grew louder and louder, drowning out the world, the kingdom, everything but her.

My Goddess. My life.

When she fell off the cliff, breaking apart, she screamed my name, and I followed her, shattering with her into a million sparks of hellfire water-fueled flames.

She collapsed onto my chest, her face in my neck as we both came back to ourselves, my hands still tangled in her chains and jewels, resting on her back.

"You said," I breathed in between desperate breaths, "if you broke apart you would form back together with pieces of me."

Cinder hummed against my neck, her lips pressing a kiss to my skin as we both shivered and shook.

"I think I fell apart," I said, knowing that I would never be the same king, the same person, now that I had her, "and you put me back together."

One of her hands came to rest on my cheek, her thumb rubbing back and forth.

"We're a part of each other now," she said.

CHAPTER 31

IMPOSSIBLE

Cinder

Waking up in the morning—after too little sleep, hours of making love the night before, which still wasn't enough—and knowing I had to let him leave me behind that day was enough to make me want a blade in my hands, and someone I was allowed to kill in front of me.

Making our way through the hurried motions of readying for his departure, the need to stab someone only grew.

It got to the point that Gus and Jacquetta didn't speak to me as they helped, just shot each other looks over my head like I wouldn't notice.

Apologies would need to happen.

Later.

Right now, I only cared about my King and the distance that waited to grow between us as it mocked my purpose in life—to protect him.

But Tristan's kiss, hot and claiming as he leaned over me outside the door to the carriage blunted the edge of my anger.

"Come home to me," I said, holding his face to mine.

His hands gripped the back of my hastily-chosen day dress, his eyes, gold laced with bright green, shined in the early morning sun in the courtyard.

Letting go of my dress with one hand, he placed his palm on my chest, right over my heart, and I grabbed it, clinging to it with all the strength in my fingers.

With his other hand, he pulled my palm from his cheek, and placed it over his own heart.

"I love you," he said, his face in grim lines, and his voice echoing the determination I felt when I went after him from Breakwater to save the kids.

"And I love you," I said, nodding, hoping he understood that I knew what he meant.

He was mine.

I was his.

We belonged together.

And we were never really apart, not when I held pieces of him and he held pieces of me, ones we would never be able to untangle from ourselves even if we tried. Neither of us would ever try.

One more kiss, this one tender and sweet, made tears collect at the backs of my eyes, and he was in the carriage, the door slamming shut.

I kept the hand that was over his to my heart, and placed the other on the cool glass of the carriage window without turning to look at him through the window. If I looked, it would have been impossible to hold back my tears.

The difference in temperature between the heat of his chest and the chilled glass was enough to make me suck in a harsh breath that seared ice into my lungs.

Dragging in air, my chest heaving, I watched as the carriage and his retinue left the courtyard.

After the last of them disappeared into the tunnel, I turned back to the steps of the palace.

My back ached just thinking about climbing all the stairs again. Looking over my shoulder at the arches that led to the shadowed training area, I thought about walking down there to throw knives, finding someone to spar with, even shooting a bow.

But images of Tristan, bow in hand, taking out Corvids as I fought in front of him on the field, bloomed behind my eyes, and I turned back to the duties I had to embrace as Queen.

Gus and Jacquetta waited just inside the massive doors, Jacquetta yanking on Gus' arm to keep her inside.

Their eyes were wide and blinking too fast, probably fighting off the same urge to weep as I was.

Whether Tristan knew it or not, my friends loved him almost as much as I did.

I gave them as much of a smile as I could muster as I made it to the top step, a wind blowing across the courtyard, making the chill around me from Tristan's absence sink further into my body.

Gus broke from Jacquetta's grip, running to my side, wrapping an arm around me while her wife's hands shook, and her eyes blew wider.

As soon as we crossed the threshold into the palace proper, Jacquetta grabbed us both and dragged us toward the grand staircase.

"Our King leaves the palace, and the first thing you two do is risk your safety outside?" Jacquetta said, shaking her head, any threat of tears gone as her face turned to one full of wrath.

"Jacquetta," I said with a sigh, "the courtyard is teeming with guards. The sky is not the enemy."

"They come from the sky, Ci—" she stopped short of calling

me by my name and not my title by letting go of me and Gus, and slapping her hands over her mouth.

Gus laughed and wrapped an arm around Jacquetta while I went to her other side to pat her shoulder.

"It's okay to call me by my name," I said, keeping my voice low because otherwise, even if Jacquetta managed not to be scandalized by my informality, someone would.

"Not out here, it's not," Jacquetta whispered through her fingers and Gus grinned, shaking her head.

"Come on, then," Gus said, "let's get somewhere we can say what we want."

We walked up the stairs, but at the point they split, I stopped.

They turned to look at me, Jacquetta with a question on her face, and Gus with sadness in her eyes before she looked past me toward the royal wing.

"He wouldn't want you to wait alone over there," Gus said, and I smiled.

"No," I said, shaking my head and taking her hand, "Rath is in there for some meeting, and I think I should go be the almost Queen while Tristan isn't here."

Well. That, and I thought if I haunted Rath's meetings, I might be able to find out more about the Chrysalis Tower, and how I could get in and out of there to kill my brother, bringing this war to an end.

"So, you're going to be the voice of reason?" Jacquetta said. Gus laughed and I rolled my eyes. "The kingdom is doomed."

"Very funny." I shook my head and turned to go do what I needed to, their laughter behind me.

But Gus grabbed my hand, and turned me around to face them again.

"Is something wrong?" A lump formed in my throat, because so much was wrong with today, with him being gone, but I shoved it aside to listen.

"Yes," Gus said, brows high as she looked me up and down. "Everything."

"What's that supposed to mean?"

"Our Queen can't go into an official meeting wearing a day dress with unkempt hair," Jacquetta said, grabbing my other hand and helping Gus pull me.

"This is what I've worn all morning." I looked down at myself, and couldn't understand what the issue was.

"Don't you want everyone to have good things to say about you when the King returns?" Jacquetta said in a singsong voice like she spoke to a child.

"He won't care about my clothes, or what they say about me."

Even as I complained, irritated at being wrenched away from what I wanted to do, I didn't fight them.

"It doesn't hurt to have another weapon to use," Gus said, smirking like she knew she got to me with that one.

Which she did.

How many times had they proved the importance of the not-subtle-art of the fashion wars?

In more ways than I could count, their knowledge and their skill helped me get here, helped me have a life far beyond what I thought I deserved, helped me marry Tristan.

Still, it would delay my plans, and I was petty enough to find that frustrating.

"Almost every person that meets with Tristan already saw me wrapped in blankets in bed and wounded." My voice was a grumble, but that just left them laughing.

"One more reason for you to start looking the part," Jacquetta said, all the singsong gone now in favor of triumph.

"Fine, but we're going Warrior Queen, and we need to be quick."

They looked across me to each other, their smiles wide, and I couldn't help grinning along with them.

But as they walked ahead of me into our apartment, already

discussing how they would dress me, I realized that they managed to do the impossible.

Within minutes of Tristan leaving, they got me smiling and laughing, my worry set aside just enough.

Maybe that was their magic.

CHAPTER 32

TOO MUCH

Tristan

"Are you sure it would not be better to bring the carriage?" General Pace asked, standing at the end of the largest guest room at the Inn, which was still too small for this meeting. "We are only supposed to go to the edge of the Marshlands."

"Yes," I said, leaning to rest my elbows on my knees where I sat on the edge of the bed. A headache pounded at the back of my skull, and I was more than tired of going over the same details again and again, "But if they want us to go further in, I need to be ready."

"Besides," Shield Elio said, lounging in the only chair, sweat on his brow, exhaustion weighing on his features, "the High Sect will have more respect for a king connected enough to nature to ride than one tucked away inside a carriage."

"Carriages are made of wood from nature." General Pace

sounded more than irritated that we were still being stubborn about this plan.

They began to go over the formation of the guards, and how Elio wanted them to be arrayed near him as I let myself stew over what was happening at home.

Everyone probably thought I was imagining what I would say, how I intended to get them on our side, and away from the fucking crows.

Or, they assumed I was too exhausted from a day of travel inside the carriage to be an active part of the discussion.

But we already went over all of this before we left the palace.

And I didn't want to stop here for the night.

Dinner was one thing. I agreed to that. Our guards and the others needed to eat, but if I had my way, we would have continued straight to the damn marshes with the fewest stops possible. We certainly wouldn't have sat our asses inside an inn until it was almost too late to do anything other than sleep.

Looking over at Elio as he coughed and took a long drink from a tankard, I realized I was being selfish.

All that thought brought me, though, was resentment.

Of Elio for being hurt, which was totally irrational, and made me even angrier.

Of myself for being unable to focus on all the things I needed to at once to make this trip worth it, and accomplish what the kingdom needed.

Of the Kingdom for the responsibilities it placed on my shoulders simply by existing, which made even less sense than blaming Elio for being hurt by the damn crows.

Of the Corvids for their part in this war.

Of Ash and all his traitors for their part.

Of the slaves Ash bought for not knowing they were already free in Onyx, and didn't have to fight for him—another one that made zero sense, and only managed to make me more livid with myself.

More than anything else, I was resentful of time itself—of a force that existed wholly outside anyone's control and ruled everyone and everything in the world without favor.

But the three days it would take for us to travel there, and the whole day at least it would take to accomplish our task if it all went well, then the three days back made me hate time with as much venom as I hated Ash.

Cinder was at the palace, safe and sound. But not with me. And still not fully healed. And she would stay that way for at least seven days.

Rubbing a hand over my face, I dragged my fingers through my hair, and looked up to see the whole room staring at me.

"What?" I asked, freezing in place and hoping I didn't say too much aloud.

"I think we should revisit a cover for your horse at least," General Pace said, bringing up one of those stupid contraptions that I hated that so many people erected over their saddles since the war started.

"No, damn it," I yelled, shoving myself up to standing, beyond done with these time-wasting, circular conversations. "We should be out there."

Pointing outside, I walked the few steps open to me in that cramped room before whirling around to go in the other direction again.

"Every stop," I ranted, "every empty conversation that only amounts to review over the same set of facts without any additional information, just delays our arrival."

"All this planning is so that we can prepare as much as possible," the General's voice was hard, and I stopped to stare at her, my blood hot in my veins, "and—"

"What, and?" I yelled, throwing my hands in the air, and looking around the room at everyone collected here. All but the General and Elio averted their eyes.

"If you let me finish," she said, only making me angrier.

"So, you can say the same things you said in the palace?" I shook my head, unable to stop the edge to my voice, or wipe the snarl I felt on my face, even though I knew this was all an over-reaction.

"King Tristan," she said, her voice taking on the same tone she used when she barked orders in battle, "we are doing all of this so we can get you home alive."

"You took me from her, and are wasting time *keeping* me away from her longer to keep me alive?" I was quieter now, but even I heard the dangerous tone hidden in my incredulity.

"How much do you love Duchess Cinder?" Elio asked, his eyes wide, mouth agape, and voice so hushed I was sure I didn't hear him correctly.

"What?" I asked.

If he wanted every single part of my attention, saying her name accomplished just that. But he couldn't have just asked me how much I loved her. That didn't make sense. I was hallucinating.

General Pace turned her furrowed brow on him, too, and I thought maybe I heard him right. Although it still lacked sense.

"Your Duchess Cinder, your Fighter," he said, voice still low but clearer in the complete lack of any other sound in the room other than the pounding beat of my heart, and the way I sucked in a breath at her name, "how much do you love her?"

How could I answer that?

Enough for the distance between us to drive me to distraction. All I could think about was her being targeted, or the injuries she was still recovering from, or the fact that she wasn't at her deadliest at a time when I couldn't be there to protect her.

"More than I thought possible to love another person," I said, telling the truth, all the fight leaving me as the ache in my chest grew. My flagging energy and physical exhaustion took over. "She is a part of me, and I am a part of her."

Shield Elio smiled a wary and concerned smile that matched

the bobbing of his throat as he swallowed before shoving himself slowly to his feet.

"That is good, King Tristan," he said, his voice still too quiet, almost not loud enough to hear at all. "Onyx is stronger with a king who loves his queen."

He looked around the room while I met General Pace's eyes.

My confusion was mirrored on her face. She shrugged, a movement I almost never saw her make, but couldn't blame her for using now.

What was going on? And why did Shield Elio ask me about Cinder at all?

Elio stopped in front of me, squinting as he stared into my eyes, studying me.

Part of me wanted to step back from him. Part of me thought I should challenge him for speaking of her, and demand to know why he wanted to know how much I loved her. But all I could do was stand my ground, waiting while his eyes bored into mine.

"If someone were to threaten her?" he whispered.

Rage flooded me, my hands balling into fists. Ash's face appeared in my mind, and my blood ran so hot I thought it might rival the heat of hellfire water.

"They would die," I said, my voice a weapon that grated on my own ears it was so harsh, "Ash *will* die. I *will* kill him."

Shield Elio's eyes widened, and he stumbled back from me, one of the guards catching him, looking just as astonished as I was.

Out of all of it, the part of his reaction I understood the least was the wide smile on his face.

"When we get to the Marshlands," he said, standing up straight again, "I need to speak first."

"But the King," General Pace started, stopping when Elio shook his head and raised his hand, turning toward her.

"You can stop all the additional planning, all the contingency plans. I am sure I know how to get the High Sect to side with us, and push out the Corvids." Elio's smile grew wider by the second, his normally boisterous voice returning even though there was some kind of tinge to it I couldn't place.

"How can you be so sure?" I asked.

"Trust me, King Tristan," he said, shaking his head, and chuckling softly before he started to leave the room.

General Pace furrowed her brow further, pursed her lips, then looked my way before nodding, and rushing after him. I hoped he would answer her questions even if he wasn't going to answer mine.

Everyone else filed out after her, leaving me in the middle of the room as I realized what that extra note was to his voice I missed earlier—reverence.

CHAPTER 33

BLUFF

Cinder

Opening the door to the public office, because even Rath wasn't about to hold a meeting in Tristan's private office without Tristan around, I held my head high, and reveled in the feel of finally having my spikes strapped onto my thighs again.

Every person in the room went silent as I walked toward the desk that Rath perched on, his legs dangling along with his jaw.

"Flame," he said, hopping off the desk, "what are you doing in here?"

I raised a brow at him, not about to answer that question.

Maybe it was the look on my face that stopped his mouth from running. Or maybe it was the way I was dressed, in a metal bustier with a leather panel under my waist that tied in the back, supporting my still-sore ribs and back muscles. But the skirt of thick silk, hanging low on my hips by a heavy, jeweled chain with slits up both my legs showing off my spikes might have also done it.

Whatever the reason for their prolonged silence, I was thankful for it as I made my way to Tristan's chair behind the desk, and took a seat.

I was also thankful for the opportunity to feel like myself in front of people other than my friends.

No matter what title I held, no matter how much I wanted to be a good queen who helped Tristan in whatever way he needed, I would always also be an accomplished assassin. And I wanted everyone to remember that. Including me.

Once seated, I took in the odd collection of people arrayed before me.

At least a few of them were farmers. That much was obvious. Even if they had cleaned up carefully for their day at the palace, they still held their brimmed hats in their hands, and dirt still lined their fingernails.

Still others looked like well-to-do merchants. They weren't the kind of people I would have assumed would come to see the King together.

Maybe Tristan worked with different groups to help them broker deals?

But that didn't make sense. It wasn't the kind of thing I would assume he would spend his time worrying about. There were deals struck every day in the country, and everyone couldn't possibly be going to the King for every single one of them…could they?

Not only did that sound like a massive waste of time, it also sounded exhausting.

Oh, if that were the case, I was not going to be a very good queen.

Well, shit.

But I tried not to let any of my thoughts show on my face as I made my way over to the seat behind the desk, making a point not to meet Rath's eyes even though I could sense his brows raised in question from where he leaned against the front of the desk.

"Duchess," Rath said while the collection of people made attempts at bows, some more successful than others.

"Please," I said, trying for a "keep going" gesture, and hoping it wasn't too informal or indecorous for this setting, "continue with your meeting."

Rath pursed his lips, his brow lowering for only a moment before he smiled, and turned back to the people waiting for us to address whatever their issue was.

One of the merchants looked to Rath who simply nodded.

"Very well," the merchant said, "as I was saying, we need to have these fields tended, prepared for the planting season."

"And with the war," another said, shaking their head in what looked to be a false show of concern—it reminded me of Ash, "many of the people who would normally work our fields have joined the guard."

"Yes," I said, not willing to let them say anything negative about the people currently fighting for the country while these people made more money than usual because of the conflict. Savvy merchants always managed to make a profit, especially since Tristan paid exorbitant prices for all the food and supplies the Crown ordered believing it was a good way to help people. "This war has been particularly taxing on those so brave as to sign up to fight to keep us all out of Corvid hands... or talons."

Many of the guards he spoke about, I trained. And I stared him down until he relented, nodding and focusing on the ground at his feet instead of saying anything else that I might not like on the subject.

Good. Maybe everyone would be so afraid of me as Queen we could just avoid certain issues. I would have to think more about that possibility later.

"We are all thankful, Duchess Cinder," the first merchant said, giving me a tight, fake smile.

It made me want to snarl. Instead, I stayed still, letting him continue.

"The challenge we face," the merchant said, turning slightly to address Rath, leaving me to wonder if I should take it as a slight, "is that those we have hired to work in the fields are so concerned about Corvids attacking from the sky that they refuse to work half the time."

Rath drew in a long breath, and made a sound like he was going to say something. But I cut him off.

"Have you tried paying them more? They are risking every-thing while others are holed up in the safety of their houses."

"Yes, Duchess," one of the farmers said, stepping forward a fraction, "but we don't have anything to help us remain concealed."

"Does that mean you do not have *anything* to protect you?" I asked, my voice low and sharp at the edges, mirroring my thoughts.

"Of course not," the merchant said, and I raised a brow at him that had him looking to Rath again. "What I mean is, there is no way to cover the entire area of the field with any kind of cover, and since the fields are only being prepped for planting, there is no way for them to cover each person in green to hide them from above, either. There is nothing we can do."

"Nothing?" I asked, hoping he heard the fury and the insult riding in the single word. This man didn't care about these people. He didn't even care about the desperate need for crops because of this war. If someone said my life depended on reading him, I probably would have been safe in assuming he only cared about the profits he stood to make.

"Maybe there is something we could come up with," Rath said, looking back at me a moment, his smile not as sure as before.

"Everything we suggest gets shot down," the farmer said, his entire being resigned and saddened.

But still, no matter how many times he was shot down, he was here. All of them were.

Wait…

Shot down.

Rath offered up some variation of the things they already tried. The merchant kept saying no, but my mind surged with a clear picture of what to do.

"You know," Rath said, careful and quiet, "the attacks have all been in strategic locations. There is no reason to assume that anything will happen in the fields to average citizens."

"I already told them all this," the merchant said, making me want to just stab him and be done with it, "they refuse to listen to reason."

He opened his mouth to continue, but I cut in before he could.

"Post archers in the trees, or in a built-up tower along the edge of the field," I said, eyebrow still high, hoping he saw the challenge on my face before he chose to keep pushing this.

"The Palace will be supplying the guard for that?" the merchant asked, grinning as if he had won something.

Cocking my head to the side, I placed my hands on the desk in front of me, and slowly pushed myself to standing.

"What part of the contract you make with your employees suggests to you that the Crown, and therefore every single citizen, should risk lowering the number of guards we have trying to win this war when there are sure to be very good hunters willing to take the paycheck to sit in a tree all day?"

Rath's eyes flashed back and forth between all of us, but I only had eyes for the merchant.

Mine were unyielding, but his were calculating and angry.

All his fury and attempts to outsmart me managed to accomplish was to make me even less likely to give in to a damn thing he wanted.

Some people were just terrible to those around them. This man was one of them.

I knew the signs, and he had them. Maybe I made too many excuses for my brother over the years, but he was the reason that I could always spot another predator when I saw one. Even if I didn't know their particular brand of cruelty, I knew what it was like to be a predator while pretending I was prey.

Ash crafted me into the predator I was, after all. And if I was going to have any success as Queen, the only way for me to do that would be through using that ability...as long as I didn't completely lose control and stab someone. At least the wrong someone.

"But, Duchess, the profit margin..." He gestured with his hand, as if that would matter to me at all.

"The profit margin will be a healthy one for you, even after hiring a few more people to keep their eyes on the skies to protect your workers."

He opened his mouth to say something again, but I just cut him off as the cold place rose in my mind, taking over, "Especially with the war. And I would think that a fine, upstanding citizen would want to contribute to us winning in any way they could."

The farmers were beaming, smiles all around, although they tried to tamp them down when they turned their faces toward the merchant.

"Well," Rath said, standing and gesturing for the group to head toward the door, "thank you for bringing this to our attention. We will be sending word to any others that might be in a similar situation, but we would always appreciate it if you could tell those you know as well."

I sat back down behind the desk, and waited for them all to leave, wondering again how Tristan did this so often.

Once the door was shut behind them, I found myself alone with Rath. He whirled to look at me, crossing his arms over his chest, his mouth turned down into a frown that looked wholly unnatural on him.

A headache stabbed me right behind my left eye as the cold place fled from me. I just knew he was comparing me to Tristan, and I was found wanting in the diplomacy department.

"Fine," I said, rubbing at my eyebrow to relieve the ache behind it, "I'm not good at these kinds of things."

"That isn't the way I would describe what you just did." His voice was careful, measured, and made me tense as it was not like the Rath I knew at all.

"How would you describe that meeting, then?"

"Your idea was sound, and so was your solution."

Opening my mouth to speak, he held up a hand with his brows raised as if asking me to please let him finish.

"But, Flame, you can't just intimidate every powerful person in this country without gaining more people who would be willing to test Onyx without the Dragon King." His voice was low and almost kind, as if that would somehow lessen the blow.

There was nothing that would have alleviated the instant regret, shame, and pain I felt at being even more of a reason for anyone to doubt Tristan as King.

My job, whether I wanted it to be or not, was at least in part to be someone who could help Tristan hold Onyx together, to help him rid us of the threat of these traitors.

So far, I failed.

"One of the merchants who was just in here is a leader of a network of merchants, and, if he wanted to, he could call in the entire network, which might cause more damage than anything some treasonous noble here or there could accomplish."

All I could do was nod, although I wanted to ask how he suggested I do this better. I wanted to understand the pitfalls of what I tried to do there, of the meetings I took, and whom I met with.

But, instead, I vowed to stay silent, and just observe for a while.

With every new group shown in after the door was once again opened, and with every new challenge that Rath helped people work through, I did learn.

I learned I was out of my depth, and I was right when I thought that someone like me had no business being a queen.

My solutions, ones I refused to voice, most often involved stabbing someone, but the truth was that I couldn't do that. Not here.

None of that truth mattered now.

Tristan and I were married. He was mine, and I was his, and I had to find some way to make this work.

For him, for me, for my friends, and for Onyx.

After a time, a new group came into the office that were so different from the rest of the people we saw that day that I found myself leaning forward in my chair.

I looked into the eyes of one rather shabby looking person after another. They eventually all filed in, arraying themselves before me.

But even my careful scan of them left me more than a little confused as to who I was looking at.

They didn't wear clothes I had ever seen before in Onyx. Instead, they wore billowing pants, or skintight pants that cut off before their ankles at an odd point, tunics tied with belts, or loose shirts that showed a lot of chest. On the men and the women, the clothes were the same.

"Carry on," I said after a moment of awkward silence.

"Flame," Rath said, twisting to look back at me, "these are some of my people, and we should have a private meeting."

He wanted me to leave, did he?

Not a chance.

Rath might have been better at diplomacy, but if these were spies and some of his people, then I could learn something that might help me do the one thing I was confident in: kill someone to end this war.

"Unless you expect anyone else to come in here," I said, waving my hand in a carry on gesture, "this *is* private."

I didn't count as someone whom they should keep things from.

Even though I knew Rath, the General, and Tristan were all keeping my brother's location from me because some error in their thinking made them feel like they were protecting me, I wanted to know everything else.

"Flame," he said, his voice lower and more insistent now.

"Rath," I said, matching his tone, "I already know about the Tower."

"What?" He reared back, stumbling off the edge of the desk, and whirling to face me.

His people sat behind him, showing no sign until that moment that they cared at all about our conversation, shared glances before they focused on me again.

"You're a terrible liar, Rath," I said, not actually believing that he was. But knowing more than he thought I did could make it harder for him to keep me out in the future. If I played this right.

Not that I had been doing that a lot, but maybe I could still salvage something from this day.

The only things I had going for me were the knowledge I gleaned from feigning sleep, my own ability to remain as blank-faced as a person could from years of practice in front of Ash's fists, and the fact that Rath was my friend and didn't want to hurt me.

Not a lot in front of a spy, but more than I had in front of most of the people Tristan had to deal with in this room.

"I'm not lying about being shocked," he said, turning entirely to me, standing too straight for our favorite pirate.

"Are you more shocked that I would ask you to tell me what you know, or that I wasn't asleep when you thought I was?"

Rath swallowed, looking to his people, but they offered nothing.

How could they?

They didn't even know me enough to call me by my name rather than one of my titles.

When he met my eyes again, he pressed his lips together as if sealing away whatever words were locked inside.

My smile made him fidget, but it was small and only one move.

Enough, though.

Placing my hands on the desk in front of me, I slowly raised myself to standing, and leaned forward, painting my face in the deaths I dealt while still my brother's sword arm.

Cold, focused, lethal.

Rath's pinky finger twitched.

"Don't underestimate what I would do for him," I said, pouring every bit of the truth of my words into my voice.

He sucked in a breath, his chest expanding. When he let out that breath, he did it slowly with an exasperated sigh hidden in it, everything about him deflating.

"King doesn't want you to know," he said, finally going to the truth of the problem.

"Tristan isn't here." My smile now was wicked, and promised all the violence I was capable of. It was the same smile I wore when I made my way into Lord Fall's home, knowing I was about to end that bastard's sorry life. "You and I both know, I'm the only one who can get in there, and do what needs to be done."

His mouth worked, trying to stifle any of the words playing on his tongue.

Maybe they were half-formed denials he knew were lies. Maybe they were more reasons why he couldn't go against Tristan's wishes. Maybe they were attempts to distract me, to talk me out of this.

Whatever the words were, they died in his mouth, and he only nodded.

I lifted my hands off the desk, standing up straight.

"Rathmoreland may not be able to speak with me about this," I said, still staring right at him. I saw his tiny nod before he turned to his people, and leaned against the desk while I turned my gaze to them, "but you are under no such orders."

Taking the seat behind the desk again, I gestured, "Please, continue what you were about to say about the traitor."

At that, one of them—a young woman who looked like she was still shy of adulthood by a few years—grinned and relaxed.

She made no attempt to hide her study of me, her grin turning into a cocky smirk.

"You're the new Queen?" she asked.

"Not officially," Rath said, and I raised a brow, not sparing him more than a glance.

"Well, well," the girl said, "all the stories about you are true."

I smiled and hoped it didn't show any of the doubt rippling through me.

The stories? What stories were they talking about?

When other people said those kinds of things, I assumed they were referring to what I did on the battlefield. But these were spies.

Maybe they knew more about me than I wanted people to.

All I could do without admitting anything in case they didn't know, was keep my face as enigmatic as possible. Which, for me, in that moment, was the flat affect of someone plotting a murder, and the grin of someone who knew more than anyone else, while I kept the eyes of the girl who couldn't show anything, my body as still as a stiffened corpse.

One of the large men at the back of the group rubbed the scruff at his chin, crossing his arms in front of his chest.

"We should tell her," the man said, his voice so low and sweet and so out of place against his looks and his body that I almost jumped at the sound, keeping myself contained only by the grace of years of practice in front of Ash.

The girl leaned forward, excitement shining in her eyes.

"Your brother is in the Chrysalis Tower," she said, telling me something I already knew, "but soon they're going to leave it for a few days to hold some kind of ceremony with the remaining twins of Mariposa."

Remaining twins? I thought Ash killed one of the twins, and the other was working for him. How many sets of twins were in Mariposa that were somehow important enough for Ash to notice?

"When he does," she said, not pausing long enough for me to ask a question, or even react in a way that might let them know I had less of an idea of what was going on than I wanted them to be aware of, "his retinue and guards will accompany him, and that would be a very good chance for someone adept at getting up high to do some damage."

"Getting up high?" I asked, "I doubt there will be any convenient crows around for me to ride my way in on."

Echoing the very conversation I eavesdropped on the other day was enough for Rath's shoulders to bunch, and it was everything I could do not to smirk behind his back.

"No," the man said, pursing his lips and studying me further, like he were trying to decide if I was capable of doing whatever it was he was about to suggest as an alternative, "but you could climb into the canopy of the winged trees while they're away from the grove, and get in there."

Climb. That was definitely something I could do.

I smiled.

CHAPTER 34

SURVIVE

Tristan

Slamming open the door to the carriage before it came to a full stop, I jumped out without looking to the skies first.

"King Tristan," General Pace yelled, her mount rearing up as she ran it too fast, and then stopped too abruptly right next to me, "you should have checked that it was safe."

I stretched, tamping down the frustration that was my permanent companion on this trip, and tried to ignore her.

My guards were everywhere. They kept their eyes above us and around us, trained for any threat coming.

Yes, normally, I did a better job of being aware of my surroundings than I did in that particular moment, but being trapped in the carriage all day wasn't helping to alleviate the simmering rage eating me alive from the inside out. I somehow knew the only thing that would solve that particular problem was returning to my Queen. Not that it made any sense to me.

"General," I said, not bothering to continue explaining.

As angry as I was the entire trip, I didn't actually want to yell at her. She didn't deserve it, and I didn't want to be the kind of person who took out my personal feelings on others who had no control over or ability to help with them.

I didn't want to be that. But every second we were on this trip it was more and more difficult to avoid.

The group was doing whatever it was they needed to at this impromptu stop on the side of the road, surrounded by thick trees, even if the leaves were too thin to be of much cover from Corvids.

Eventually, someone would call me to come get my share of whatever they were going to serve for lunch. Until then, I decided to wander over to the bank of a little stream, trying to find peace in the sound of the water moving along.

Peace flowed away from me faster than the water did, leaving even more impatience in its wake.

Not even the damn stream was worried about making good time getting to wherever it headed.

"King Tristan," Shield Elio said, coming to my side, and handing me a basket of food before sitting on the damp grass and muddy bank with his own basket.

I looked around, trying to find somewhere else to be so I could eat by myself, but the entire area was flooded with our people.

So much for keeping this trip a low profile kind of affair.

Hopefully, the entire country wouldn't be buzzing with the news that the King left the Obsidian Palace. Again. Especially not right then when the major front of the fighting was waiting there just outside Bridgeton.

People understood when we were in Breakwater, that's where the fighting was at the time. They didn't know I was gone when Cinder and I were traveling to the valley, but this?

No one would understand. Not unless I managed to accomplish something from the trip. But, staring at the back of Elio's head, I doubted I would be able to accomplish much of anything at all.

"Come eat," Elio said, breaking into my thoughts, making me shake my head to regain focus.

There really was nowhere else for me to be at that moment, so I took a seat next to him in the muck, careful not to drop my basket full of food.

"Did you jump the line to get our food so fast?" I asked, bitterness growing within me at the thought of his actions making me guilty by association. Suddenly the food in front of me was less appetizing.

"No," he said, leaving it at that as I bristled next to him, waiting for some kind of explanation.

When none was forthcoming, I surrendered, and started to eat my simple basket of food from the supply and kitchen carriages.

"How much do you know about your parents' relationship?" Shield Elio asked from nowhere.

I looked around us to make sure he was speaking to me, and then just opened my mouth, trying to find the words to answer a question I never expected him to ask.

"My parents?" My question was as empty as my mind.

"Yes." He turned to look at me before taking another bite of his food, smiling as if nothing out of the ordinary was happening. "Are you aware they didn't know each other before they married?"

"Oh," I said, shaking my head not because I didn't know, but because I knew it all too well. "I am well aware that they did not have the kind of love for each other that Cinder and I have."

Everything, even his offhand comment, always came back to her.

And that's what I wanted to do. Go back to her.

"Do you know how I became a Shield?" he asked, taking a smacking bite out of an apple that made me jump.

"No, I never heard." Was I about to? There might have been only a handful of things he could have offered to tell me that would make me want to listen. That was one of them.

He was the only Shield in ages. And he was from Onyx. He could have come from any of the other countries on the continent…why didn't I know this story already?

But, with all that was happening with the High Sect, maybe it didn't matter what happened to label him so. Maybe it was better to just focus on this trip, to figure out what to say to get them to side with us.

"I was in Lehar at the last battle of the last war," he said, and I sucked in a breath, unable to breathe much at all after that.

Of all the things I thought he would say, that wasn't one of them.

"Did you see what happened?" I asked, through a throat closed tight, and lungs screaming for me to breathe again.

"What I can tell you," he said, "is that it happened fast, and your Duchess shouldn't be alive."

That snapped me out of whatever spell his initial revelation had worked on me, and I tried to surge to my feet, to do what—I had no idea. Probably go back to her, regardless of what the High Sect thought.

But I didn't even fully stand before Elio shot out a hand to stop me. Something that felt like a cord of steel as strong as a sword wrapped around me, holding me in place.

My eyes widened, and my mouth fell open as I realized that he somehow wielded magic.

One of my own Onyx citizens was using magic when I thought the only person in the entire country who had the ability to even attempt it was someone descended from the Dragon Kings.

"Are you…" I couldn't finish the question.

Was I looking at a relation somehow?

"No," he said, shaking his head as if he read my mind, and letting go of my arm. The cords of magic retracted, releasing me, "They asked me the same thing when the clergy who saw me do it brought me to the High Sect where they declared me Shield."

"You did...that to become Shield?" What was I even supposed to call that magic? And no wonder they asked. Many of them were from here, too, and understood that we didn't have magic here.

Usually, we didn't.

"When the explosion happened," he said, and my mind sprinted in circles trying to keep up with his change of topic as if trying to keep up with Cinder on a battlefield, "I was trapped with some others, hiding from the line of Amethyst guards surrounding the manor."

Something didn't make sense.

I tried to imagine how it was that, according to Cinder, the manor her family lived in was reduced to ruins, the guards surrounding it turned to nothing, and she was blown off the wall surrounding the house, along with others—most of whom didn't survive.

"But how did you live through the blast out there when people further from it were killed?" I asked, my voice hushed, thinking of how much everyone in Lehar went through, how much she did.

"And that," he turned to look into my eyes, his losing all the usual joviality they had, "is why I am a Shield. So..."

When he turned, I turned with him, staring at the little brook trickling by, wondering if this one was sacred to the clergy or not. If he even knew.

But following his lead, too stunned to do much more, wore off fast.

"You said she shouldn't have survived." I grabbed the sleeve of his cloak, wrapping it tight in my fist, drawing his eyes my way, his brows high. "You know what caused it."

He shook his head, his brow knitting together, and my hopes for something to tell her fell, maybe some additional clue that could help us understand the blast, and, therefore, how to recover the air.

"I *believe* I know what caused it. That isn't the same as knowing. And, no, I can't tell you my speculations yet. But, no, she shouldn't be alive."

My hand loosened, dropping his sleeve before I folded my fingers around my untouched food.

"Because she was on the walls, and others were also killed there?" I asked. Thinking of her death, of never getting to meet her, know her, love her, left something open, gaping, and raw at the edges in my chest. I pressed a hand to it to keep it from bleeding.

"King Tristan," calling me by name drew my focus back to him, and I swallowed as he seemed to be waiting for my permission to tell me this, as if he were checking to see that I could handle it.

Honestly, I wasn't sure I could. But I also needed to know. Now that it was laid out in front of me like a nightmare, not remembering the details only made everything worse.

I nodded, pressing harder against my chest.

"A ball of blazing hellfire water hit right where she was standing, killing the people next to her, and shattering the wall out from under her. I saw it happen."

CHAPTER 35

NOT YOU

Cinder

I didn't bother to check with Rath, or Jacquetta, or Gus. Not when I finally had a mission, a way to help. Besides, they would all try to talk me out of it.

No matter what they would say if they knew—and it was obvious what their reaction would be—I was doing this.

All I had to do was get there in time. All I had to do was use the opportunity of this thing Ash was planning against him.

Once I managed that...well...I could handle the rest.

He made sure of that. This time, I would find the cold place. I wouldn't hesitate. This time...I would be exactly who I was trained to be.

The hardest part of preparing to go was finding something to wear that wasn't too ostentatious. The last thing I needed on this little trip was to stand out.

Just like all the times before I went to Madam's, I needed to be as forgettable as the wind, as dark as a Corvid's wing, and remain as hidden as the sun at night.

Finally, I wore the kind of clothes I was most comfortable in, clothes to kill in. My black cloak hid me entirely, my weapons clung to me, and a small bag of easy traveling rations from the kitchens was tucked onto my belt.

I wasn't sure, however, if I could get there or not.

Not without finding someone in Mariposa to give me directions.

What were the chances I would be able to find someone who not only knew how to get there, but also how to get into an impenetrable tower? Someone who wouldn't rat me out the first chance they got?

Slim.

But I had to try.

Releasing a long breath, I took to my final task.

In a perfect world, I would be back before this letter would even be an issue.

Jacquetta and Gus wouldn't turn me in to anyone, and, even if they did, no one would be heading after me or risking anything to get me back.

No, this letter, while addressing all of them, focused on Tristan.

My world was far from perfect. I didn't trust that he wouldn't surprise everyone, and hurry back here for one reason or another, making short work of his meetings in the Marshlands. If that happened, then he might return before I did. And, as much as the mission undoubtedly posed risks that he wouldn't want me taking, I had to do it.

That also meant I needed to leave him with some answers about my intentions because my King would turn the world inside out looking for me. He would never give up hope I would come back if my whereabouts were nothing but a huge question in his mind. This way, if I met with Jocelyn instead of Ash for some unforeseen reason, and she killed me...

If that happened, Tristan needed to know.

Not just because I thought he would need the encouragement to focus all his rage and pain on my brother to avenge me. But because I wanted him to know that his love, his vow in my heart, and his faith that I was fit to wear the crown spurred me to do this.

Writing it all out, though, no matter how short and clear I wanted to make it, made tears threaten at the backs of my eyes.

Fighting them didn't work.

One broke free of my lashes, dropping onto the paper, smearing the ink.

But that was more than fitting. I pressed a kiss to the wet smudge, leaving behind a faint imprint of my lips.

A rogue shiver of fear raced through me, and I took a deep breath. Was this a sign that I wasn't coming back? I squeezed my eyes shut as I shoved the thought away, and set down the letter.

"No," Jacquetta said behind me, sending me whirling around to face her, my heart hammering away in my throat. The swift move replaced the shiver with a low ache through my back.

She stood in the doorway, her hands fisted at her sides, her face in sharp lines of fury, her entire body trembling while Gus stood behind her, looking back and forth between us.

For all the rage pouring off Jacquetta, Gus was the picture of confusion. I didn't have time to explain this. Nor did I want to. But the anger rose up within me in me without any conscious decision on my part as if it were called to answer Jacquetta's fury.

"What do you mean, 'No?'" I asked, my voice low and harsh, even as my body remained loose. They weren't a threat to me in any real way.

If they managed somehow to stop me from leaving right now, they both had to know it would be a short-lived victory.

After all, Tristan's office was right down the hall, his window still available for me to use should I need it.

But I didn't want to do that. I much preferred my initial plan to just walk down the stairs, across the courtyard to the stables, get on a horse, and ride it hard out of here without a word to anyone.

Maybe it wasn't the best plan in the world, but if anyone other than these two had tried to stop me, I could just pull rank. Being Fighter Cinder and the King's chosen Queen came with perks.

These two though…

"You know what I mean," Jacquetta yelled. "How dare you think you're just going to run out after him. He told you to stay here."

"What?" For a minute I almost laughed, but managed to hold it back. Laughing at her definitely wouldn't help. "Jacquetta, I'm going to the Chrysalis Tower to kill my brother. Rath's spies told me about a rare chance to slip past Ash and his people."

"Cinder," Gus groaned, dropping her head back like as if imploring the ceiling to give her some kind of help with me, to which I rolled my eyes, "only people who know how to get in there are ever going to."

"No one else is me." Why did everyone keep underestimating me? "Every time something like this comes up, someone tells me I can't do it. Well, how do you know?"

"People have tried." Jacquetta threw her arms in the air, and looked to her wife to help her come up with some other way to talk me out of it.

But I wasn't about to be deterred because someone else failed.

"Other people have tried to break into the Obsidian Palace, too," I reminded them, gesturing to the walls around us. They knew I had broken out, and then back in again—to say nothing of me almost getting inside before the search for a bride started.

"Damn it, Cinder," Jacquetta said, "it isn't the same. There is no way into the Tower without dying unless you go right through the front door."

"That's not possible." No place was that secure. I shook my head, frowning at the strange belief they all seemed to have in this place.

For the first time since we learned that Ash took refuge there, I began to wonder if I could actually do this, get in to kill my brother without needing to meet Jocelyn first.

"Unless you think you can get into the winged trees without anyone seeing you," Gus said, crossing her arms, and looking down at the floor so she didn't see Jacquetta round on her with her mouth hanging open. "There is no other way in."

"Gus," Jacquetta hissed making her wife duck her head even further.

"How do you know that, Gus?" I asked, voice low and careful so I didn't get her in any more trouble with Jacquetta.

She raised her eyes, slow and tentative in her movements, her red hair somehow diminished in the light of rage coming off Jacquetta.

But after biting her lip, Gus said, "I used to work in Mariposa."

I smiled, and Jacquetta buried her face in her hands.

"Does that mean what I think it does?" I asked, staring at Gus, willing her to say that it did.

"No," Jacquetta screamed, erasing my smile in a second with her shrill, out-of-control wail, "you are bad enough."

Jacquetta pointed at me, and I was powerless to respond. My friend was more irate than I had ever seen her. She shook with fear. Even when we saw each other after Gus was wounded, Jacquetta never acted like this.

"What do you mean, I'm bad enough?" I tried to make my voice even and calm. Instead, it sounded calculating, even to my own ears.

"You throwing yourself into battle all the damn time," Jacquetta yanked at her hair, her eyes growing wilder by the second as she lost focus on anything in front of her. It made me want to wrap her up in my arms, and tell her sweet lies until she stopped. It robbed the fight from me. "I have to accept that it's part of who you are, but not Gus. Not my Flower. This wasn't supposed to happen again. No one is supposed to go outside again. I can't lose…not again."

"Oh, Star," Gus said, wrapping her wife up and whispering sweet words like I had wanted to as I sat in the chair with a thud, my legs giving out.

Madam. She was worried we weren't going to come back to her just like Madam Valentin hadn't.

I don't know how long we stayed in those same positions, me as helpless as I had ever been in my life.

A friend, someone as close to me as family, needed me, and I didn't have the ability to do anything about it. There was nothing I could do to help her, to alleviate this pain, and make everything okay for her…

Well. There was one thing.

Her sobs—guttural tearing of her lungs and vocal cords—eventually subsided, and I licked my lips to prepare myself to speak. I was still worried my hoarse whisper would only make things worse no matter how much I knew what I was about to do, what I was about to risk, was the only thing I could offer Jacquetta.

"Gus," I said, and Gus' eyes, rimmed in red although no tears shown on her face, met mine, "you need to stay here."

CHAPTER 36

A REASON

Tristan

Just imagining Cinder being hit by that blazing ball of hellfire water, the heat of it, the force of it, was enough to make my blood turn as hot in my veins as the air around Cinder must have been that day. My arms shook as my fists tightened until my knuckles popped.

My Cinder. My Queen. She almost didn't make it. She was almost reduced to ashes like so many others that day, including her parents and mine.

Pressing my trembling fist to my mouth, I tried to hold back the anguished cries that wanted to tear out of me. I forced myself not to order everyone back to the palace just so I could hold her, and remind myself that she was alive, that she was real.

I opened my mouth…maybe to ask Elio how she survived…I wasn't sure. But the only thing that came out was a choking noise as my throat closed to contain the emotions hammering through me.

"To this day," he said with a nod, as if he heard what I wanted to say even if I wasn't sure what it was, "although I have replayed it in my mind more times than I can count, I don't know how she survived."

Bile, thick, noxious, and hot, rose in the back of my throat, and I pressed my shaking hands into my chest trying to force it back down.

"What you need to know is that your Duchess will be fine. The rest of us may burn just like Lehar did in the last war, but I believe she was spared for the same reason I was."

Snapping my head in his direction, my body stilled, the heat in me stalled for a moment, the violence of my body's reaction to knowing just how close I came to never having her in my life temporarily silenced by his words.

"What is that reason?" My voice was a hoarse rasp, a threat I couldn't hide riding within the innocuous words.

"I believe we both have our parts to play in this war." He turned to look straight at me, his eyes boring into mine, every bit of the large personality that was so subdued since he came back to us from Corvid captivity was focused in those eyes, pouring through me as if there was no hiding under that gaze. He looked into every dark place in my soul, and I was powerless to stop him.

"Do you—" I couldn't finish the question. The bile was back, wanting to splatter all over him. I pressed against my chest and stomach, my eyes squeezed shut, the force of the swallow and the attempt to hold back almost too much.

"No." His voice was gentle this time. "I don't know what that role will be, only that I am certain we were both meant to play a part in saving Onyx from this threat."

My eyes opened as air eked past my throat in small, insubstantial breaths.

Just as he searched through me a moment before, I attempted to do the same. I needed to know if he was lying, if he thought Cinder was somehow supposed to die this time around.

I didn't find that in his gaze, but I didn't find anything that reassured me either.

"King Tristan," he said, and something about his voice reverberated through the air with a strange feeling through it that made me think it was magic, "you have already had a success your parents did not when they were your age."

Shaking my head, I tried to understand and couldn't. Whatever he meant lay beyond me, but I held it in my mind, knowing I would pour over this conversation for as long as it took for me to come to understand what he was trying to tell me.

"You love your queen, and she loves you. Hold onto that, and let it keep you going until we win this war."

Was that the success my parents didn't have? How was that some kind of marker in my ability to save my country? What was he talking about?

Of course, I would hold onto Cinder, and she would hold onto me. It was all we could do. We fought for each other as much, if not more, than we fought for our country, our friends, and our family. We fought in order to have the life we both wanted with each other someday. We wanted more life. We wanted a chance to see each other grow old, to spend more time than we had so far loving each other.

All of that was obvious, so why was he pointing it out as if it were a revelation?

I shook my head, and my forehead hurt with how hard I furrowed my brow.

He patted me on the shoulder as he slowly got to his feet.

"You need to eat and rest. This is going to be a challenge at the Marshlands, I think."

That was all he said before he left me sitting on the side of the road, staring into my food, trying to suss out the true reason he told me what little he had.

After all of his words, I still didn't know exactly what he did to survive the attack on Lehar, or exactly how it was enough to make him a Shield. I didn't know how Cinder survived either.

So, what did that leave me with?

What did I have now that I didn't before Shield Elio decided to tell me things I already thought I knew in cryptic half sentences?

Not realizing what I was doing, I finished my meal, the feeling of being sick long gone from me as I poured over everything again.

General Pace made her way to my side, and sat down where Elio was moments before.

"Are you less likely to bite my head off now?" she asked, her voice clipped, although not careful, or even particularly kind in the accusation.

I took a deep breath, and thought about how she was right. Ever since we left the Palace, my entire body was alight with rage and fear. I itched with it, as if it ran along just under my skin, burrowing through my veins.

Rage because I wanted this war over, because I wanted to be with my wife, because she still wasn't healed fully, because there was nothing I could do about it, because I had to leave her before I knew for sure she could fight back as much as she would need to if something happened.

Fear because I wasn't sure if I would ever see her again.

But the way Elio spoke, it seemed as if he thought we would be reunited, that I would see my wife again, and…

Oh.

"I am sorry," I said, running a hand through my hair as my heart sank. "Leaving Cinder right now has been harder than I thought it would be. And I knew it was not going to be easy."

She pursed her lips the smallest amount, but her eyes softened.

"Understood. Now, do you think your concern for her will continue to block our ability to do what we need to? Or may we speak about the plan for the Marshlands?"

General Pace was a lot of things, but, after Madam Valentin's death, I knew she was also someone who had to go into battle with no assurances, and leave behind the person she loved.

If General Pace could still manage to do what she needed to, then how could I allow the fire of rage to cloud my judgement, blocking me from doing all that I knew I should do for the success of the mission?

"Does it ever get easier?" My voice was little more than a whisper, and she was still for so long that I thought she might not have heard me. But she finally answered.

"Part of me wants to lie to you." Her voice matched mine, low and hollow. "I want to tell you that eventually it becomes part of life in a way that will never leave you breathless and shaking."

At those words, the fire raged within me again, making me itch to slaughter anyone that prevented me from returning to Cinder.

Because General Pace had lived my nightmare, and I didn't think I was strong enough to survive it as she had.

"I do not lie to my king," she said, and I forced myself to remain seated, to run through Elio's belief again, to try and let it become something that I believed in too in a way that would give me hope.

"No matter how many times I left, I never got used to it. It never got easier. But every time I came back, every time she was there, waiting for me, healthy and whole, it did make me less likely to snap in half under the pressure of not knowing."

Letting out a long, shaking breath, I put my head in my

hands, and tried to imagine what it would feel like when I finally got home to Cinder.

After the battles we had already been through, I knew what it was to hold her while she clung to life. I knew what it was to drown myself in her to remind myself we were both still alive. And I knew what the joy of seeing her smile after all the pain and heartache was, too.

Raising my head, I got to my feet and nodded at the General. "Thank you."

Without so much as another word, she stood next to me, and walked away expecting me to follow to discuss strategy.

It wasn't easier. Nothing about this was easy. And I didn't expect it to be. But as long as we got to the end of it, and I could hold my Cinder again…that's all that mattered. I had to remember that.

CHAPTER 37

FOREVER IN DARKNESS

Cinder

"You won't make it in without me," Gus said, her voice hard.

"No fortress is that strong," I said, trying not to just shove them both in a bathroom, lock the door, and alert a guard as to their whereabouts on my way out of the palace.

"See?" Jacquetta wailed, waving a hand my way, and crying even harder into Gus.

"As much as I'm sure that's usually true for you, Cinder, not this time. This place has exactly one way in that anyone knows about, and it's heavily guarded."

I ran through the complications of that, of how I could manage to quietly make it past the heavy contingent of guards… there had to be a way. I just needed to find it. Maybe I could have Gus explain the layout of it all to me.

"Then how do you think that you being there with me will make a difference?" The one part of her plan that really didn't make any sense to me was this. And it was driving me mad trying to understand what I was up against.

"Because I know the one way in that isn't right in front of their faces." Gus gave me a shaky smile as she ran her hands over Jacquetta's back again and again, and grimaced at the pain her wife was in.

"Won't it be guarded, too?" I asked.

"Not usually with more than a couple guards, which you can take care of easily."

"That doesn't make sense. Why would anyone leave that avenue so open when the other way is so carefully watched?" Nothing about this place gave me a burning desire to visit. The only information I was getting was more specter than fact, more nonsensical than anything I thought I could forge a battle plan from.

"Let me draw it," Gus said. "That way both of you can understand what I mean, and maybe it will make you feel better about this, Star. Maybe you'll understand why I have to take her."

"But…" Jacquetta, her face covered in tears, peeked up at us from her crumpled place in Gus' chest.

"Come on, Star," Gus whispered, kissing her on the forehead. I tried not to sigh and bite my lip, not wanting to make it too obvious that I was impatient to go even if I didn't understand a thing about what I was walking into.

Somehow, Gus managed to corral Jacquetta, and I trailed behind them to the table where she found one of the ordering papers to write on.

The image that formed under Gus' swift strokes on the page left my stomach falling further and further into my toes.

"You've got to be joking," I said, my breath thin.

"Impenetrable," Jacquetta muttered, sounding just as daunted as I was.

Why in all the hellfire in Onyx was the Obsidian Palace not inside that instead of on an island in the middle of a river?

Before us was a rough sketch of a bare mountain, largely devoid of vegetation, that was hollow in the center where tall trees surrounded a tower built into one of them that had rooms far up in the canopy of branches.

"How the fuck do I get in there? Even climbing?" I was thinking out loud now, muttering half-formed thoughts, and trying to work through a plan to get myself over the bare, stone face of the mountain without being taken out by the guards. It would be so easy to post them there just to stop people like me.

"Do any trees on the outside of the mountain rise any real distance up its side?" I asked, leaning closer to the little drawing, trying to think of some way to connect the trees on the outside with the ones on the inside.

Gus just laughed. I swallowed.

She doodled trees on the outside of the mountain, at its base, spreading out flat out from it. They were dwarfed in size by the side of the mountain.

"Fuck."

No wonder this wasn't someplace I had been before. There was no point in sending someone to do an assassination in this place. It really was impenetrable.

I sagged where I stood.

Looking at Jacquetta and I, her head turning back and forth, Gus made a dark dot at the base of the mountain.

"What's that?" Jacquetta asked, her voice haunted as if she were looking at something as darkly magical and terrifying as the crows when we first saw them shift.

"That is the only way in that isn't guarded by way too many people," Gus said, pointing at the dot, and wrapping her arms tighter around Jacquetta's waist where she stood next to her.

"Okay, so tell me how to find that spot. I'll get in, and you can stay here. Problem solved." Really, this was the best-case scenario. A back door conveniently marked by the guards posted to watch over it? Easy.

"But why do they have that way in?" Jacquetta muttered, clinging to Gus as if her grip alone would be enough to stop anything bad from happening to her wife.

"Finding the spot isn't the problem," Gus said, and I couldn't help but wonder why she was answering me first, and not Jacquetta. "It's the way in for the servants. No one cares if one of them goes missing every once in a while."

"What?" My voice was a snap, the blood in my head pounding with rage as I clenched my fists. Jacquetta sucked in a breath beside me.

"Not everyone in the nobility thinks like you, Cinder," Gus said, and Jacquetta looked at me with only a touch less anger than when she first walked in.

"They're about to learn, then." Being Queen was going to be useful after all. There was no way Tristan knew about this. He would never allow it to go on, and I didn't intend to let it either.

"But…Flower," Jacquetta said, biting her lip and nodding to the paper in front of Gus again, "what does the way the twins of Mariposa treat their servants have to do with the way into the mountain?"

Good. At least one of us was staying on task, because I was about to find out the name of the nobles who treated the servants that way, and relieve them of their titles as a wedding gift to myself. As soon as Tristan came back from the Marshlands, and I returned with one less brother, I was going to make sure no one treated people that way in Onyx again.

"The tunnel through the mountain is Corvid black, and it's like a maze in there." Gus' voice was low and grave, and it sent a shiver through me wondering exactly how many people were lost forever inside the mountain in the dark.

"No one thought to put hellfire lights or even torches down there?" I asked, trying to understand what I was about to walk into. Even with Gus' information, I was going to use the tunnel. It was the best option.

"If it was easy to navigate, then it wouldn't be impenetrable." Gus shrugged as if anything she said warranted a reaction so small.

Looking back and forth between Jacquetta, whose panic still showed in both her eyes and in the grip she had on Gus, and Gus, whose eyes were wide and pleading toward her wife, I didn't know what to do.

Yes, it was clear what to do about the nobles and the way they treated people, regardless of how it would cement my place in their minds as a bad queen. And it was clear what to do about the tunnel once we took back Mariposa from Ash. But the problem still sat in the quickly-scratched drawing sitting in front of Gus.

Maybe I could have her draw me a map, and take a stone light with me to use in the tunnel. But what if the way she navigated it in the dark didn't translate to the light? It was possible she would tell me to turn right at the second offshoot, when there was an offshoot there she didn't know about because she couldn't see it. However she had measured distance in there, I doubted I could recreate it on my own without her guidance.

But I couldn't take her with me. Taking her and leaving Jacquetta behind to stew in her worry felt like slapping Jacquetta in the face, and spitting on Madam Valentin's memory.

Real or not, even the idea of disrespecting Madam by upsetting Jacquetta so much after we lost Madam felt like running myself through with my own dagger.

"Do the best you can, Gus," I said, forcing my voice to hold only conviction and belief that it would be fine, even as my mind screamed and thrashed that this was a bad idea. "Draw me a map of the tunnel, and write directions."

"You can't still be planning on going through with this," Jacquetta turned that fierce look on me again, and I could only nod. Before the explosion brewing inside her could rip into me, I scrambled to explain myself.

"Killing Ash could save too many lives for me not to take this chance." It was the only thing I could say, and it helped that it was true. I may not have the same level of confidence I did before that I would be able to make it into the tower, but if I did, I knew it would be worth it.

Gus stood up and turned around, gripping tight to Jacquetta's hand, and looking into her eyes as she said, "Then I have to go with you, Cinder."

"No," Jacquetta and I said at the same time, my voice tinged with sadness, and Jacquetta's with horrified shock that made me cringe.

Whipping around and standing to gather Jacquetta to her until their foreheads were pressed together, Gus bracketed her wife's face with her hands while Jacquetta pushed back against her.

"Star," Gus said, her voice pleading, making me want to run, but rooting me to my spot as I stared at the floor, lost, "please. I don't want to leave you right now. I know how hard this is. But Cinder's right. If Ash is gone, half the war is over, and we are all safer. *You* are safer."

"I don't care about me," Jacquetta said, her voice a shaking whisper, her hands no longer trying to shove Gus away. Instead, she clung to Gus' dress at the waist in a grip that threatened to rip the fabric.

Gus groaned, the sound echoing the wrench of my heart at witnessing my friend in so much pain.

Pain that I caused. Pain I wasn't going to stop making for her.

"Jacquetta," Gus said, "I promise. I will come home to you. We have too much life left to live together for this to be the end. I haven't had enough time with you."

Tears threatened the backs of my eyes, and I swallowed

down the guilt-riddled sob that built in my chest as I lifted my eyes from the floor. I sent an apology to Tristan in my mind for what I was about to do.

"No," I said, Gus and Jacquetta snapped their focus to me, as if they had forgotten I was in the room.

Jacquetta looked like she was hoping for me to offer her relief, and Gus looked betrayed. Based on the looks on their faces, neither of them were about to get what they thought they were.

"*I* promise. Gus will come home to you, and you will live long lives together. I brought her home before. I will do it again."

Regardless of what I wanted out of my life with Tristan, that I wanted to be here when he got back to the palace, and call him mine forever, if it came down to it, it would be Gus over me. That was what I was promising, and they both knew it.

All the red in Gus' cheeks drained from her face leaving her pale and gasping.

Jacquetta's shaking escalated, her sobs choking her as if they turned her inside out until she wrapped one hand around Gus' waist, pulled Gus tightly into her, and reached a hand out for me.

I slammed all the doors in my mind that connected my emotions to my face and body like I had so many other times in Ash's presence over the years, not willing to add to her heartache, as I slipped my hand into hers, both of us holding on tight.

"Both of you come home," she didn't sound like herself anymore. She sounded like Madam Valentin. It was almost enough to break through my resolve, but I sucked in a breath to hang on. She was putting herself through so much for my plan, the least I could do was show her someone she could trust in. The assassin. The Fighter.

"If there is any chance that making a move would mean you

can't both make it home, just turn around. We will find another way."

Jacquetta let go of me, and kissed her wife while I pressed against all the shut doors in my mind, begging the Gods and Goddesses I never prayed to that this would work out, that I could bring Gus home.

To my parents—the ones I always prayed to but couldn't when it came to my brother—I prayed that, no matter what happened, Jacquetta and Tristan would forgive me.

CHAPTER 38

ONE MORE REASON

Tristan

Two days. Two days since I left Cinder. Two days of traveling. Two days headed toward a potential disaster of monumental proportions. Two days headed away from the absolute greatest moment of my life to that point.

How fast it all changed.

In an attempt to not be a giant asshole to everyone around me, I spent far too much of my time in the carriage replaying that last night with her in my mind.

Only once had thinking about her lead to me with my pants open, cock in hand, imagining the grip was hers, and my fingers were on her pussy, her cries in my ears as her legs shook around my arm.

But, of course, the damn carriage stopped, leaving me fumbling with my laces before someone could fling the carriage door open just to tell me something "urgent."

None of the things they came to me with had been pressing, let alone urgent. None of them.

And with every minute that my cock sat in my pants, pressed too tightly for the twitching hardness it had become, without any release and zero hope that I would see her for days still, it became even more difficult for me to reign in the raging inferno in my veins that made me so awful to everyone.

More often than not, when we stopped, I wound up saying something nasty only to apologize right after.

It wasn't fair to any of them. And it wasn't like me at all.

Normally, I was better able to compartmentalize enough not to inflict my issues upon the people who were doing everything to help me hold the damn country together.

So far, General Pace and Shield Elio had managed to keep most of the rest of those traveling with us from dealing with me directly.

They were doing it to protect the others from my shit disposition, but that just made me feel even worse.

I was the King. I was supposed to be better than this. I was supposed to treat my people well…

Maybe the traitors had a point.

Everyone knew the Dragon Kings were done.

Body heat notwithstanding, I didn't have any special ability.

Neither did Cinder's brother.

The only thing special about me that wasn't an accident of birth was back at the palace waiting for me, wearing my ring, with my heart in her hold.

Finally, after far too long in the carriage by myself with my thoughts, both divine and full of love and morose and filled with self-doubt, the wheels rattled to a stop beneath me.

A second later the door of the carriage whipped open just like it had so many times before, and I let out a sigh that was half groan as I shoved myself out into the world.

Here, not far outside of the edges of the Marshlands, with

the sun setting, I could smell the profuse moisture in the stale wind already.

The air was thick, as if it laid across my shoulders as I shrugged them within my immediately-sticky shirt. It was almost as oppressive as the weight of the kingdom on my shoulders.

Somehow, the wet air made me realize another reason why I needed Cinder so much.

"You have that look on your face again," Elio said from beside me as we both looked out over the vast plain in front of us full of one of the crops that actually enjoyed the more saturated soil.

"What look would that be?" I tried to make my voice not sound so biting, but only managed to make myself sound flat and dismissive.

"King Tristan," he said, drawing my gaze his way, surprising me as I watched a grin play with the corner of his mouth, "one day, you are going to have to learn to hide when your mind is full of her. And that day will come much faster than you think."

He managed to pull a gust of a humorless laugh from me as I turned to look at the inn that we would be taking over. It had no business here other than for the people who made trips to the Marshlands.

"Cinder makes it all lighter, easier," I said, the words as thick in my mouth as the swamp-filled air.

"Love is supposed to do that, make you feel like you can do anything." He clapped me on the shoulder with one of his giant, paw-like hands, and I stiffened so I didn't stumble under the friendly blow.

"One more reason for me to be with her right now," I muttered under my breath as I took a step toward the Inn, and the undoubtedly endless review of the preparations for our meeting with the High Sect tomorrow.

"Maybe wanting to return to her will spur you on to have a

successful encounter with the High Sect, and turn them away from their fake, purple-haired Shield, and his suggested path."

Elio made the comment in an off-handed fashion, as if it wouldn't matter all that much to me. But it halted my forward momentum, stopping me from even thinking about walking into the inn, and grinding my teeth through another meeting.

Instead, I turned back to the field and the setting sun, realizing that the days had grown longer again without me realizing it. I couldn't look beyond Cinder's injuries and the war on our doorstep. Knowing Cinder, loving her, was making time itself flash past me, should I have been surprised that her influence managed to make me oblivious to the way she made me better, too?

But, would it be better for me to hide all of my thoughts of her when we met with the High Sect?

Trying to push her from my mind was hard enough. When she was so far from me that I wasn't sure of her physical state, the effort made my stomach churn, and my fists clench at my sides. Nothing about the idea was natural, and everything about even attempting it for a moment left me gasping, hoping for someone to punch.

"King Tristan," General Pace said, coming to stand next to me, her voice low and her eyes scanning the skies, her focus never wavering, "we should get inside."

"I never saw it, you know," I said, my voice hard as I fought back the ugly urge to lash out at people who were not at fault for the furious reaction in me, and the ever-roiling emotions that I needed to get a better grasp of.

"Never saw what?" she said, dropping her eyes to meet mine for a moment before returning to the skies.

"For years, I was with you almost every day, and I never saw you lose control when you were apart."

She sucked in a breath, dropped her gaze to the ground, and a shudder ran over her shoulders.

Everything about her reaction made guilt rise inside me to swim with the seemingly unending anger and fear. It all left me scrambling for something to say, some way to make this better for her, to cover my own stupidity.

"I'm sorry, I didn't mean—" Reaching out a hand to maybe pat her shoulder...or something...she turned to look at me, and stopped me from muttering more half-formed thoughts. I couldn't even complete my awkward gesture.

"For so long—because of circumstances beyond our control, and choices we continued to make—I could not openly express anything, ever. Practice made it easier. It will with you, too." She shook her head, and, as if clearing the matter from the air around us, offered me a tight smile. "We should get inside."

"Can I..." After she managed not to be derailed by her grief, was it fair of me to ask?

"Go ahead. Ask me." Her face returned to its normal, neutral stance, her shoulders back, her head high. Every bit the General she was, she looked like she was staring down a field before a battle, instead of just her friend wanting to understand.

It made my step falter, causing me to question whether I should truly continue with this conversation. But, maybe, it would help me understand. And if I understood, would that help us win this war?

Maybe that made it worth it. Or, maybe, I was just being selfish.

"What decisions and circumstances kept you at such distance from each other?" I finally managed to release the fundamental mystery of her relationship to Madam into the air. I thought I knew. I could make educated guesses. But I wasn't certain. Yes, I knew the General better than most other people in the world. She had been a fixture in my life as long as I could remember. But, I knew little of Madam Valentin aside from my interactions with her in the most formal settings, and what I knew of her in relation to Cinder.

"None of them matter now. We both had duties and paths that we did not want to deviate from, and we both chose to put them ahead of our relationship."

"But..." it didn't make sense, "...you did still have a relationship?"

She smiled, her eyes looking at something past me, and I could only imagine she was reliving some moment or other in her mind. I would have done the same if asked of my relationship with Cinder.

"Yes. We had a devoted relationship that we always returned to when it was convenient for both of us." The General shook her shoulders again, and headed toward the inn. She was apparently done with my questions, and done waiting for me to move.

I tried to imagine having to live like that, with Cinder continuing to be the assassin, traveling all over to kill someone while I focused on the kingdom and waited at home.

Maybe it would have had more appeal to have an emissary as formidable as her doing Onyx's bidding based on information Rath provided—if I wasn't trembling with worry and need of her after merely days apart.

One day, perhaps, it would be something we would be able to try, Cinder and I. For now, I just wanted her to be healthy again, and to return to her as soon as possible.

CHAPTER 39

DIFFERENT TIME

Cinder

"I can't believe it was that easy to leave the palace," Gus said as we made our way through a copse of trees on the outskirts of a town at the edge of the Kaleidoscope Fields.

"When you're known by all the guards, why would it be difficult? They probably just think we're headed out to the training grounds." My eyes scanned our surroundings, my voice low, and my ears set to pick up on anything in the woods around us, even as I pretended nonchalance. "But we should pick a different topic."

Gus startled from her place on her saddle, and looked around before urging her mount to move a little faster.

She knew how to get us where we were going as far as directions went, but I was the one more adept at getting somewhere without rousing alarm or suspicion. And talking openly about the palace or the guards was a quick way to be noticed by anyone who happened to overhear us.

"Maybe we should have left at a different time," Gus said, her voice lower, matching my volume.

"This is fine." Leaving just after noon, on a trip that was supposed to take a day, worked better than she thought. Going by myself, the timing would be different. But with Gus along, and traveling a vastly different path than the one I intended, this would afford us enough time to avoid arriving first thing in the morning. We were therefore less likely to encounter anyone on high alert, and hopefully fewer other servants using the passage.

"Are we going to be traveling during the night?"

Looking at the thin forest and the sky beyond, I tried to answer her, but came up empty.

"Whether we do or not is dependent on too many factors for me to answer you right now."

Gus nodded, but she chewed on her bottom lip as she glanced at me, making me wish I could explain more to her. But I didn't trust our surroundings. If I tried to explain, the chances were too high that someone overhearing us could make something from my words.

This was exactly why I traveled alone on all my assignments for my brother.

Somehow, I needed to be able to communicate enough with her to reassure her, and not so much that I would give us away. Not to mention the fact that I couldn't allow myself to completely fall into assassin mode, and forget how to talk to her at all.

Already hours in, it was a more difficult challenge than any I had faced on my other kills.

Passing through trees, fields, and the edges of small towns, the sun finally began to sink below the horizon, and we found ourselves in a thicker area of trees.

"Is this a full forest?" I asked, bringing my mount closer to Gus' side.

"Full? You mean large?" she asked, her brows raised.

"Yes. Is this large? And how long until we get there?"

By "there," I meant the path under the mountain, and I hoped she knew it. I didn't want to risk saying more.

"Maybe four or five hours yet?" She scanned around us, blinking into the deepening shadows of the trees, her eyes finally looking beyond the thick canopy toward the waning light. "And this forest goes all the way."

Good. Her careful wording gave me what I needed, but I didn't think any spies that might be about would be able to glean much from it, unless they were aware of how long the journey was to the mountain.

"We should stop for the night, bring the horses away from the road, and then camp a little further in."

She craned her head around again with an odd look on her face as I turned my horse towards the trees, allowing the mare to pick her way through the vegetation.

"Road?" Gus finally asked from behind me.

"Track, path, same thing." There was a smile in my voice as I rolled my eyes, but she couldn't see from her position.

Inside this forest, the path she led us down was little more than a deer trail between the trunks, but it was well-trodden enough that we shouldn't camp out right next to it all night long.

Finally, some distance from the path, I swung my leg over the mare's head, and dropped down to the ground, flinging the reins over a branch before helping Gus dismount.

"Why do you get off your horse that way?" Gus asked over her shoulder as I helped her down, bracing myself not to hurt my back, already sore from hours in the saddle.

A grin formed on my face unbidden as I imagined Gus

taking up my style of dismount, and how Jacquetta would be scandalized by it.

"That way my back is exposed for less time to someone who might think of sneaking up on me."

Horror. The look on her face was horror.

Maybe I should have been more careful in the way I explained it. I thought she might find it funny. Apparently not.

"Right." I said, letting my smile drop and moving back to my own horse. "Well, hobble your horse, and we'll take the bags a little further away."

Doing the same to my mount that I instructed her to do to hers, I grabbed the saddlebag, and moved off into the trees in the deepening gloom of the oncoming night.

Whether it was normal or horrifying for every move I made to be dictated by the years I spent training and kills I made, I didn't know. There were scars from my past I was unable to hide as much as the dead were scarred by my blades. But every time something like this came up, it reminded me that, queen or not, some things about me would be hard sells for the people. And that was a very real pressure I needed to think about now.

A fire was out of the question. But between our cloaks and the warmth returning to the area, we didn't need it. I handed Gus a small stone light I kept tucked deep in my saddle bag, and showed her how to shadow it with her hand so it only shone in the little area she might need it to.

No matter what anyone thought of their assassin queen and her habits, right now, the only thing that deserved my attention was getting us both through this. To accomplish that, no one could spot us.

To my relief, after Gus pulled her food and water skin from her bag, she shoved the stone light deep inside it.

"I'm surprised you didn't want to travel through the night," she whispered, her voice startling in the pattern of soft sounds in the forest.

"With my injury, I don't have the stamina." It was hard for me to admit, which was stupid, but true.

For so long, I prided myself on the level of training I did, and the shape I was in. That first time at the palace, without the regiment I was used to, it made me so weak that I passed out after the first battle against the crows. After training the guards so much, by the time I needed to rescue Gus, I was in top form again.

At this moment, even if I assumed the best of my physical abilities, I didn't trust I would be able to get either of us out alive before falling apart if we didn't rest.

Gus, to my unending gratitude, didn't comment again, and soon the sound of eating was replaced with the shuffling of her pack, and, presumably, laying down for the night.

Part of me wanted to remain awake. But soon after I finished eating, her breathing evened out, and my eyelids became too heavy to lift.

Waking in the forest to a hand over my mouth meant one silent move before my eyes opened again.

Gus sat over me, her face trembling, her jaw clenched, looking completely unaware that my spike was at her side, ready to end her in the early morning light barely seeping through the trees overhead.

Her wide eyes met mine as she lifted her hand from my mouth, and placed a finger over her lips in an unneeded reminder to be quiet. She tilted her head back toward the way we came. Back toward the horses.

Nodding, I moved silently to a crouch, keeping my spike ready, and peered through the trees.

One of the horses whinnied. A second later, the mare appeared, stomping backward, throwing her head while someone in ill-fitting pants and a dark cloak hung onto her reins, grunting with the effort to pull her in.

With a hand held out to Gus in a signal to stay here, and a

grin blooming on my face, I darted through the trees on my toes, careful not to step on sticks or through the underbrush, giving myself away.

Although every step I took closer to where we left our horses the night before proved I didn't need to be so cautious as the three people trying and failing to control our horses trampled the ground around them, causing a racket.

"Be quiet," one of them said, their voice a rough growl as they danced away from what would have been a powerful blow of a hoof to their chest.

"You do it, then," one of the others shot back, almost losing their grip on the reins. "It would be easier just to find the riders, and take their purses."

"These horses are worth more than what their riders have in their purses," the first one scoffed, and my grin turned into a smirk.

Just regular thieves. Not guards, not one of Ash's zealots. We were warned that this kind of thing was becoming a problem because of the war.

Well, it was time to test the limits of my recovery.

CHAPTER 40

FACE OF A KING

Tristan

The carriage slowed, the wheels long since gone silent as we traveled, making me wonder about the state of the road here.

How far out from the edge of the Marshlands did the ground remain soggy and soft all year?

For the seconds between coming to a stop and the door swinging open, I allowed myself to think of Cinder, to worry, knowing I would have to set it aside, and remain focused on what my goal was during this time away from her.

As soon as the door swung open, the smell of the thick, wet air filled the carriage, forcing my focus to narrow in on my task there as tightly as possible.

Once, many years ago, my parents had an argument that I overheard. I remember tucking myself behind a potted plant in the great room in the royal wing, pulling at a hole I had managed to tear into the knee of my hose as the fashion in those days for small boys was to wear our hems above our knees.

But more than anything else about that moment, I remember the accusation my mother flung at my father: she said it was too easy for him to focus completely on his duties as King, and forget about duties he had at home, to us.

At the time, I didn't know what it meant, only that the way she said it made it clear her accusation was certainly not a compliment.

Looking back, I realized what she meant. Even if I wasn't sure it was as true as she thought it to be, I knew at least enough to understand what she tried to say.

So many years later, though, I wondered if anything could have prepared me for the new and comprehensive way that her words were a part of me.

Because no matter how hard I tried to hide it, I knew that nothing about focusing on the needs of the Kingdom as completely as it required me to would ever be easy again—if I managed at all.

Cinder was too much a part of me.

As I stepped out of the carriage, and looked around the perpetually strange, shifting environment of the Marshlands, I realized that I had to make everyone around me believe that my mind was entirely present here, and not back in the palace with her. No matter how hard it was.

The ground beneath my feet was a thick, muddy paste, but someone had covered it with planks of wood.

All around me, our party placed the planks along the mud, leaving their transports behind.

Further in the Marshlands there were few to no trees. Some remained there at the edges. Those that did grew heavy with moss that managed to weigh the branches down until they dragged their tendrils through the mud. Still, they remained light enough to sway in the mild breeze which was the only respite from the pressure of the moisture in the air.

"We will leave a small contingent of guards here with the transports," General Pace said, appearing so quickly at my side that I jumped, swallowing an undignified squawk.

Doing so made sense, but part of me wondered if it wasn't dual purpose. By leaving the transports there at the ready with a small contingent of guards, we would be able to beat a hasty retreat if necessary.

Nothing about this plan inspired confidence in the General either, it would seem.

I nodded. Neither my misgivings nor hers could stop us from trying to make this work.

Something besides Cinder had to go our way in this war.

Waiting around, I allowed my body a chance to get used to breathing in the hot air around me, and wondered what she was doing.

Hopefully, she was slowly working her back to full health. I tightened my jaw thinking about how hard she might have been pushing herself. Thank all the Gods and Goddesses that she had Jacquetta and Augustina there to help keep her from doing anything too reckless.

"That's better," Shield Elio said, coming to stand beside me, "but I can still see it."

A small laugh and a sigh were all I could offer him in response to his observation. Especially since the itch under my skin remained. I was just trying to be better about controlling my reaction to it.

"It's normal to worry," he turned away from the group swiftly gathering to grin at me, "but someone like her will never be the kind of queen who doesn't give you cause to. Even if we weren't at war, her version of caring about the country and the people will always involve her blades."

He slapped that heavy hand on my shoulder, then walked away. At least I didn't flinch under the weight that time.

No matter how hard it was for me to do as he suggested, I had to admit, he was right.

My own worry, my own need to be with her, wouldn't—and shouldn't—stop her from being who she was. Who I fell in love with. And most of all, what I thought the kingdom needed from her.

"King Tristan," General Pace called to me, and I moved into place alongside her. "We are ready."

Taking a deep breath, I started walking with everyone else. My eyes were trained forward while some of them still had to look upward, watching for attacks.

At the front of our column, a rotating line of guards placed more planks of wood to give us a better walking platform through the muck and mud.

"How much wood did we bring?" I asked under my breath, not expecting anyone to answer.

It had to be one of the details the group worked out when I wasn't paying enough attention. No matter how hard I tried to recall them talking about it, or even mentioning the need for it, I couldn't.

Cinder would be angry with me if she knew how distracted I had been, and, even more so, if she knew that pining after her was the reason for that distraction. It would be one more thing that would make her doubt her place, her role, as Queen by my side.

"We have enough," Elio said next to me, ripping me from my thoughts to answer my rhetorical question while leaving me with more.

Enough for what? How did he know if we had enough wood to get to the place the High Sect would intercept us?

As far as I knew, the plan was not to meet them at a specific place within the Marshlands. It was just to arrive, and expect them to find us. For some reason I couldn't imagine, everyone just accepted as fact that they would find us in the vastness of the Marshlands, and that it wouldn't take long for them to do so.

At every one of our planning sessions, I emphasized that we should send word once we got to the outskirts so that they would know we were coming. Either that or set up a specific location for us to meet them.

No matter how many times I voiced my opinion, they just kept assuring me that it was unnecessary.

Part of me wanted to point out to them that if we ran out of boards and had to drag ourselves through the mud, it would be because they underestimated how long it would take the High Sect to find us and confront us.

But I wasn't allowed to be that petty. Not as a king.

All I could do was try desperately to keep my face from betraying every one of my concerns, and maintain some control of the constant, raging inferno in my blood, as well as the itch under my skin that echoed Cinder's name.

At the rate we moved, slow and plodding, along the boards in two lines of people carefully contemplating their next steps even as they scanned the sky and the soggy terrain around us, it might take us days to get far enough into the marshes for the High Sect to find us.

It didn't take long for the trees to disappear entirely, leaving our lines weaving through narrow strips of mud between vast stretches of what looked like shallow lakes. But it was impossible to tell.

The swamps went on far off into the distance, swallowed by a fog that seemed to float everywhere as if the weighted, murky air was simply too much not to form into low mists. The way the low, gray wisps were mirrored in the overly-still water of the swamp created an echo of the sky that left me concerned that we would be lost in this place, and never know which way was up, let alone how to get out again.

Clenching my hands into fists until my blunted nails drove into my skin, sending shards of pain lancing through my palms was the only thing that stopped that thought from making me rage aloud.

How many wild chases down rabbit holes into the darkness would we engage in during this damned war? It seemed all we did, aside from losing guards and friends and family, was fail to make forward progress.

Elio touched my arm, and I shook off the melancholy which some twisted part of my mind was trying to veil all my anger, worry, and frustration in. It wasn't like me, but a lot of things that weren't like me had been happening.

Maybe what was and wasn't like me was changing just like this world…I wasn't sure I liked where I was headed.

"You have to do better than that," Elio muttered.

"Sorry," I said back, even if it sounded as wooden as the planks beneath my feet, it was something.

He made a derisive snorting noise, and I took a deep breath, trying to prepare myself to be what they all needed me to be again—someone who was together, who was as even-minded and prepared for anything and everything that this war might attack us with.

I told Cinder she was ready for her role. So, I needed to at least pretend convincingly that I was ready for mine.

As I opened my mouth to say something to make Elio think better of me, his hand shot out, grasping the edge of my cloak in a tight fist.

"King Tristan, you're out of time," he said, his voice low and grave. "They're here."

GOOD MORNING

Cinder

Skirting my way around a tree trunk, I made a quick study of the three thieves battling with our horses, and couldn't help the smile on my face.

The one closest to me, facing the horse, was an easy task—one swift step, a raise of my spike, and a clean thrust between his ribs.

For the few seconds it took for me to complete the move, I kept eye contact with the horse, its nostrils flared as it snorted and grunted in distress, its hooves stamping the ground.

But as soon as I finished the kill, his hands going slack on the reins, the horse simply shook its head free, and stayed in the same place.

The agitation didn't leave it, but it allowed me to step over the thief's body, and place a soft hand to its muzzle.

"Shhh," I whispered, "I'll finish this in a second."

"What in the hellfire? Calvin!" One of the other thieves

seemed to be smart enough to notice their fallen friend, and finally met my eyes.

"You shouldn't take what isn't yours," I said, stepping away from the horse as it danced backward.

"Like you, little girly?" The other thief gave me a smarmy once-over, a grin forming on his face, making it clear that he thought he was getting somewhere with it.

To be fair, he wasn't bad looking, and he probably did fine with women. But those women didn't see him like this.

Like prey that thought itself a predator.

In a swift move, I reached forward as I jumped, yanking the reins away from them, and wrapping them around my forearm.

Not wanting to get myself hurt, I let the horse buck, allowing a jump of my own, and the momentum of the yank on my forearm to fling me into the air so I could kick his slimy grin right off his face.

He fell back with a dazed thud and a groan, his companion's mouth dropping open.

"Gus, the horse," I called as I whipped the reins off my arm, and dropped to the ground, surging up at his friend, shoving my spike between his ribs, and whirling around to stab the one on the ground in the throat before his friend had even toppled over.

"Cinder," Gus said, her voice strained as she tried to hold both horses, patting them and staying out of the way of their stamping hooves, "did you have to kill them all?"

"Why?" I turned to her, wiping my spike on my leg before I slipped it into the sheath. "Do you think I should just let them roam around hurting people on the roads?"

Taking one of the horses from her, patting its nose and giving it a quick kiss, I looked up at her.

Her mouth hung open, her eyes darting back and forth between me and the horse before she looked over her shoulder at the dead around us. Her face twisted up in disgust while her eyes dropped in what looked like sadness.

"Gus?" My voice was small. Even though I couldn't understand what her thought process was, for some reason it seemed like I should feel bad.

"You don't make sense sometimes," she said, almost low enough that she seemed to be talking to herself.

"And how don't I make sense?" I needed to understand this.

"Just yesterday you were upset about the way people treat servants. Now here you are, caring for the horses," she waved a hand at me and the horse I was petting, "but you just killed those people without once wondering if stealing was worth being killed over."

"Reports of a lot worse crimes than stealing are coming in from people all over the country, especially on the roads." What did she expect me to do, sit down with them and have a nice chat?

I prepared the horse to ride, and swung myself up into the saddle, paying little attention to the continuous stream of disconcerted looks she shot my way. It was clear to me I wasn't going to understand her point.

Finally, she mounted next to me, and we began to make our way through the forest again.

"Cinder," she whispered, her eyes on the trees in front of us as I raised a brow her way in lieu of a question, "if you were to attack someone in my defense, and someone came along who didn't know what was happening, what would you think of them killing you for killing my attacker?"

"They're welcome to try."

She huffed out a sigh, and shook her head.

"Let's pretend they could, and you were dying...slowly... what would you think?"

Playing out the scenario in my head brought one thought to mind.

"As long as you were safe, I would only be upset about leaving everyone I love, and angry at myself for losing."

"Of course you would." She let out another long sigh, and I tried to find where I went wrong. Clearly, I wasn't giving her the answer she was looking for.

We lapsed into silence as I continued to puzzle out what she meant. But it didn't matter how I turned it around in my head, I couldn't understand her.

If someone were a threat to someone I loved, they were dead. If someone were a threat to my country or my lands, they were dead. If someone were in my way of protecting either someone I loved or Onyx or Lehar, they were dead. Those things seemed obvious to me. And I didn't worry about them after they were no longer a threat.

"Have you ever been to a trial?" she asked after a time. I furrowed my brow thinking about it.

"No. We didn't have them after the last war in Lehar. Or..." I tried to remember the ways things changed, and all I could remember was Ash and his guards—including Brix acting as their leader—being in charge of everything to do with law and punishment. "At least, I don't think we had them. My brother and his monster of a best friend took care of that kind of thing."

Gus swallowed hard, and I grimaced thinking about what memory must have been set off by mentioning him.

"Sorry." My voice was low, but she shook her head, waving a hand toward me as if wiping my words away from the air around us.

"Just so you understand," she said, and I tried to figure out what we were talking about now, "in the rest of the country, there are trials and jails that deal with people when they break laws. Normally, when someone steals something, they're punished with jail time through the courts instead of ending up dead."

"But we don't have time to bring those thieves to the nearest

Guard station, and this mission is important." I understood what she was saying, but even if I thought about taking them to a Guard station before I stabbed them, I still would have killed them. We didn't have time for anything else, and this chance could save Onyx.

Gus blew air out through puckered lips and puffed cheeks, her eyes wide. I frowned.

How did we not agree on this? It was so obvious to me.

"At the end of this war," her voice was low, slow, and deliberate in a way that made me feel like I was being scolded by my mother or Madam Valentin even if I didn't understand why, "you are going to be Queen, which means that you are going to be the embodiment of those laws, and those trials will be held, in part, in your name."

I knew that. It made me grind my teeth together that she thought somehow that fact should change my actions. I still didn't see it.

Before I could open my mouth and argue with her, she raised a hand and pulled the reins on her horse, bringing it to a stop.

Lifting herself in the saddle, she scanned the trees around us, holding a finger to her lips while I scanned the trees myself looking for a threat, my free hand on my spike.

Gus gestured with her head, and turned her horse to one side. Without a word between us, I followed after her.

She led us past some more trees until we were in a little circle of them, mostly blocked from the outside with a grassy, sun-dappled center to the small copse.

Once she began to dismount, I did the same, swinging my leg over the horse's head, and beginning to hobble the horse.

But Gus put her hand on mine, stopping me.

"I don't know if we should tie them up." She chewed on her lip, and looked around us as if an answer would materialize from the air.

"Then we leave them to find their own way home." I stood up, and took the bridle and saddle off the horse instead, setting them aside, slinging the saddle bags over my shoulder. If we were going to leave them here to make their own way home, then I wanted them to have the best chance to avoid being grabbed by someone else.

A pat on the horse's nose, a few moments to help Gus do the same for hers, and I followed her out from between the trees.

"Not far now," she whispered, her breath warm as she leaned over to speak directly into my ear.

With a nod, I slowed my steps so I could follow behind her even though I wanted to be at the front in case of trouble.

It took longer than I expected to get to the point where Gus held her hand up, signaling to stop.

Even then, she led carefully around another couple of trees as I made myself her shadow, so I didn't accidentally expose myself to the guards she said were always posted around the servant's entrance.

Once she turned around and leaned her back against the tree trunk with a jerk of her head behind her, I knew we were in a place where I could take the lead.

No matter what Gus thought about the way I dealt with the thieves, I was about to deal with these guards exactly the same way.

Grabbing Gus by the shoulders, I maneuvered us so we switched places. Then I leaned around the tree, letting my head brush along the rough bark, the smell of sap thick this close to it.

Even in the second it took to assess the situation at the entrance to the way through the mountain, I knew my initial plan had to be adjusted.

There were a lot more than a few guards posted here...did I pack enough blades for this?

CHAPTER 42
TRICK

Tristan

For a second, I was confused. I looked around the people in front of me on the boards. Everyone seemed to be going on about the plan to head forward. No one that checked the skies stopped or set up an alarm. None of the people in front of me stopped their forward momentum. No one looking to one side or the other called out a warning.

Turning back to Elio, my frown deepened to find him with his eyes closed and hands raised, palms out in front of him.

How did he think anyone had found us when he wasn't even looking?

An image of Cinder, blindfolded and crouched on the training ground floor, perfectly still, rose in my mind.

"Fuck," I muttered, crouching down, placing one hand on the board at my feet as I unslung my bow from my shoulder, and closed my eyes.

I took a deep breath, trying to focus on the world around

me, listening for the sound of the proverbial rope swinging through the air.

The first thing I felt wasn't anything that helped me. It was the reverberation through the board of the feet of those behind me that stopped in their forward movement, shuffling in place as they couldn't get around me and Elio.

Next, the air was split by a cry for everyone to stop.

Finally, beyond the sound of bows being readied, and swords being drawn, I felt it.

Under the boards we walked on, somehow within the swampy, muddy mess of the trail we were making through the low, endless pools of too-still water, something was moving.

At first, it felt like the natural ebb and flow of a pond. But this was discordant in a way that wasn't out of pattern enough. If it were a sound, it would have been an out-of-synch army.

Standing in a second, still in a loose, battle-ready stance, I readied my own bow, and turned to the side that I felt the ripples coming from.

In front of me, as everyone shifted to cover their predetermined area around us, I tried to see beyond the gray, flat water reflecting the mists that hung unperturbed along the occasional thin piece of mud or swamp grass.

But...nothing.

Somehow, I felt the thrumming under the boards, and could even tell the direction it was coming from. But I still couldn't see it on the surface.

The water should have shown ripples, betraying any attempt to get near us.

"What is this place?" The low murmur came from someone in our line, but no one offered an answer. What answer was there to give?

If any of the guards had ever been here, to pay their respects to the clergy, they didn't offer up any wisdom either.

Did anyone come this far into the Marshlands?

For a moment, I felt like I was trespassing. But I shoved that to the side, and let it be impaled on Cinder's spike in my mind. It wouldn't get us anywhere to allow myself to believe we had no standing here.

My eyes never left the water or the mist right in front of me, waiting for that moment when it finally showed movement. But I was still aware of the moment Elio snapped his eyes open, and stepped up to my side, staring straight ahead as I was.

The fog in front of us began to coalesce, to stir and eddy.

All along the winding line, muscles tensed, whispers moved, and anticipation connected every frantic beat of our hearts. The flowing rage of hellfire in my blood turned up the heat, and my focus expanded.

We were spread out too far here. We were in a strange place, outside of the rules the rest of Onyx's lands followed. At the end of the day, I needed to bring home everyone there with us.

I let out a breath to force my hands not to tighten too much on my bow as the ripples finally appeared in the water before us, smaller than I expected, and then stopped.

Narrowing my eyes, I waited, holding my breath, hearing nothing except the pounding of my own heart in my ears.

The moment stretched too thin, the air in my lungs running out, the fire in my veins flaring, the itch under my skin growing.

Between one rapid heartbeat and the next, the thick cloud in front of us disappeared, and a wave, too large to be called a ripple, surged toward us as a massive dock filled with people appeared in the middle of what was moments before simply a stretch of water.

Reaching us quickly, the wave crested over the small path of mud, over the boards we stood on, soaking our shoes.

In the middle of the lines of people in front of us, not wearing anything that made him stand out in any real way, was the leader of the High Sect, the Vane. Just to his right was another robed person, this one with bright, purple hair, his lip curled up.

"King Tristan," the Vane called out, "it's been too long."

There was no way I was going to respond to that obvious taunt. If he thought that I was going to explain with everyone standing here the perilous balance between Onyx and the Marshlands, he was a fool. Then again...he was standing with the fake Shield from Amethyst.

"You know why we're here," Elio said from next to me, his hands still out.

Across from us, the new Shield flashed a sneering smile to Elio, his brow raising.

"Of course," Reol said, his voice low and rumbling, as if trying to imitate a growl, an attempt that almost made me roll my eyes, "you all think you have any say at all in what happens within the Marshlands."

"No," I said, and he flinched when a very real growl was present in my own voice, "we are here to remind you of your promises."

"Interesting," the Shield snarled, as if his mere words would somehow inspire a fear in me that would cause me to listen to anything he had to say, "a monarch that never upholds his end of the bargain is expecting others to hold true to theirs."

"Expecting you to uphold your end of the bargain long in place, as I have, is not the same as not caving to your requests to change long-standing tradition." That was the politest way of telling him he could go fuck himself because I had done nothing to renege on the commitments Onyx made to the High Sect.

"Coming from Amethyst," Elio said, "you don't seem to have a very good grasp on the realities of Onyx and the Marshlands. Normally, that could be forgiven, but not when it is so very clear that you're using your usurped position for your own ends." His voice boomed even though he kept it far from yelling. His natural volume and power simply drowned out the other, making the new Shield look more like a petulant child than a threat.

"Usurped?" The Shield bristled, his purple hair rising on his head like that of a boar.

Whether he was a real Shield or not, he had some kind of magic in him.

"Don't use your cheap tricks on me, boy," Elio said. "You forget, I am truly a Shield, and I can feel the illusionary power of your damned Amethyst leaking all over you. A real Shield wouldn't need that purple."

It took everything in me not to turn to Elio and ask him what in the hellfire he was talking about.

Did all Amethyst people have some kind of illusion power? Was there something in their hair that gave them some kind of ability? Was it in their blood? And could Elio only tell because he was a Shield? Nothing made sense.

"Cheap tricks?" The Vane screeched as the members of the High Sect behind him cut their gazes away from us, darting looks back and forth between them.

At that point, I considered breaking their concentration to be a small victory, even if I didn't have a clue why it was happening.

"Regardless of this person's ability," I said, trying to give them something they could point to where we weren't involving ourselves, in a last bit of hope to accomplish what we came here for without risking the clergy getting their claws into Onyx's inner workings, "the Marshlands should remain free of any person or creature taking part in this war. That would be true neutrality. By allowing the Corvids, or Amethysts, or any of Ash's people to use the Marshlands as refuge, you are declaring yourself for a side."

"What are we doing by allowing you to come in here now?" the Amethyst sneered.

"This is a peaceful meeting to request that you remember

your commitments, and we will be leaving the Marshlands at its conclusion." Meeting with me was incredibly benign compared to the terrible betrayal they were engaging in, and they knew it. There was no point in pretending I saw it differently. They knew why we were here.

"And now we get to the crux of the matter," the Vane said, tipping his chin up as if he were about to play a winning hand.

Nothing about their stances shifted. Nothing about them suggested we were going to like what happened next here. I braced myself for whatever happened, once again taking stock of the serpentine line of our people.

"Perhaps neutrality is no longer beneficial to us," the Amethyst Shield said, raising his hands and letting loose a strangled sounding scream.

From the still-misty, gray depths of the marshes, massive black shapes darted our way.

"Corvids," the cry went up from our line, echoed by other voices, all of them swallowed by the swirling fog as our foes approached.

CHAPTER 43
ONE OF US

Cinder

They made no attempt to be quiet, clearly more than secure in their belief that no one was even thinking of challenging them.

And why would anyone?

No one else had a Gus to guide them through the tunnel in the mountain.

The guards roamed, sat, chatted, and generally loafed about. Off to one side were some tents and a campfire.

Good, they must have been assigned here long enough to make camp. That meant that if we dragged all their bodies into the tents when we were done, none of the servants would think to look, and the alarm wouldn't go up for a while.

Silently setting my saddle bags down, I turned back to Gus.

I flashed the fingers on my hands twice indicating to her how many guards we had to deal with.

Gus chewed on her bottom lip, preparing a throwing knife and her short sword.

My hand raised without me even thinking about it, setting my palm on the hilt of her sword as I shook my head.

Yes, there were a lot of guards. But I made a promise to Jacquetta, and I meant to keep it. I could still handle this many guards on my own. It wasn't ideal, attacking in the open, risking them somehow having a way to contact backup, having little cover from which to make my move…but I could make it work.

Peeking out from around the tree, I missed it. My mistake was that look, that extra second to try and calculate what move I was going to make.

"Fuck," I muttered as Gus popped out, and waved a hand over her head, drawing the attention of every single set of eyes, including mine.

"Hello," she said, her voice far too bright for the occasion.

Jacquetta was going to kill me. I needed to make it work, there was no other choice.

Darting back to another tree, weaving through the trunks, I made my way around to come up behind the guards as they advanced on Gus.

"What are you doing here? How did you get here? Who are you?" One of them peppered her with questions, not even giving her enough time to answer, as I made my way to the back of the group.

Only part of me listened as Gus played like she was just lost in the woods, and oh my how strange finding all these people posted here so heavily armed. Were they guards? Was something wrong? No, of course that isn't a sword strapped to her side…

I added the bit about the sword in my head as I managed to slit the throats of four of the guards while she rambled on in her most exuberant voice, wearing her normal good cheer as armor along with a heavy dose of stupid that she most definitely didn't possess.

But we were running on borrowed seconds. This ruse couldn't hold. Finally, one of the damn guards turned as I laid his fiftth dead friend on the soft detritus of the forest floor.

"Fuck, no." He lunged at me, blade first, while the people around us began to echo his confused outburst.

It was easy enough to duck below his blade, blocking it with one of my spikes, and ramming the other between his ribs.

Yanking it out and letting him drop to the ground unceremoniously, I whirled to stab the person coming for me from behind. One spike drove through his eye, kicking him off as I slashed out with the other spike, meeting the oncoming blade of another attacker before I stabbed that one in the neck.

"Perry," someone yelled from behind me, giving me a name to at least one of the dead near my feet, while their hands wrapped tight around my neck, choking me, pooling the blood in my brain as they blocked the flow in my body.

Another guard ran at my front, their weapon drawn.

I kicked my foot out behind me in a sweep as I stabbed a spike into one of the arms that cut off my air, and flipped the heavy body over top of me, all in one swift collection of simultaneous movements. Ripping my spike out, I used the momentum and a shove to throw one attacker into another, impaling my would-be strangler on his friend's sword.

My back ached and I snarled, angry at the situation, my own body, and pain in general.

With a leap, I slashed the throat of the guard blubbering over running his own friend through, and spun to catch the blade of another attacker screaming as they ran up behind me.

A surge upward, and that one was dead, too.

Three attackers tried me at once, so I flung myself inside the guard of one of them, knocking their blade to the side, into their friend, and stabbing them in the neck.

Using the limp body of that one as I shield, I pivoted, throwing them between me and their other friend.

Dropping the body, it yanked down on the sword of the one who tried to get to me, and I jabbed my spike into their neck over the top of their friend's head. Their bodies fell to the ground together, one on top of the other.

More came at me, stepping carefully around the bodies—which was a mistake.

In seconds, I stepped on their friends as they screamed at me before I slashed one throat, slammed my spike home in another's ribcage, and gutted yet another one.

Their bodies fell on top of their dead friends.

Finally, the crowd was thin enough for me to glance toward Gus.

One guard was dead at her feet, and she fought a second, while a third came at her from the side. From the look of it, she didn't know it yet.

Pulling one of my throwing knives, I ducked under the wild swing of a wailing attacker, and flung the knife out. It found its home in the neck of the guard pursuing Gus.

They made the fatal mistake of yanking the blade out, increasing the torrent of blood pouring from their wound.

With a quick count, I knew I only had two left. One took a step one way, and back the other, trying to fake their movements and confuse me.

At least this one tried something. But my back was angry now, and so was I. There was too much to do, and bigger targets for me. I didn't have time to play their games.

More quick-footed changes of direction, but it seemed to distract the two guards facing me more than it did me.

I pulled another throwing knife out, and readied it while the other guard seemed to want to back up her friend—who was doing a lot for not accomplishing much—was frozen by the wild movements in front of her.

The dancing one pivoted to the left, but they kept their weight balanced on their toes in a way that bunched their muscles, and I knew.

With a swift move, she headed to the right, arm preparing to swing her sword at me, but I halted any question of how she would move next by burying my throwing knife in her eye.

Her friend gasped, looked at me, raising her sword, and darted toward the trees.

Sometimes, people made my job too easy.

Another throwing knife, another toss with a turn for momentum, and she was down.

Now, all that was left was helping Gus.

But Gus had two bodies at her feet now, and she was wiping her blade off on the moss of the trees she had backed herself against.

"Did you use the trees?" I asked, not realizing before when I looked her way that she basically narrowed the access to herself with them, forcing the rest of the guards to go after me.

"One of us had to think it through instead of running into the open, blades first," she fired back, her mouth in a thin line.

"I'm going to choose to ignore that," I said, wiping off my own weapons, and collecting my throwing knives.

"Why are there extra knives?" I asked, pulling two more knives out of the back and arm of bodies.

"Because they got too close a couple times," Gus said, taking her blades back from me.

For a moment, my back felt just fine as I grinned at her.

"Stop it," she said, her cheeks turning rosy as she smiled back, "we need to get through to the other side."

With a nod, I turned toward the tunnel, and took a deep breath, stretching out my back.

Yes, we still needed to make our way through the dark maze of unmoving rock, a challenge I didn't think any of my blind-folded training prepared me for.

CHAPTER 44

TIME OF KINGS

Tristan

I pulled my bow up, taking aim at the dark shapes still hiding in the fog.

"Drawing weapons here does the opposite of proving your point," the Vane yelled, his voice shaking. I refused to look his way and risk missing the Corvids moving into the open.

"Allowing the crows to stay in the Marshlands does the opposite of proving yours. Did you really think we wouldn't defend ourselves?"

"Well, it's nice to see you drop all pretense of formality." The Amethyst Shield had a smile in his voice, but I refused to look at him, either.

The real threat was no longer the men on their power trips on the ground. The real threat was now in the dark shapes swooping through the mist behind them.

"I suppose I should thank you all for dropping any pretense that you're neutral. You know Ash will never let you have any place of power, no matter what promises he made you. He'll turn his troops on you as soon as he can. The clergy will cease to exist."

Cries went up at once from the many voices lined up across from us. They were so loud and so discordant that I wasn't able to discern whether they were arguing or agreeing with me. But it didn't matter, because I was telling the truth.

"He'll kill off the High Sect first." My voice was hard, but I used all the years of speech making in front of large crowds to project it to every set of ears among them, past the muting quality of the fog and swamp surrounding us all.

"You know nothing. He'll expand our reach once he takes over Amethyst," the purple-haired asshole screeched.

Great, he was a true believer. How had the High Sect allowed him to infiltrate their ranks, and lead their decision making? Was that really only based on his status as Shield? And if it was, how had he managed to be declared one? And why didn't Elio wield as much power where they were concerned?

"Of all the people here, you're the one who knows the least," Elio bellowed, lifting his hands, and waving them in some kind of pattern I couldn't clearly see from my peripheral vision.

The clouds split, billowing away in seconds, to reveal the Corvids beating their giant wings without moving forward, as if the same force that blew away the clouds also restrained the crows.

"How dare you question me. I am a Shield. I am here to protect the High Sect. You involve yourself with a court. You started this." The Amethyst Shield was spouting nonsense. Nothing he said resonated with anything Elio had ever said. Nor did it sound anything like the stance of the High Sect before his arrival.

"Shields, you fucking idiot, are separate from the High Sect because they are supposed to serve the people." Elio's deep, loud rumble of a voice shook, and even the fire in my veins stuttered for a moment, as if my insides were afraid of what an angry Shield was capable of.

"Serving a weak Dragon King—who is missing the 'Dragon'—does not serve the people."

That managed to drag my attention away from the crows for a second. A growling sound of warning came out of my throat. Part of me wanted to drop my bow, and let fly an arrow right into his purple-tinged face.

But Elio's yell of indignation next to me made me take my eyes off the purple-haired faker, with his clenched fists and face flushed in rage, and focus again on the flying figures above us.

"You fucking idiot. The lot of you are for following his lead. The former Duke Asshole is the weak pretender. He practices no magic aside from lies." Elio slammed one of his big palms on my back, and I almost let my arrow fly accidentally. "The time of the Dragon Kings is not over."

One of the crows released an almost human cry before diving.

Taking a breath, I was about to end the bird when another one slammed into it from the side, sending it careening before ducking its head, and falling to the back of the pack.

"Fucking crows," someone muttered near me. I couldn't agree more.

It was news to me too that Elio thought the Dragon King line meant anything other than my warm blood, and the accident of birth into the royal line. But I didn't want to start any actual shooting here.

Beyond the Marshlands, I was more than willing to kill every last feather arrayed against us. But right then and there, it would have been suicide with our line the way it was, and our limited number of guards.

No one could come to our aid. No one was prepared to fight in this muck, and we were nothing more than easy targets in a convenient row.

"What do you know, Shield Elio?" the Vane called, his voice holding a hint of what I guessed was excitement. It made the itch under my skin worse, like it was nagging at me.

"King Tristan is the Dragon King, just like the Kings of old. He will push back this onslaught, and any others that come against Onyx. If the Corvids were smart, they would end their role in this war right now."

He could have said anything. Instead, he chose to use the exact words that would give all these people hope for something that I couldn't possibly live up to while not giving them any specific information at all.

Clearly, Elio was lying. He was saying what needed to be said to get us through this crisis.

I couldn't even be angry with him, not when the Corvids moved into a tighter formation before one of them dropped down to the dock, landed next to the High Sect's Vane, and shifted into a human woman in a flowing, black gown.

She was as dark as the night sky, her skin and long hair all a similar color. In the gray, muted tones of the swamp, her darkness was just as striking as the shock of bright, purple hair on the Amethyst Shield next to her.

Keeping my arrow trained on her, I took in the staring eyes of the entire High Sect standing before us, all of them looking on me in awe.

"The return of the Dragon..." she said, her voice soft and silky, so different from the odd half-bird, half-human croaking the crows spoke in that it sent the hair on my arms standing on end.

Her eyes roamed over me, seemingly looking right past the arrow aimed at her heart. There was a clear calculation in her eyes, but I didn't know what she was looking for.

Of all the arguments Elio could have made, how was I supposed to prove this to them if they challenged his assertions?

Better not to move, to keep my arrow aimed, not to let her

see me flinch. It might not make any of them believe, but it was better than doing something that would result in failing to convince anyone of anything, or stumbling into making them believe Elio was a liar and I was willing to go along with his lies.

She smiled, tipping her head our way.

"We did not think it would happen. No matter how bold your Fighter." Her eyes left me, and I suppressed a shudder as she turned that deep gaze to Elio. "It is her, is it not?"

Elio only let out a huffing noise that didn't give me any more information than did his cryptic words on the road here.

The Corvid woman waved a hand, saying, "Do not tell me, then," and turned her back to us which was enough of a surprise for me to raise a brow.

Above them, the crows, flying back and forth, keeping themselves aloft as they shifted their positions, squawked amongst themselves in low noises that must have been the crow equivalent of whispering.

"I must bring this news to my people." She tipped her head at the Vane. The Amethyst next to her let his mouth hang open.

"No, you said you would end this today." The Amethyst grabbed her arm.

Within a second, a flashing of feathers and spreading of wings forced the Amethyst to stumble back from her, protecting his eyes.

"Do not presume to tell me what my people will do." The strange crow voice she used was only more unnerving when thick with anger. "You made promises to us. We made no such promises to you. If you wish to court the Dragon's wrath, be my guest. But I will not burn my people on the pyre of your idiocy. We will bring this news to our monarchs, and make decisions then. You have no hold over Corvid, or any of her people. Including me."

With a great flap of her wings, she launched herself into the sky.

Most of the other Corvids followed, except the one that tried to dive at me. That one let out a loud call, and circled as if looking for the best angle of attack.

One of the retreating crows turned back, picking up speed before slamming into their wayward fellow again, snapping their massive beak at the wings of the other, but drawing them off to follow the rest of the group.

Letting out a breath, I was careful not to show my relief at the retreat of the crows, even based on a lie.

I doubted most of the High Sect could shoot the way my archers could. As long as the crows didn't return and there were no hidden troops in the swamp around us, we were no longer the easy targets we had been.

"You've lost your attack dogs," Elio called across the water as I lowered my bow.

"They will be back, and then your King's reign will be over," the Amethyst Shield yelled, the purple tint returning to his cheeks.

Next to the Shield, the Vane turned to scan the conflicted looks of the rest of the High Sect, and stood taller, straightening as he turned to face us.

"What happened here today changes nothing," he said, raising his chin as if doing so made his words true.

If the Corvid woman brought the lie home, and it made the crows back out of this war, today changed everything.

"Are you still going to back this charlatan?" Elio bellowed, waving a hand toward the purple pretender whose grin was far too wide now.

"He is a Shield, and, as such, will win the clergy real power in the new court."

There it was, the power play, laid bare for all to see. The Vane didn't care whether the Amethyst next to him was a real Shield, or not.

"You are a fool." Elio's voice shook, and the water in front of us rippled with the force of it.

"Raise the water," the leader screamed, and all the members of the High Sect behind him started to raise their hands.

All around us, the murky water of the swamp began to creep toward our thin strip of muddy ground.

"Fuck," I muttered, looking down the line of our people toward the way out, watching them scramble to go back the way we came.

But we each had to wait for the person in front of us to move, which would take far too long.

I had no idea how many of our people could swim. If the High Sect could control the marshes like this, would swimming even matter?

Were the Dragon King and most of his guards about to drown?

After worrying for so long about an attack from above, I might be destroyed by an attack from beneath my feet, despite winning some kind of hope with the Corvids today.

Nothing about the layers of irony in this moment were lost on me, even as I scanned the area, looking for some way out of this situation and seeing none.

CHAPTER 45

TRUTH

Cinder

Inside the cavern, we could only see for the first few steps before the sheer rock face of the tunnel turned a corner, leaving a darkness so absolute it felt like death.

If Gus wasn't holding my hand, if I couldn't smell the increasingly mineral scent of the air in here, and if our footsteps weren't giving off soft echoes while I felt the strength of the stone beneath my feet, then I might have believed we were actually dead.

After simply walking in silence far too long, a thought worked its way into my bones, making the sound of my own breath irritating enough to make me itch like I slept in hay. I whispered, "You didn't seem to have a problem with me killing all those guards."

No matter how many times I ran through any difference between the guards and the thieves, I couldn't understand why killing the thieves had bothered her, yet she participated in killing the others, and hiding their bodies.

She sighed, a heavy sound that dropped out of her mouth with such weight that no echo followed it.

"Those guards knew what they signed up for. Every single one of them were willing to risk their lives for your brother, or his wife, or the Corvids, something. None of them really just needed money to survive."

I opened my mouth to retort with my standard justification for using a blade to clear my path, but I hesitated.

Running her words through my mind, I thought I might have finally managed to come to understand on some level what upset her. The problem was, I still didn't feel bad about it.

"At one point, I was paid—well, my brother was—to kill people."

She squeezed my hand as I paused to take a breath, neither of us stopping our progress forward. The thought of all those kills had hit me before. But I had to shove it all far away from me, and lock it in a dark room in my mind in order to continue on. I didn't have time to look back. Not while we were at war, and my blades were necessary to end it, to protect everyone I loved.

But now…that room was open in my mind, and garish light was shining on all the dark thoughts there.

"He always told me a story to go along with each one, just a sentence or two that made me believe the killings were all on behalf someone. Like my cousin. Her bastard husband hurt her."

"You did a very good thing in ending that man."

I nodded even though she couldn't see it. I did it because she was right, nothing would ever make me feel bad about killing Lord Fall.

"The problem is, I don't know anything about the rest. I can't even tell you at this point how many there were. Well…I can tell you how many there were today…"

She laughed, and it loosened something inside me.

"Cinder, what happened before, there is nothing you can do to change it, and there's no way to go back and find out if what your brother said was true or not. That's not your fault. Please don't beat yourself up over all of that."

"But, that's the thing, Gus. Even if I do run them all through my head, over and over, and try and understand—even if I found out that for sure some were innocent—I don't think I would cry over it. I've never hurt a child, and I never would. But, beyond that…only the people I care about would make me lose any sleep."

"Then I am even more thankful for being one of the people you care about."

Her voice was thick with the same sarcastic, laughing tone she teased me about Tristan with, but I still heard something hiding in her words that I couldn't decipher.

"Why do I hear a caveat in your voice?" We were already in the dark with nothing else to keep us company other than the sound of each other's voices. It was as good a time as any to confront whatever she was thinking.

"You're lying to yourself," she said after a long stretch of silence. Her words almost made me stumble.

"Lying about what?" My voice was as small as it was when I spoke to Ash, and I hated it.

"All that time you were convincing yourself that you shouldn't be Queen. Why was that? And don't say because King Tristan deserves better. Give me the real reason."

Somehow, chewing on my bottom lip made a sound in this place. Maybe she couldn't hear it, and maybe there was no echo. But I heard it. And it was loud.

"Because…" I took a deep, ragged breath, "Onyx deserves better than someone who can kill without mercy, without feeling. The people deserve a protector that won't slaughter them without a thought if they pose a threat to the King or her friends."

There. That was the truth. It was more than the blood on my hands. It was more than the goodness of my King. I knew, tucked away in that room with all the memories of all of the killings I committed because my lying brother told me to, it was the truth. The people and the country deserved someone who could protect them the right way. And I would only ever know how to do that with my blade leading.

"Don't you think you could become that?" she asked, her voice soft and sure in the same way it was when I told her and Jacquetta the truth of me.

"No. I don't." That was also the truth of me.

Along the way, maybe it was that first kill Ash ordered me to perform, taking the life of the man I thought I loved, someone who had only been kind to me in the fucked-up way in which he could, I lost the part of myself that could be what she suggested.

I would always be this. This was the best that I was capable of.

Gus let us both walk in the silence of the graveyard of my past, among the bodies of the people I killed, among the nights I spent happy and contented in Tristan's arms not thinking about all the other nights I stole from so many others. She waited so long to say something else that the quiet seeped into my bones again, made me itch again.

"How would you deal with your brother's slaves if they were to turn themselves in?"

"The same way I dealt with the ones I've met so far. If they come to understand he isn't their savior, and lay down their arms, I would bring them to the guards, and let them handle the situation. If I managed to get them subdued without their weapons, same thing. But if they still refused to see they had been duped, if they still fought me, I wouldn't feel bad about taking them out of equation."

She lapsed into silence again, and I wasn't sure if there was any more to say. It was all true, and no matter her arguments, seeing any other way seemed impossible to me.

"You're already closer to the person you think the country needs than you think."

Was I? I didn't see how she thought that.

"I still enjoy it, Gus."

Her steps stuttered as if she tripped on something, but she kept on moving. I pretended it wasn't because of what I said. I didn't want to bring her home to Jacquetta just to lose my friendships with both. I would accept it if that's what they wanted, but I didn't want this trip to wound Gus emotionally as it was already wounding her wife.

The damage in my wake wasn't just measured in dead bodies.

"Exactly what part of it do you enjoy?" she finally asked after leaving me with the sounds of just our footsteps and breath for too long.

"After spending so long training, I enjoy being able to use my skills. Fighting is fun. Being able to move my body in ways that took me years in some cases to perfect...it's like a master painter showing off their masterpiece. It sounds bizarre, probably, but the way we just took out those guards and the thieves before that, being able to do that without dying or getting seriously wounded, that's my version of a masterpiece."

"Only difference is yours are in blood."

I laughed, and, even though it was strained, she did, too.

"Yes, mine are in blood and stench, organs and pain, and they are ugly, but they are what I was trained to do. And being better at it than almost anyone else is a source of pride for me."

"Hmmm..."

That noise wasn't encouraging, but I didn't know how else

to describe what I was talking about. Part of the reason I could never just be a queen in a pretty dress in the throne room no matter how long Onyx was at peace—which we would hopefully be for quite a while after the war—was because I would miss the work. I would miss being so good at something. Especially something I knew took me so long to perfect, and most people would never be able to do no matter how hard they trained.

Most people had some piece of them that would destroy them from the inside out after seeing all I had seen, and killing as many people as I had killed. Even I knew that.

Some of the people in Lehar that saw too much death during the last war, were broken deep within, haunted by all of it. Even some of the ones who never killed anyone.

But I wasn't. And I never would be.

"Did you enjoy training the guards?" she asked, making me widen my eyes even though it didn't help me see any better. But I didn't expect her to speak again.

"Yes, that was amazing. I felt like I was doing something wholly good with my skills, I was as proud of that as I am for killing Lord Fall, and freeing my cousin."

Gus squeezed my hand again, and I tried to catch up to her thinking. She clearly had a point, and I missed it.

"See? You're already better for Onyx than you think. Maybe, well, maybe just be careful when you kill thieves from now on. See if you can disarm them first."

I laughed. I couldn't help it.

After all of that, she was just dropping the subject of her concern over extraneous death. She seemed not to worry about it further.

Even if I didn't agree with her that I was somehow more magnanimous than I thought, I knew who and what I was. I did think about the training of the guards.

Maybe, once we found peace, that *was* something I could do.

Maybe we could have additional training in the training grounds after the guards were put through their initial paces. I didn't want to upend their regular training after all. But perhaps it would be good to have an elite group trained to a level of skill closer to my own. It would give me a chance not to get discombobulated by too many pretty gowns, and too much time sitting around the palace.

Hmmm…Gus was a genius.

She picked up another conversation, this one about what we should expect on the inside of the mountain, and I listened appropriately.

Our words became our companions as we made our way in the dark. I hoped that every turn she made was the right one.

Finally, hours later, long enough that I was starving for some of our lousy traveling food, a faint light grew up ahead, and I took a deep breath. We were nearing the end of this perpetual blackness.

But before we reached the faint glow along the floor up ahead, a body tackled me from the side, ripping my hand out of Gus'.

CHAPTER 46

FLIP

Tristan

"Don't push anyone in," General Pace yelled from somewhere closer to the front of our line.

"Hurry, hurry, hurry," the guard in front of me muttered under her breath.

I agreed with her, but the repetition was doing nothing to lessen the boiling in my veins, or alleviate the itch.

The Vane cackled from his secure perch on his thick, floating dock as water touched the edges of the boards under our feet.

"You can still give the High Sect the powers it deserves, King Tristan," the Vane taunted.

Shaking my head, grinding my teeth together, I tried not to give in to the urge to raise my bow and just shoot him.

"No," the Amethyst screamed, "he doesn't deserve to be King. He chose the wrong queen."

Unable to hold it in anymore, I let loose a wild snarling growl of a yell.

"Speak whatever twisted lie you want about me, but you don't deserve to speak of her." I wasn't about to say her name, and invite this worthless liar to do the same.

"Enough," Elio bellowed, flinging his arms out.

The water lapping at our toes flowed out away from us, gathering every drop of water from the muddy swamp beneath it, cracking the ground as it went. It collected into a massive wave that towered over the High Sect on the other side.

"Come on, Shield." Elio's voice boomed, the wave frozen in front of us, shaking with every word he said. "If you really are one, you can stop this. You can fight me."

"Go on, show them. Fight back," the Vane cried. At least I thought it was the Vane. His voice sounded strangled, the water between us filtering it in a way that made it seem as if he wasn't even in the same world, but was somehow calling out to us from the other side of death.

"You do something," the fake Shield screamed back.

"Even with all of them working together," Elio said, waving his hands, sending the water swirling into a rotating serpent that arced above the clergy huddled together on the dock, clear now except for the few obscured by the whirling tube of water, "even with their own sacred water, they don't have the power."

Stifling a smile, I studied the clergy as they crouched down, looking everywhere with wide eyes, as if they couldn't see a way out of this one, and all of them thought they were going to be drowned by Elio's magical water snake.

"I'm sorry!" The faker surged to his feet, hands clasped as if begging. "If you let me go back to Amethyst, you'll never need to see me again. You—you're right. I am a fraud. All I have is my stone from home, my illusion. I'm sorry. Let me go. Please."

"Before we go..." Elio's mouth twisted into some mad

version of his normal, wide and open smile. This one was as dangerous looking as the snake of water.

He lowered the water from the snake slowly back into the swamp, allowing it to settle perfectly still again.

"You," he said, lowering his hands only to raise one finger, and point it at the false Amethyst Shield, "get out of Onyx and never come back."

"If any of my people catch you," I added, slinging my bow over my shoulder, and settling the arrow into the quiver at my back, "I will pardon any crime they commit against you, as a warning to others."

"Thank you. Thank you." He bowed his head, refusing to lift his eyes, and took a deep breath, relaxing his shoulders.

"How long did you know he wasn't a real Shield?"

"How long have you been lying to us?"

"We trusted you."

Accusation after accusation flew from the members of the clergy to their leader, and, for the first time since we arrived, I no longer worried that this situation with the High Sect would be repeated years from now.

Part of me hoped for new leadership among them, but I didn't have a say in what they did amongst themselves. Nor did I want a say. It was better to walk away now, and leave this small win just as it was.

Elio had different ideas.

He raised his hands and bellowed, "Hey. The faker isn't the only one who decided to forego their sacred duty, and the role they voluntarily undertook."

"The High Sect should have a say in the running of the country." Even now, while being snarled at by his own people, humiliated by his ill-conceived plans, abandoned by the crows, and outsmarted and outdone by Elio, he just kept on.

"No," I said, not about to let his rantings grow.

"You have the Marshlands, and should be happy you even

have that." Elio waved his hands, and a splash shot out of the water, right into the leader's face, making him hiss and jump.

"Shield Elio," the Vane screamed, wiping his face without managing to make him look less like he was slapped with water, complete with hair wildly sticking out on the side of his head, "I will revoke your status as Shield."

I sucked in a breath, about to scream back at the Vane, my want to get out of the High Sect's focus be damned, but Elio touched a hand to my arm.

"My recognition, because it came with eyewitness testimony at a formal meeting of the clergy from outside the High Sect itself, is for life. There is nothing you can hope to do to me. And, if you tried, it would be even more proof of your corruption." Elio grinned, his voice returning to that boisterous and jovial way he usually had.

After his injuries and everything that happened, I wasn't sure I would ever see him like this again. It was strange that it came when he was issuing threats, but if I were in his position, putting the Vane of the High Sect in his place would have made me happy, too.

Elio turned toward me, and I took it as my cue to face toward our exit. Our people had almost gotten to the point that he and I could begin moving ourselves.

The members of the clergy on the dock across from us began arguing with each other again, most of the complaints lodged at the Vane.

For a second, I wondered why they weren't leaving the same mysterious way they came so they could argue privately, but then decided that I didn't care what their reasoning was.

Maybe they were too distracted by their failure here to accomplish any of the goals they must have started with. It didn't matter. I had no role to play with them, and they had no role to play with me. Just as it always was.

Actually, that was even better because the power plays and

subtle ways they tried to exert influence in the past would no longer work at all. From this moment on, I was free of at least this challenge.

"But first," Elio said, turning again toward the dock, drawing my own focus there. I couldn't imagine what else needed to be covered.

He didn't go on to finish his sentence. He merely lifted his hands out to the sides, palms down as, almost in a single voice, the clergy all leapt to their feet and screamed, "No."

Elio flipped his hands over, and slammed his arms down to his sides.

The dock, and every last person on it, flipped into the air, and slammed back into the water, sending up a splash that forced ripples to wash over the bank of our walkway, dousing my toes again.

All the clergy were left to scramble through the water and muck, reeds and other swamp goo dripping from them as they made their way to grab onto the edge of their overturned and broken dock.

"None of their parlor tricks will work now. They deserve to get wet," he said, voice loud and full of laughter.

My mouth dropped open at the sight, and small, choked chuckles broke out along our line.

But there was nothing else to do aside from turning back the way we came. Taking my first steps along the boards, I followed our people home.

CHAPTER 47

ALONE IN THE DARK

Cinder

In the blinding darkness, I landed hard on my side, the weight of the person who tackled me and the saddlebags coming down on me, too.

"Fuck," I grunted, pain flaring through me as I pushed against the weight of the person.

"Don't go in there. They took them. They're killing them. Don't go in there." The person's rant just continued, the same words over and over again, their voice raw and raspy while they scrambled to grasp onto me.

"Get off me," I snarled, shoving at them, and reaching for my spike.

"Wait, Cinder, wait," Gus said, her footsteps marking her place for me even if I couldn't see her at all.

I continued to struggle with the person on top of me as they tried to keep hold of me until Gus reached us, poking her finger in my ear.

"Ow, Gus," I hissed, pulling my head away.

"Sorry, can't see," she said, her hand landing on my shoulder a second later.

"Friend," she said, and I rolled my eyes because this person was not our friend, "how long have you been in here?"

Among all the questions she could have asked, that was the first one?

"Three days. I don't know the way. Had to hide. They're killing them. Don't go in there. They took them."

"Oh, good, we're back to this," I said, maneuvering myself so that at least they weren't on top of me anymore, even though Gus' hold on my shoulder kept me from grabbing her hand and running for the faint light.

"Cinder," Gus scolded as I ground my teeth.

If she wanted to stay here and deal with this person and their bizarre actions, then she could. But it would be easier just to kill them, and keep it moving. I should have done it right away before they had a chance to tickle her empathy. We didn't have time for this.

"We know the way," Gus said, and I slapped my hand over hers on my shoulder, shaking my head in the dark. "I will take you to the way out. The guards aren't there, so they can't bother you. Then I will meet up with my friend on the way back in."

"Gus, no. I can't let you go alone. What if you get attacked? Jacquetta will kill me." Now I sounded like the random person from the darkness, rattling off too many words too quickly.

"Friend, do you need some water?" She just ignored me as she fished a water skein and food from the saddlebags, continuing to speak to them as if they weren't raving, and I didn't make a damn good point.

All I could do at that moment was sit there and stew while she helped them. Sure, it was a nice thing to do, and I would normally be fine with it. But my elbow and my hip hurt so badly from the impact that I was just thankful it didn't lead to more aching in my back. And we needed to get this done so we wouldn't get caught just as we were getting into position with nothing to show for our troubles so far.

"Cinder," she finally said as their shuffling alerted me to the fact that they were getting to their feet, "stay here. Check out the mouth of the tunnel, and I will be back in no time."

"No, Gus. I have to come with you." Even though I didn't want to. I wanted to go on with our mission.

"Fine, but it would be faster if you stayed here."

"Damn it." Running my hands over my face, I tried to think it through.

Yes, it would be faster for her to lead this one strange person out, and then hustle back herself, instead of leading two people out, and one on the way back.

"I want you to scream as loud and as long as possible if something goes wrong, do you hear me?" I finally said, deciding to check out the end of the tunnel as soon as she was gone.

"This won't take that long," she said, and I grabbed her hand, finding it without a problem. I knew where they were both standing from the sounds of their feet, and I knew that Gus was facing me from the sound of her voice.

"Bring yourself back here. I don't want to die at the hands of your wife." I squeezed her hand and let go, already worried about her.

Gus handled herself better in the last fight with the guards than I had ever seen her do before, but that didn't mean that it wouldn't have been better for me to be there with her. This went against everything I promised to Jacquetta.

"You be careful," she said. "Don't do anything foolish while I'm gone."

I couldn't do much. If she thought I was going to run in there, leave her behind, accomplish the mission, but then risk getting chased on my way out without being able to find her, then her mind was scrambled from being in the dark too long.

Listening to her steps as she walked away, it was everything I could not to run after her.

But she was right, this was faster. I kept reminding myself of that.

At least this close to the end of the tunnel, I could still see the faint traces of light. Following that enticing glow, I made my way toward the opening that would lead to the hollow bowl in the middle of the mountain.

Gus said there were trees in here, the winged trees, and that the place we needed to go was somehow high up in one of those trees in the center of this strange place. She said these trees were as tall as the mountain, and dwarfed all those on the outside. But part of me still didn't believe those details.

She had to at least be wrong about the height of the trees, right?

Making my way toward the light, I tried to step as silently as possible.

Right at the edge of it, I dropped the saddlebags slowly to the ground, the edge of one just barely visible in the low bit of glow here.

The last thing I wanted to do was lose our rations. But I needed to be able to move quietly to check out the opening of the cave on this side, and they were in my way.

On the balls of my feet, I slunk along the edge of the tunnel that led out, the light growing in intensity. The cave turned here as it had at the other entrance, but it was far more gradual and longer. Before I reached the end, I could see beyond the entrance to a vast, dark, green space.

It seemed the light here was muted, and all I could think about was how thick the tree canopy must be. There was no dappling of the ground from the sun overhead, just gauzy, green light filtering down.

Finally, the green shifted, and I realized that I was actually seeing through some of the branches. Their leaves were huge, creating a curtain that almost seemed translucent over the entrance.

The leaves wouldn't care that I was there. Giving up on my subterfuge, I stood up taller and moved, still staying as silent as possible as I made my way toward the end.

How was I going to see to the other side of the huge leaves without giving myself away. How was I going to climb such massive things?

Normal trees were pretty easy to climb. The space of the branches between leaves, or boughs, or needles offered plenty of places to grab onto. Those things were massive. I wasn't sure how the leaves were even attached, nor could I fathom how big the branches must have been to hold them up.

Once I reached the leaves, I closed my eyes, and got as close to them as possible, listening for any sign of people on the other side.

I didn't hear anything, even though I waited for a while. I moved along the edge of the leaf, where there was only space enough for a single body between it and the rock wall of the interior of the mountain.

Finally, I came to the end of the leaf where it overlapped along the edge with another one.

But at the bottom of the line of overlap, there was a small gap.

Getting down on the ground, I was careful to keep my hands and everything else from the small gap until I lowered my head to peek through it.

On the other side of the leaf, the light was just as green, but even more muted. It was almost like being in a field during a full moon, just a touch brighter, and a lot greener.

Watching a little longer, moving my head even further into the gap, revealed nothing but green and absolutely ridiculously huge tree trunks in the distance.

How big was this place?

And did they really take everyone out of the area for this thing they were doing, this killing of the twins that Rath talked about?

That seemed foolish. But I supposed that any place so well positioned and so well known for being impenetrable might give people a false sense of security.

What was that like?

I loved my home, but long before the last war, I was aware that being on top of the hellfire source held an inherent level of risk. And after the war…well…nothing really felt completely safe again.

Even in the palace, there was an attack. People died.

Shoving myself up to my feet again, I stepped back to the entrance of the tunnel, and tried to spot the branch that held the leaf only to come up with no information. A quick stroll down one side of the canopy, and another the other direction, gave me no clue as to the branch I would need to climb.

After all this, I wasn't sure how to accomplish my goal.

All I could do was head back to the saddlebag, and wait for Gus.

Moments later, I sat, fetched up against the wall of the tunnel, just at the edge of the light, leaning on the saddlebags, waiting for Gus as sleep claimed me.

Rolling pebbles woke me, and I pulled my spike as I surged to my feet, stopping my momentum before I drove it home into Gus' side.

"Good morning to you, too," she said, grinning at me, and shaking her head.

"You don't seem to mind me pulling a blade on you," I said as I slipped my spike back into its place along my thigh.

"Because you won't kill me. Come on, get up." She hauled me to my feet, and I wondered about her faith in me.

"I looked out there. Didn't see anyone. And, what's worse is I have no idea how we're going to climb on those leaves." We collected the saddle bags, and made our way to the entrance.

Gus leaned over, whispering in my ear, "The leaves are strong enough. And if we use their weird fuzz, we should be able to climb right up them. Once we get higher, there are multiple layers of leaves that we should be able to climb between. I'll lead the way."

She walked over to one of the broad leaves, and looked back at where I stood with my eyebrow raised. I was willing to just watch her show me what she meant because her words made no sense.

With a grin, she turned back to the leaf, reached out to grasp around the thick vein running down the center of it, and simply climbed on like she was climbing a rope, her feet walking along beneath her like they were more hands.

"Are you serious?" I muttered under my breath, unable to hold back my shock.

It didn't take her long to get high enough to transfer to another leaf, simply repeating the same moves. In all she did, the leaves barely even shuddered under her weight.

There was no choice, I was about to trust the strangest trees I had ever seen with our lives.

Placing my hand around the large vein, fuzzy tendrils grabbed me back. They were only present on the vein, and not on the rest of the leaf.

Letting go and pulling my hand up to my face, rubbing my fingers together, I found no residue left behind by the tendrils.

With a wild grin, I adjusted the saddle bags on my shoulder, and grabbed the vein again. These strange trees could not have been better for our purposes. All I had to do was finish the mission.

CHAPTER 48

LIES

Tristan

"That could not have gone better," General Pace said as we got back to the transports.

"Not even in my dreams did I imagine that working out so well," I agreed, but looking over to where Elio was, I couldn't stave off the concerns that followed my relief. "Although, I do wonder if there will be fallout when they find out he lied."

"Lied?" she asked, her attention wholly on me now, leaving behind her half perusal of the action all around us while she spoke.

"We both know the time of the Dragon is over." My voice was low, as quiet as possible while still being audible to the General. The last thing I wanted to do was confirm the assumption for some poor guard, causing him to question his devotion to the country.

"King Tristan," her voice was loud, making no attempt to

hide whatever it was she was about to say to me. That alone was enough for me to give her my full attention in return, "None of us are sure of that. Anything could happen."

She turned away from me, and took two steps before my senses returned.

Even if I didn't agree with her, or understand why she would think that when the truth seemed obvious to me—no one even remembered what the Dragon King's powers were—I still needed her for something before we all took off.

"General," I said, catching up to her, and stopping her with a hand on her arm, "I would like to travel light so that I can get back to the palace faster."

The truth was, I wasn't asking. I had zero intention of taking three days to get back to the palace when I could make the trip in two if I pushed.

Cinder was waiting for me.

Just thinking about her was enough for my blood to heat up again, but at least the itch beneath my skin was gone. The sweat that coated me after the confrontation still clung to me in that thick, muggy air. Feeling the itch beneath the perspiration would have been enough to drive me to distraction.

General Pace sighed, knowing full well that she was going to have to adjust whatever plans she had in order to make this happen.

"I will accompany you along with a small contingent of guards." Her voice suggested it would be unwise to argue with her, but I couldn't help it.

"You are suggesting I ride in the carriage even though it would be faster to travel on horseback?" It might even cut a few hours off our time getting back. If my plan to get back as fast as possible wasn't going to be derailed by her penchant for posting up inside inns, and talking me to death, then I needed to make it clear right now that I was serious.

"It would be easier for us to have the guards ride in shifts with people sleeping in the carriage in turns so we wouldn't have to stop at inns but once to exchange horses." Her jaw clenched, and I knew she was irritated with me.

And damn it, she made a good point.

"Then I will ride, and do shifts as well."

"King Tristan, that isn't wise." She shook her head.

"We just sent the Corvids back to their people to talk about calling off the war. Why would we have to be so worried about attacks from above?" She had to agree to this. I didn't want her against me on the subject. It could cause delays, but I hated to order her around. Pulling rank on a friend made me hate my crown even as I felt like I abused it.

She let out a sigh that sounded long-suffering, and I suppressed my urge to smile.

"Fine, but that means you are part of the Guard for that time, and will not be riding ahead. You need to be watching like everyone else." She turned on her heel, and walked away to organize what I asked of her. I couldn't keep the smile off my face anymore.

Cinder, I'll be there soon.

Maybe I could keep myself focused on the job at hand if I just spoke to her in my mind, pretending she was next to me the whole time.

Once this war was over and all the ensuing public events were complete, I imagined touring the country with her.

The last time we rode side by side for days, I was furious with her. It would be nice to try again, to have a good time with her on the road.

Looking to where General Pace was issuing orders and collecting the guards she wanted along with us, I wondered if she would ever let us do such a thing without a full retinue slowing us down so much that it would just be a collection of boring days plodding along.

Somehow, I needed to set up a chance for us to ride together freely for at least a day or two.

"Rath," I whispered to myself. That was the answer. He would know how we could lie our way to freedom, and where we could go after. He was always a worthy conspirator.

"King Tristan," Elio called, looking grayer behind his beard than he did when we got here, even as his eyes seemed brighter, "I heard you're pulling ahead."

"Yes," I peered closer at him, trying to understand the strange look about him, "forgive me, Shield. You did a great thing today, but are you alright?"

He laughed, that loud laugh as big as he was, and I smiled again, glad to hear it back even if he looked a little sick.

"Doing that much with my shield drains me physically, but I am better now than I have been since my surprise return."

I nodded, although I didn't really understand what it was like to have magic, let alone how it would be draining to use it.

"Getting back to her will be good for you," he said with another grin that pulled one from me in return.

"She is always good for me. But I need to ask you, why did you lie to them about the powers?" I leaned in so I could whisper to him. "I am not the Dragon in any way that matters."

He laughed again, slapped me on the back—a tendency that was as endearing as it was irritating—and leaned in to whisper to me. Although, I worried that with his loud voice he wouldn't be able to be quiet enough to keep this conversation to ourselves.

"Are you sure?" he asked, and moved past me without explaining what that was supposed to mean.

Nothing about this day felt real.

Regardless of Elio's strange insistence that I had the Dragon King powers, his ruse did manage to accomplish everything that we wanted to. We were about to head back to Cinder faster than we traveled so far from her.

Cinder was my wife, which was enough for me to feel blessed. She would hopefully be a lot healthier by the time we got back. We made enormous strides toward potentially ending this war.

I took a deep breath, and looked around at all our people, all of them healthy. We were bringing everyone back.

Even if our wins today were in large part due to a lie, I was thankful for them.

Making my way to General Pace and the collection of guards she had assembled around a small carriage that would travel faster than the large ones, or even the official royal carriage I rode down in, I couldn't help but feel like I was doing a decent job as King for the first time in a while, and more hopeful than I had been since I met Cinder.

She was my hope. And now I felt like I could finally bring some to her.

DROPPING IN UNANNOUNCED

Cinder

If I managed to do this, I could bring so much hope home for Tristan when he returned. I needed to keep that in mind as my arms and my back screamed at me even as most of my weight was supported by the way my legs were wrapped in the length of the rope.

Gus was wrapped in her own rope above me, both of us anchored to one of the bits of branch that attached the leaves to the main branch of the tree.

The main branch of the tree was too damn big to wrap our ropes around, but it was plenty large enough for us to sleep on with our saddlebags.

After two days of sleeping on the branch, Ash and his full retinue returned to the tower, and all I could do was wait until they gave me an opening.

But I couldn't make my move too soon. I couldn't risk it.

My best chance would be to get Ash alone. I didn't want to test myself fighting against Jocelyn. She was too good.

Fighting Jocelyn alone would be impossible enough, but to do it while I also had to fend off attacks from a dozen of Ash's guard...there was zero chance I would survive that scenario. The ones he kept closest to him wouldn't be as easy as the ones I killed on the way in. I would never be that lucky, and he would never be that stupid.

In a perfect world, I would wait until he was alone, and take care of him without needing to face Jocelyn at all. Maybe all I had to do was wait a little longer, look for the right time, no matter how much the ticking clock heightened my anxiety with each passing second, as if counting down the minutes of my life, not just the time until attack.

His personal guards might have been slaves. I was willing to bet at least a few were. But most of them were probably well-trained, accomplished fighters. Maybe they were from the Marquessa's side. Maybe he hired mercenaries for the job. Maybe Jocelyn called in reinforcements from the Protectorate.

The problem was that I didn't know the skill level of the people sworn to protect my brother.

Watching them stand around while he made plans with the Marquessa and some of their people who were busy destroying the lives of any Mariposa people who dared to challenge their rule was not helping me in gaining any knowledge about my opponents.

My brother's personal guards were easy to spot. Every last one of them wore a helm with that stupid, terrible, purple sigil on the side. But trying to glean any real information about them beyond the fact that they were all disciplined enough to stand still while their fake king held a useless, self-important meeting wasn't working.

"But, King Ash," one of the people sitting near him said, his voice obsequious and a hair away from whining, "it's growing more difficult to keep the Mariposa people in line."

"We should just sell the ones who argue with us," the Marquessa said, running her hand along my brother's arm, her face twisted into a sneer that was at odds with her actions in a way that made me want to punch her until her face shifted permanently.

Someday, I would get her alone. Someday, after I took care of the more dangerous hands in this war, I would cut hers off her body, and make her pay for her part in giving my brother the means to do so much evil.

Onyx, Amethyst, and Corvid were wrapped in the embrace of battle and death because she handed my brother the means to train his slaves and plot a war without anyone else knowing what was happening. Her hands had more blood on them than mine, and she couldn't even wield a blade.

"I think," Ash said, and it was everything I could do to remain still, the sound of his voice so clear this close that the idea of hearing his thoughts made me shudder, "we should throw them in the theater, and make them listen to the prophecy."

The fucking Protectorate prophecy?

When was he told what it was? I didn't know what it was, even after all these years, and so many cryptic mentions of it from Jocelyn. I was never told what exactly the prophecy was, only that it was the reason she and her partner showed up during the last war, and why she trained me.

What the fuck did the prophecy have to do with any of this?

"Every person in the country should know the prophecy," one of the others said. "It could end the war. No one would fight for the Dragon if they knew."

For the Dragon? Was that how they referred to Tristan? He was the Dragon *King*, their king. They were traitors, and whatever the prophecy said, however they manipulated it to tell the story they wanted to hear, when this war was over, Tristan would still be the Dragon King. Tristan would still rule over Onyx. No matter what I had to do to make it happen.

I didn't even believe that the Dragon King magic was real beyond the heat of Tristan's warm blood, but now I wanted him to manifest that fabled, unknown power that supposedly formed the Obsidian Palace.

More than I ever cared about the stories before in my life, I wanted them to be true right then with a desperation that rang through me. If I could have willed it into being, I would have done so just to prove all of those traitors wrong.

My King, my Dragon, needed to snap them in half.

Containing the snarling fury building in me allowed the strain in my muscles to fade into the background as I continued to wait for my perfect opportunity.

Finally, they agreed on some kind of plan for the people in Mariposa who didn't believe in Ash and his lies.

All in a line, the visitors began to leave.

"King Ash," Marquessa Ziya whined, "you need to come to bed soon."

He gave her a perfunctory kiss on the cheek, and turned her toward the door along with the others leaving.

"I'll be along soon, Queen of Ahmya." The way he said her false title was like he was talking to a pet. "I just need to speak with Jocelyn."

She pouted over her shoulder at him as she walked away.

"We'll have an heir soon enough," he called out, and she smiled.

Gross.

Everyone else couldn't leave fast enough. I needed to get down there, and end his twisted game of make-believe before they had a child on the way to make it all worse.

Could I kill her when she was pregnant?

The Marquessa sashayed her hips on her way out the door,

her head high, and the guards falling into step with her as if they were actually her personal guard. Yes, I could kill a pregnant version of her. Although I would prefer her not to be heavy with child by the time I got the chance. I didn't need to feel sorry for the growing spawn of evil in her belly.

Finally, the door closed behind them, and Ash turned to Jocelyn, the only two left in the room.

"You should not be telling everyone of the prophecy," Jocelyn said. "That could expose some of what the Protectorate knows to the rest of the world."

Ash waved a hand in dismissal, and I didn't care anymore about listening. The way he grinned at her, the way he was manipulating everyone, it made me want to drop down right now and attack.

The only one staying my hand was Jocelyn. I still didn't think I could beat her in a fight, least of all in my current condition. I was better, but not at full capacity.

"We both know that it's only to weaken the Dragon," Ash said, draping himself again in his seat. "Anything to get that bastard dead, and my sister out of this fight before she's the one with an heir on the way. Maybe it would help to tell the whole country about Cinder's work for me. Maybe I should tell everyone he's raping her, or blackmailing her with her past."

My mind went blank with white hot rage. He could tell the country whatever he wanted about me and my past, but if he tried to use a lie about assault, if he tried to sully my relationship with Tristan with that ugliness, I would keep him in a cell as my personal sparring dummy for a year before I killed him.

"Are you going to give the Marquessa an heir?" Jocelyn asked, changing topics completely and making me squint.

Why did she call her the Marquessa and not the Queen?

"Of course not," Ash laughed, and it made my rage return, "she is a means to an end, and it's unlikely she will survive the war."

The look he shot toward Jocelyn told me that he wasn't intending for the Marquessa to survive.

"I drink the tea every day. She has no idea. Now, I need you to get them ready for the next battle." He waved a hand, and Jocelyn headed toward the door, making me lean forward.

As soon as she was gone, the door swinging shut behind her, a grin split my face.

Letting go of the choke on the rope, it whirred as I dropped from my hiding place in the branches near the ceiling.

Ash leapt to his feet, his mouth agape.

I landed on the tiles of the room, pulling enough to strain the rope as I unwound the last of it, unsheathing my spike and my sword.

"Instead of lies or twisted prophecies," I said, "how about we start with some truth. And you tell everyone that you're a coward who will never be King of anything except his own sick fantasies."

"Sister," Ash said, flinging his hands out to the sides in a mockery of opening himself up for an embrace as he took a few steps away from me, and grinned a humorless, sharp-edged grin, "how nice of you to join me...and save me some time."

Pointing my spike at him, I said, "You and me. We end this now. No one else needs to be involved."

"Oh, Cinder," Ash said, "we won't be doing that."

He flung himself back to the door. Before I could catch him, he ripped it open.

Jocelyn walked in, pulling her sword as she did.

Damn it. This was exactly what I didn't want. Why didn't I realize he was too close to the fucking door?

"She doesn't need to be involved, Ash. This is between me and you." All I could do was hope she wouldn't fight me again, that I could keep it between him and I. Because fighting her was a nightmare.

"Oh, but Jocelyn does need to be involved now." His smile

was wild, his eyes too wide and menacing. "She won't be backing down again."

Fuck. She refused to fight me before. What changed?

I was behind. I didn't know the fucking prophecy they talked about. They said I didn't need to know. Well, I needed to know now.

There was no running from this. No matter the condition of my back—which I wasn't sure of—no matter how low my odds, this was what I had to do. I ruined my chance by getting too angry, and confronting him while she was too damn close. But there was no other choice, I dropped into fighting stance.

"What changed?" I asked, not expecting them to answer. "What does your precious, fucking prophecy say?"

"It says," Ash's smile was soft, almost fond, as if the prophecy from so long ago handed down in the Protectorate Mountains from some unknown priestess in some mysterious ceremony was actually worth a damn in this world, and Jocelyn and I weren't about to cross real steel, "that you're going to die."

CHAPTER 50

SWIFT

Tristan

We made good time. The decision to sleep in rotating shifts, and trade out our horses at an inn halfway proved to be the best decision so far.

Maybe it made for a slightly less comfortable ride for me and the other guard who rode my assigned horse while I was sleeping, because the horse I got, the one I refused to give to anyone else, had such a bony back that the saddle didn't sit quite right—but I didn't care.

After we got to the palace, I intended to retire this poor old horse, and let her live out her days pampered with no more loads to bear, human or otherwise.

She was most likely some kind of pack or farm horse before. But for her service as a temporary mount for the King, she would be a spoiled member of the royal stable in whatever years remained in her.

"The world works in strange ways," I muttered, patting the

horse on the neck without breaking my attention from the road around us or the sky above us.

No matter how unnecessary I thought it was, I promised General Pace. And I would keep that promise. At least for another few hours.

With so little time left before I saw her again, I was equal parts frustrated at being away from her the entire trip, and thrilled we were so close to being together again. It was a mix of emotions that I could barely put to words.

Spotting General Pace shifting her position with another rider so she was in the front of the arrangement of guards, I spurred my horse on, gesturing with my head to the guard I passed for him to take my place as I took up a position next to the General.

"Only a little while left," she said, as if we were already in the middle of a conversation, which almost made me laugh because there had been very little conversation at all since leaving the Marshlands.

Maybe it was her way of making up for all the needless ones we had on the way down.

"Do you think that any word of what happened reached her yet?" I asked, grinning at what she would say about how well it all worked out. For some reason I thought she would just laugh at the image of all the clergy in the water, and the pathetically begging Amethyst.

Oh, no, that was wrong.

Cinder's reaction to the Amethyst's lies would be rage. She wouldn't be happy at all that I let him go. She would probably say she wished she could have been there to kill him. But she would absolutely take a few shots at all of Amethyst once I told her about the begging.

Second Prince Nevan aside, she hated them.

Now that I thought about it, I needed to have her explain to me why she liked Second Prince Nevan so much. At first, she hated him more than most people with purple hair, except maybe the Marquessa.

My Queen hated her brother's wife more than most people in any country, let alone Amethyst.

"Word probably has yet to reach the palace," she said, bringing me out of my thoughts about Cinder. "We are traveling swiftly." General Pace's voice was calm, and she seemed more relaxed than she had on the rest of the trip. The proximity to home must have done her some good, too.

There was so little—aside from a couple of weddings—for us to celebrate since the war started that even getting home seemed like an occasion that should come with some kind of grand gesture of levity.

"Lady Augustina and Lady Jacquetta will probably suggest this after they hear about the trip," I said, smiling already about what their reactions would be, "but maybe we should have some kind of celebration for the whole palace, and the guards that came with us on this expedition."

General Pace raised her brows and turned to look at me, breaking her own concentration on the task of watching for any attacks and making my smile widen.

"Part of me wants to say no. That it would be inappropriate for the situation in the country at large, and that we might be too presumptuous."

"Only a part of you wants to say that?" I couldn't help looking back at her, and she allowed herself a small laugh before returning her focus to the road.

"Yes, because the rest of me thinks that this is a victory in some ways, one we very much needed. And, regardless of whether it brings peace with the Corvids, it was still a large win against the creeping power grab of the High Sect."

"The High Sect will never take over control of Onyx. We will not be like other nations where worship blocks rulers from doing what's best for the country, or where beliefs are so ingrained in the concept of the country itself that just worshipping is seen as doing good for the country. That will never be enough for Onyx, and I will not let people think it is simply because their faith leaders have told them so."

Maybe my impassioned declaration was more fervent than the situation called for, but it was the truth.

"You sound like your father," General Pace said, her voice low as if trying to soften a blow.

Normally, it would have felt like that to be likened to him, even if he was a good king. In that moment, it didn't as much.

"He was a lot of things. Not always a great father, and a worse husband. But he was a good king, and he was completely, utterly, right about the role of the High Sect."

"I want to tell you something about your father. I have wanted to for a long time, but I am still unsure if it is the right time for it."

Looking at her again, I studied the way she held herself stiffly, even for her, and as much as I maybe didn't want to hear it, I wanted her to unburden herself.

"This is the right time. Please, tell me."

She waited, the sounds of the horse and the carriage traveling over the road the only thing breaking the silence again, luring me back to thoughts of Cinder and home that had been my constant companions since we left the Marshlands.

"Your father..." she trailed off, but now she had my undivided attention.

After promising General Pace, I should have been paying attention to our surroundings, but for some reason—morbid curiosity maybe, or some vestige of blind hope from my childhood—I wanted to hear what she had to say.

My parents were long dead, but she knew them better than I did in many ways. Maybe she would be able to tell me something that would change the way I reflected on them. Hopefully for the better.

It was a lot of power to put on words, on a long-held thought about the two people who made me, but it was something that I didn't have the last seven years. Nor was it something I had to help me process my confused grief just after they died. Maybe it would have been beneficial. All I could do was listen, and hope it turned out to be positive for me this time.

"During the last war, I believe they actually fell in love," she finally said, and I didn't need her to clarify whom she meant.

"So, you're saying the last war brought them together, and taught them to love each other?"

Only for it to end in their deaths.

"Yes. I have thought that for a long time. They were fond of each other, had respect for each other, but you know they were not in love with each other. Not like you and your bride."

General Pace deliberately didn't call Cinder by her name or her title, nor did she call her my wife.

All of the guards behind us could think she meant fiancée. Everyone knew we were engaged. But she agreed, as did the rest of us, that no one needed to know we were already married. The country would feel cheated.

But the revelation about my parents surprised me more than I wanted to admit. Well, more than one revelation.

"He always treated her with respect when other people were around, and I never heard about either of them being cruel in private. But I know he had affairs."

She widened her eyes, but she nodded.

Maybe she didn't know that I was aware of my father's dalliances while I was young.

"They had a complicated relationship, but they always cared about each other. I am probably one of the few people who knew them well enough to know when it changed."

At that, I nodded. It was true. She was close to them both, although she was not quite a general then.

"Before they went on that last mission into Lehar and everything went bad, I started to think that by the end of the war we would have a second prince."

I almost fell off my horse. They got that close at the end?

Only to have it all ripped away.

We couldn't get to the palace fast enough.

CHAPTER 51

HARDER THEY FALL

Cinder

I laughed loudly, enjoying the fury that passed over Ash's features, his eyes hardening and mouth morphing into a snarl. I used it to keep me from giving up in the face of Jocelyn's skill.

"Some Protectorate priestess took the time to foretell the exact moment of my death?" I laughed again before dropping any pretense of humor, circling to the side, mirroring Jocelyn's moves across the room from me. "Waste of time."

"No," Jocelyn said, her voice as close to anger as it ever came. It seemed that insulting her homeland and its mystical ways wasn't something she liked. I could use that. "The prophecy said that, for Onyx to gain its place in history, I had to go to Lehar, protect the new Duke, and train his sister until she flies. Then my blades may be wet with blood, dripping on the wings of Onyx. Only then will the magic return. The magic must return for Onyx and Lehar to thrive, no matter how many others may die."

"That's it?" I screamed, looking to Ash for a second, which left me open for the chance Jocelyn was quick to take.

She darted forward and swung at me, her blade only a flash in the light shining from the hellfire pits that lined the room.

Even as fast as she was, I was ready enough to block her strike, whirling, facing her again from the other side of the room.

"Your prophecy is nonsense. It could mean anything," I yelled.

"It means everything," Ash screamed, backing away to tuck himself behind the chairs, closer to the exit. "Everything."

"Oh," I said, not taking my eyes from Jocelyn this time, even as the foundations of my world shifted under my feet, creating a whole new vista that spread out before me. As if the ashes falling on Lehar, the destruction of my home during the last war, had blocked the real world from view all this time. When I finally saw it, I learned I had studied all the wrong weapons, and the only ones left for me to fight with were made of clay.

"You did all this because of that fucking vague prophecy?" I screamed, no longer sure if I was more furious with Ash, Jocelyn, or myself.

"Nothing is vague," he screamed back, gripping the chair in front of him like he was about to hurl it at me. "For Lehar and Onyx to have magic like it used to, you have to kill, and die, and I have to claim power."

I shook my head, still not letting my attention waver.

Jocelyn tried to come at me again with her single sword, in strikes so fast I had to parry them with both my blades, one on either side of my body, up high and down low, and still I barely caught them in time.

But the second she finished, she backed off again.

"Stop playing with her," Ash yelled. "Kill her now. Wet Onyx with her blood."

"What changed?" I asked, looking to Jocelyn as she ground her teeth together at Ash's command. "You wouldn't kill me before, when he ordered you to in the courtyard at home."

An eerie silence swept over all of us as she stared at me and I stared back, Ash forgotten to the side until I dealt with her.

"Jocelyn," I said, her name tasting like a lie, "why now?"

"You flew at the last battle," she said, and then she attacked.

We slammed our blades together, back and forth. I tried to close the gap between us, narrowing the fighting space to slow her down, but she stepped back.

Again and again, I blocked, slamming our steel against each other, the force ringing through my spike and my sword, flying up my arms, into my still-weakened back.

I didn't have time to think about what she said. I didn't have time to go on offense. I didn't have time to do anything except survive each thrust and swing of her blade.

Something needed to happen. Somehow, I had to come up with a way to attack her.

My back screamed, the muscles too tight and too sore from the work of getting in here in the first place. I should have trained harder. I should have waited to do this. I shouldn't have left the palace until I was healed completely.

Doubling my efforts, with a guttural cry, I finally caught her sword with my own, our handles tangled, and I jabbed at her with my spike, aiming for the killing blow.

But she spun away, stepping back further, looking down at blood that dripped from a slice in her left arm.

"No." Ash's voice was loud and panic-stricken. He was closer to the door, and I was running out of time before I lost my chance to kill him, too. "For the magic to come back, for me to win, she has to die. Now. She flew. Do it now."

"I didn't fucking fly," I yelled, pointing my spike to Jocelyn. "I was on a bird's back, and you know it."

"That's the same thing," she said and jumped back at me, I whirled to the side this time, blocking her blade, trying again to stab her with my spike.

But she ducked, jumping beyond my reach.

We circled each other. She showed no signs of wavering or slowing. My breath remained steady, if too deep, and full of rage.

"All of this because of some vague words that could mean anything. Stop this." My voice was hard, and somehow over my own blood rushing angrily in my ears, I still heard Ash muttering.

"No. I will be King. I will save Onyx. No." He shook his head. It sounded like a mantra he told himself, something he desperately wanted to be true.

"*You* are destroying Onyx because you wanted that fucking prophecy to mean you would be in power." There was nothing left in me that recognized a hint of the brother I grew up with.

When we were kids, he wasn't warm or particularly nice, but he wasn't this. And this was all that was left. Any shred of desire I still had to save him, to talk sense into him, was swallowed up in his mutterings about how right his wrongs were.

"Says the woman who fucks the Dragon, and flew with crows like she was one of them." He pointed at me, and I snorted a half laugh.

"You're working with them," I said. "You accuse me of things that are true of you. You're the one flying with crows."

Didn't they see how their prophecy could be interpreted however someone wanted to? It didn't make sense to base any actions on it, let alone attack your own country, and turn traitor in an attempt to take over the whole continent.

"Cinder is wrong," Ash screamed, and I paid closer attention to the way Jocelyn moved herself to a place she could look at him and I at the same time. Her look was studied, calculating. "She flew. I was the Duke. Kill her now."

Jocelyn attacked again, her blade low and out to the side. I turned and blocked it with my spike, using my sword this time to try and hit her.

She was too fast. She turned and ducked, continuing her turn close to the floor, and forcing me to leap back—up and over her swinging blade, to avoid being cut down.

I landed in a crouch, absorbing as much of the impact with the floor in my leg muscles to save my crying back. To give my arms a rest, I even dropped the tips of my blades to the tiles at my sides, letting the ground hold them up for me.

But, as Jocelyn ran toward me again, sword raised, a knife came out of nowhere, slammed into the back of her hand making her wince, suck in a breath, and change trajectory to face me and the person who threw the knife.

"Gus," I said, my breath leaving me in a rush on her name as I raised my blades, dropping back into stance.

"You're both fools," Gus said, a short sword and another knife ready in her hands.

No matter how fierce she looked, no matter how good her stance or her hold on the weapons, I couldn't let her face Jocelyn. Not on her own. She wouldn't survive five seconds.

I moved closer to my brave, idiotic friend who should have stayed where I told her to. She should have stayed there, and been able to return to Jacquetta no matter what happened to me. Now, I had to find a way to beat Jocelyn, and ensure Gus' return to Jacquetta.

Part of me thought that if Gus died here today, Jacquetta would make sure Madam Valentin's spirit would haunt me if I died, too. And I knew that if Gus died, Jacquetta would never forgive me for taking her from the palace to help me on this mission.

Both my friends might be lost to me today.

Adjusting my hold on my short sword and my spike, I moved to stand a little in front of Gus.

Jocelyn would have to hit me first.

My old trainer shifted her weight, and I knew she understood how this was going to go. Even if she lunged at Gus, tried to engage her, I would be the one she was really fighting.

Gus refused to let any of us forget about her presence, though.

"I am no fool," Ash said, taking a single step forward as if that should be intimidating to anyone even as he remained close to the door, away from the fight without a blade in his hands.

"You are," Gus said with a derisive laugh, "you both keep saying she flew at the last battle, but—"

She was cut off by a cry from Jocelyn as she ran at us. I parried with my sword. Unwilling to turn and try for the jab with my spike which would leave Gus open, I drove my spike toward her leg instead.

Jocelyn whirled, only to have Gus slam her sword against Jocelyn's.

With a scream to distract them both, I swung my sword, my steel clanging against Jocelyn's block, as I jabbed out with my spike, aiming to hit the portion of her arm not covered by her armor.

Gus threw a knife as Jocelyn kicked out at me. Her boot hit me in the chest, and sent me careening toward the floor as the blow and the impact ricocheted pain through my ribs around toward my back.

Jocelyn spun. Her short, armored cloak caught, ripping the knife from the air as I barely stopped myself from falling.

A grunt, a searing breath through my healing ribs, and I shoved forward to attack again.

But Jocelyn stepped back, studying me and Gus.

Fuck. I knew that look. She was trying to gauge Gus. She was trying to understand how much my friend knew, and how she fought.

I couldn't let her see that Gus had an injured leg. I couldn't let her notice the odd gait, and use it to her advantage. Somehow, I had to come up with a way to distract them.

Gus did it for me.

"Yes," she yelled, looking toward my brother like she was trying to figure out if she could throw her knife that far. I didn't think she could. "You're both fools."

Oh, I knew where she was going with this.

With a growl low in her throat, Jocelyn attacked again.

A strike, a block, a parry, a slam of her free arm past my guard, and directly into my ribs along my side. She sent me to the floor again, then advanced on Gus.

"No," I screamed as Gus smiled, raising her sword to block Jocelyn's swing.

Their blades clanged together as Gus said, "Cinder flew at the first battle."

Jocelyn fumbled as I scrambled to my feet behind her. Ash paled, shaking his head.

In a move far too fast for Gus to counter it, Jocelyn swung her sword around and down, right into Gus' leg where it clanged against her boot.

"Say hello to Jonesy," Gus said as I grabbed Jocelyn's throat from behind, and stabbed my spike between her ribs right into her heart.

"You should have killed me in the courtyard," I said, right before I dropped her lifeless body.

All her knowledge, all her skill, all the years she spent training me to be as much like her as possible while she let my brother hurt me laid out before me in the splay of her hair across the tiles, and the grim smile on Gus' face as she looked down on her.

Whirling around at the sound of pounding feet, I watched the back of Ash's head disappear beyond the shoulders of his guards as they poured into the room.

CHAPTER 52

MIDNIGHT

Tristan

Reigning myself in, trying not to pull too far ahead as we made our way through Bridgeton was one of the most frustrating things I had ever been through.

After what the General told me, all I could think about was how I refused to let history repeat itself. Nothing would tear Cinder away from me. We both went through too much to get to where we were together. We deserved the chance at happiness that my parents lost.

Once we reached the bridge, I couldn't hold back anymore, and spurred the horse to pick up the pace.

"King Tristan," General Pace called from behind me as I flew, bent over the knobby horse's head, through the tunnel, into the courtyard.

One of the guards at the doors darted inside as others poured into the courtyard.

Nothing seemed different, other than the sheer number of guards that came out to greet our arrival.

I flung the reigns of the horse to one of the guards, hopped off its back, patting it on the neck in the process, and hurried up the steps as the General and the others came through the tunnel.

Running up the steps, I would have lost the kingdom if I had to wipe the smile off my face to save it.

Before I reached the door, it swung open, Rath jumping out with Lady Jacquetta right behind him.

Their faces fell when they saw me, which sent a shard of molten hellfire water down my spine, stealing the smile from my face.

"What's wrong?" I asked, my voice hard. "Where's Cinder?"

Lady Jacquetta's lower lip trembled as she stole a glance at Rath, and ran back inside the threshold of the door.

"Rath?" I asked, my heart in my throat, pounding harder than the horse's hooves as I rode across the bridge.

"King, I'm glad you're back." He stood up straighter, and took a deep breath, his face impassive, nothing about his demeanor doing anything to make me less suspicious of their actions.

"Lady Jacquetta?" I pushed past Rath, and faced her. Every second they avoided telling me what was going on made me itch more with the need to destroy something for making me worry this much. Something was wrong. So wrong that I felt history's blade hanging over my head.

"Queen Cinder is..." she sucked in a shaking breath, a shudder running through her, and I reached out a hand to touch her arm, needing an anchor as much as offering her support to finally be able to tell me, "Cinder and Gus went to break into the Chrysalis Tower."

"What?" I roared as I whirled around to face Rath.

"She found out that her brother was leaving the tower for a

short time, but long enough for her to think she could break in, and lie in wait to kill him."

"No one can get in there. They'll kill her." I was too loud. Every set of eyes in the courtyard, including the General's turned to me, a palpable fear, the look and stench of it, rippling through the crowd.

"Gus," Lady Jacquetta added, her voice cracking, "went with her to show her the hidden way in."

"How long ago? We can stop them before they get there." I shoved Rath out of the way, and stomped down the steps, trying to think about how many guards I could bring with me for a full-on assault on the Chrysalis Tower.

It would be a bloodbath, but I couldn't think about that now.

"You can't," Rath called behind me, grabbing onto my arm and yanking me to a stop.

"Believe it, or not, Rath, I'm still the fucking King, and I can." My words were clipped, rumbling low in my throat, but I knew he heard me as he came around my side to look into my face.

"No, King. They left days ago."

My legs gave out, and I crashed to my knees on the steps. One leg twisted under me, but I didn't feel any pain. That moment was dominated by the blinding heat of fear and rage, all of it so dark it blocked out the sun. I screamed.

"This can't be happening." Somehow in my breakdown, I heard words. They came from me, but they didn't sound like me. I wasn't even sure how I was moving my mouth.

"King, she'll be back. Any minute, they'll come back." Rath kept talking, kept assuring me that there was no reason for me to lose my head.

But he was too late, every part of me was lost in a haze of my worst nightmares.

"She could already be dead, and I would never know." Again, my voice came through the darkness of my unseeing eyes, a pleading evident in my trembling voice. Without addressing them, I begged the Gods and Goddesses not to make me live through losing her. Not to repeat what happened to my parents. To find happiness only to have it shattered like so much glass.

"Please, please, please." Any other words I might have said dissolved into begging, mindless and repetitive. They flooded through me along with a painful degree of heat in my blood.

It was tearing me apart, this possibility of grief, the unknowing.

A sharp, smacking thud landed on my face, sending me backward onto the steps, sprawled out as the world blinked back into existence around me until I could see again.

Lifting my head from the steps, I stared into the narrowed eyes of General Pace.

"Gather yourself. There is something we can do, and you are going to get up, and fucking do it. She is not dead yet." The General turned on her heel as Rath helped me up, his face pale and wan. My friend was just as worried as I was.

"We move out in ten minutes," General Pace barked to the stunned and staring guards gathered in the courtyard. "Duchess Cinder is inside Mariposa."

A collective gasp went up. Some people muttered unintelligibly, while many put their hands on their weapons, their grips tight.

They were ready to help her. They wanted her back, too.

My Queen was their Fighter, and none of us wanted to imagine losing her.

"She went to break into the Chrysalis Tower in an attempt to kill the traitor."

Jaws dropped all over the courtyard. They all knew it was impenetrable, just as I did.

"Lady Augustina showed her a secret way in."

That was enough for their jaws to drop further.

All except one person who laughed, loud and wild.

"Only Fighter Cinder would be able to break into the impossible tower," they yelled from somewhere in the back of the crowd, and, although I couldn't see them, their words managed to lessen the temperature of the inferno inside me a degree or two.

Cinder was the only person alive who would ever even think to try, and she was the only one I would ever say had even a fraction of a chance.

It wasn't a large one. But it existed.

"Right," General Pace said, and she pointed toward Mariposa and the Kaleidoscope Fields, "but *when* she needs to come back, she will need help escaping."

"How are we going to help?" Rath asked, looking from me to Lady Jacquetta who haunted the doorway. "We can't attack the tower itself."

Shoving myself to my feet, I wanted to punch him like the General punched me. I was willing to attack anything if doing so would bring Cinder back to me.

"No," the General said, and I whirled to face her, ready to order her to do just that, guilt over pulling rank be damned. "But we can be ready for her to come out of the forest. We can cover her retreat across the Kaleidoscope Fields."

"Yes," I said, finally my voice sounded like I was in control again. It was only a single word, but it was better than being on my knees begging the Gods and Goddesses for their intervention.

"Go. Ten minutes." General Pace looked back at me with a single nod that I returned.

It was time to get my Queen back safely.

CHAPTER 53

FLIGHT

Cinder

I yanked the armored cloak off Jocelyn's body, and spun it to protect myself from any attacks shot toward me from my brother's guards as I wrapped the rope around my legs.

Gus was ahead of me, working her way up the rope, doing the moves I showed her to make it easier and faster for her. But she wasn't practiced like I was. She was much slower, and I couldn't let her be lower than me. I couldn't let her be a target.

"Faster, Gus," I called, whirling and twisting, using the armored cloak to knock away a thrown knife.

But as I did, another knife flew past me, and sank into one of the guard's necks.

"Nice shot," I yelled, "Keep getting higher. I'll take the shots now." She gave me an idea. I used the cloak, then threw a knife, checked her progress, and twisted myself higher only to repeat the process, over and over.

"They're too high," one of the guards yelled, their knife dropping down to the floor of the hollowed-out trunk that made up the big room in the top of the tower.

"Get downstairs. We can stop them. They can't get out of the mountain."

All the guards filed out of the room, and I wondered about their surety.

But without time to dwell on that, I flipped myself further until I reached the small branch, pulling myself over the edge of it.

"Cinder," Gus said, at my side in a second, helping me untangle myself from the rope.

"They're going to be on the ground. I think getting out the way we came in is no longer an option," I said, stretching out my aching back. Like usual, getting in was the easy part, but getting out after the alarm went up about an assassin around was fucking hard.

"I'm not very good at rock climbing," she said, chewing on her lip.

"What are you talking about?" Somehow what she said had to refer to a way out of this, but I couldn't figure out how.

"Getting word or reinforcements to the guards along the top of the mountain will be hard for them before we reach the edge of the trees," she said, and her doodled image of the mountain popped into my mind.

"How far is the jump from the edge of the leaves to the top of the mountain?" With Gus tied to me it would be a lot harder, but I could make this work.

"It isn't a jump, but the top of the leaves are still a house's height away from the top." She shook her head as she went to stuff the ropes into the saddlebags again.

"No, we aren't taking the saddlebags. We're just taking the ropes. And don't worry about the climb. I know what to do."

She looked at me hard, but just handed me one of the looped

ropes that I slipped over one of my shoulders as she did the same with the other, and we set off.

Crawling through the leaves of the winged trees was easy enough. We just crouched down, and went as fast as possible. A sort of hunched run that wasn't really crawling. But we couldn't stand all the way up without moving the leaves above us enough to set up an alarm among the guards stationed on top of the mountain.

It didn't take as long as I thought it would to reach the edge of the trees.

But the guards attempting to alert everyone that we were there would have to go all the way down the tower tree, run throughout the forest floor, then take the steep, switchback stairs that went up the inside of the mountain wall.

If my brother was idiotic enough to insist he go along with them, him being carried in the chairs carried by servants some of the higher ups rode the stairs in would slow them down even further. And my brother was exactly the kind of asshole who would request it for special treatment instead of a valid reason.

We had to get to the top of the mountain first.

Finally, what must have been an hour of running was behind us, and I peeked between two leaves at the wall just beyond their edge.

I reached out and easily found a handhold before turning back to where Gus was perched.

"Tie this rope around yourself," I whispered, tying off the other end around my middle and creating a harness of the rope around myself. "Do it just like this."

She nodded and got to work, handing me the other rope, which I just looped over one shoulder, tucking the armored cloak into it, making sure I could still move.

Of all the things that concerned me about what we were doing, my movement being restricted when I could least afford it was highest on my list.

Gus nodded when she was done, and I looked her over. It all looked right.

I gestured for her to go first, and braced myself, waiting until she was secure on the wall, before following after her.

With hand movements, I showed her how I wanted her to follow me, put her hands where I put mine, put her feet where I put mine.

She nodded, and I moved into place above her. Every move made my back ache, but in a way that told me it was getting better by being forced to do this. I was going to be sore tomorrow, but I had to make it there first. And I had no intention of dying when we were so close to getting home.

Looking down at her, I kept my progress slow, deliberately picking handholds and footholds that would be easier on her, not forcing her to stretch herself too far, or make the use of her booted leg difficult.

Finally, I reached the top of the mountain. Looking around the massive circle, I saw no guards at all.

Did they not look inside the mountain? Were they that complacent?

Impenetrable.

Why would they ever think to look inside when they believed like everyone else did that no one could break into the mountain?

Smiling, I tapped the rock in front of me until Gus looked up at me.

With a gesture, I showed her that I was going to move to the side so she could keep following my path to my current position.

Carefully, I made my move, and began to untie myself from the rope.

A couple minutes later, she was in the place I just vacated, breathing hard as I grinned and gestured for her to untie herself.

Her brow furrowed. I used my hands to show her we were about to go over the edge, and she would need her hands for her weapons.

She bit her lip and nodded, beginning to untie herself.

I moved my feet to higher places, using my legs to slowly raise myself, and look over the edge.

A guard sat on the rather flat bit of the top of the mountain, looking out at the trees, not far from us on my side.

Looking along the rim both ways, I spotted a lot of guards. There was too much space between them, and most were lounging lazily. One even leaned on the tip of his sword where he dug it into the rock near his feet.

Gus popped up next to me, looking around, her hands on the edge of the flat part itself before she leaned forward on one of her forearms, and drew in the dirt.

Her drawing told me that we weren't close enough to the stairs to use them, but that the stable of horse for the royals and nobles that were inside the tower sat between us and the stairs.

Almost perfect.

I nodded and launched myself onto the flat top of the mountain. The guard in front of us barely had time to turn at the noise I made before I slit his throat with my spike, dropping him.

In that short time, the alert went up from one of the other guards.

Grabbing Gus, I hauled her up beside me, an arrow slamming into the rock right where she was a second before.

"Come on," I yelled, yanking Jocelyn's cloak from the rope around my shoulder, and wrapping it around her hands as I wrapped it around mine.

She followed me, ducking her head to look over the edge of the far-too-steep slope that we needed to descend somehow.

"We can't climb down. We'll be too slow," I said as I kneeled at the edge and placed my wrapped hands on the rock in front of me. "We slide. Do what I do."

Gus was fast as she followed my lead, more arrows coming way too close.

Once she was in position, I said, "Now!" and we shoved off.

The slope took us in a second, sending us sliding down on our toes, knees, and hands wrapped in the unique Protectorate cloak.

It wasn't made for this, but it held up fine while I had to grit my teeth at the way the rock scraped my knees even through my leather.

"Cinder," Gus yelled, her voice as strained as I thought mine would be.

But the guards above us didn't stand a chance. By the time they reached our previous position, their arrows didn't reach far enough down the side of the mountain to hit us.

Looking to my side at the swiftly approaching ground, I prepared for a hard landing.

"Dig your toes and hands into it. Slow us down, now," I yelled. Gus dug in right before I did which meant I slammed into the ground first, and allowed myself to crumple so the cloak wouldn't be ripped away from her.

"Everything hurts," Gus groaned.

"Feel the pain later," I said, scrambling as a twinge went through one of my knees and my feet throbbed while I hauled her to standing.

We both looked up the side of the impossibly high mountain to where the guards scrambled, although they were too far away for me to be sure what they were doing. Then we ran toward the stables.

"I'll kill any guards we run into. You get a horse," I whispered, although I didn't want to be using my voice at all in case there were guards close to us.

"Only one?" she asked, as quiet as I was even though she was breathing heavily.

"Quicker that way."

We neared the stables, and there was a horse right near the fence closest to us. I pointed him out to Gus as I focused on the guard sitting on the fence, staring into the trees away from us.

This part, at least, would be easy.

I threw a knife, ending the guard. But somehow in my focus, I missed that there were three more not far inside the paddock, and a cry went up just as Gus jumped the fence with the horse, stopping in front of me.

She didn't have to say a word as I swung myself up behind her, no saddle, and she kicked the horse into motion again.

All the while guards poured out of the stable after us.

CHAPTER 54

UNBELIEVABLE

Rathmoreland

King and I had known each other all our lives. But this guy was different.

He never broke down.

Not like this.

It didn't make sense to me. He didn't even do this when he thought she betrayed him.

All I could do was shake my head, and silently beg as we sat on our horses, side by side, at the edge of the Kaleidoscope Fields.

Their guards were everywhere around us, but none of them were in front of us.

No. The couple that tried had a snarling King pointed their way until they moved.

Come on, Flame.

It became a chant in my head. Beneath any of the other words I thought or said, a plea into the world for her to show up repeated over and over again.

Hours. We waited fucking hours while hardly moving.

King got more agitated with every hour that past.

Finally, near dusk, a huge flock of birds burst through the trees on the other side of the fields, flapping, cawing, and careening madly as they went.

People around me jumped at their noise, but then settled as if it didn't mean anything.

I leaned forward, squinting through the tree trunks, looking for another sign.

Something shook the top of a tree, its limbs shuddering, and I kicked my horse into movement screaming, "King."

I spent too long on the water not to know how to listen to nature's signals.

Not a second later, he was passing me. All the other guards caught up to our wild stampede seconds after that.

And a few minutes later, as we stormed across the fields, a horse with two people on it burst through the trees riding harder than was ever safe.

The person with the reigns had bright red hair, and it was enough for King to scream, "Cinder."

If Gus was there, and someone was riding behind her on the horse, it was Flame.

Grinning, I whooped and rode harder.

As they drew closer, arrows flew from the tree line as riders poured out, firing at our Queen.

"Halt," General Pace called, and all the horses did, well-trained as they were, even when their rider urged them on.

Poor King tried twice to get his horse to move.

"Fuck," he yelled, jumping down and running forward.

"Stop, King," I yelled, following him.

He was a lot of things, including a damn good shot. But I was faster.

Right after he let an arrow fly that almost made it to the line of pursuers, I tackled him to the ground, and started to drag him back.

"Let me go," he snarled, fighting me to a standstill, neither of us getting anything other than a coating of dirt.

"No. Don't die right before she gets to you." Fucking idiot.

"She needs me." He just wouldn't stop. I wanted the General to punch him in the face again, give him another black eye.

"Wait," I said, watching something unbelievable, "what is she doing?"

He paused long enough to watch with me as she twisted in her place at Gus' back, Gus moving her hands to hang onto Cinder's legs where they were wrapped around her, while Cinder flung something around like she did with her dress that night we danced together.

The flinging thing, some kind of fabric, knocked an arrow from the sky that would have slammed into her back.

A second later, King used my distraction to surge to his feet. At least he didn't run again.

No. This time he readied his bow, and took out one of the pursuers, his shot longer than theirs.

Well. Looking back and forth between him and the riders after Flame and Gus, I realized that shot was farther than anyone I knew could make.

He fired again and again, raining arrows down on the ones after his Flame.

They were smarter than they looked because they turned and headed back the way they came. Meanwhile Gus didn't slow one bit.

As they came closer, I could see the horse foaming at the mouth, eyes wild, chest heaving. She brought it to a quick stop in front of us, and Flame leapt at King as he lunged at her.

They fell into each other, a mess of bodies and limbs and murmured words of love on the ground.

I shook my head as I stepped around them to help Gus climb

down. She winced as she dismounted, breathing hard and patting the poor horse that had a layer of sweat all over it.

"Jacquetta?" she asked, and I smiled.

"Right over there," I said, pointing to the carriage that sat completely out of place at the edge of the fields.

Gus started limping that way, but a second later guards were pushed aside as Jacquetta barreled through them, running into her wife's arms.

Looking back and forth between my friends on the ground, and the ones standing in front of me, I figured I wouldn't hear the story of the last few days for a while.

With a sigh, I turned back toward my abandoned horse.

I really missed my mates.

AFTERWORD

Thank you for reading!
If you enjoyed this book, please leave a review at your favorite bookseller.
Don't forget to go to jdarleneeverly.com and sign up for the newsletter to be the first to know about all the updates on this series. The sixth book, After Ashes Fall is coming soon.
As a special exclusive for those who sign up for the newsletter, the author is giving away a prequel in this series, only found with sign up, as well as an exclusive free book in another story world and more.

ACKNOWLEDGMENTS

A whole hearted thank you to Bean, the Rottens, and all of my friends and family. Again, huge thanks to Jupiter Alley and Krystal for their help in making this happen, Heather Cardona for all she does, Miblart for the gorgeous cover, Lucy at Jupiter Alley for the absolutely brilliant sigil covers for the interior of the hardcovers, as well as the team at Wishing Well.

But also, for you all, the readers.

During the work on this book, after it was written and while I was in the editing process, something happened that derailed my health to such an extent that I was unable to do any work. It all ground to a halt.

Those of you who checked on me, checked on the book, checked on the characters you loved, and stuck with the story and my broken body until I could grind through what I needed to, I will never be able to thank you enough.

It will always be one of the great achievements of my life to see this book complete and be able to share it with you.

Maybe this is our magic.

ABOUT THE AUTHOR

J. Darlene Everly is an author of fantasy stories. The Cinders in Midnight Glass series will wrap up soon. Her serial, Crossroad Inn, is available on Vella, and the first season will soon be available in book form. Her debut trilogy, The Grimm Star Saga: First Light is available everywhere, and two more series will begin soon. Keep an eye out for Major Arcana to go on preorder, and The Grimm Star Saga's first release coming up. And keep reading for all of Cinder's story. There are a lot more stories to tell in this same story world. They will be coming soon.